THE MANHATTAN SPLIT

FUSION

CHRIS KENNY

Cover designed by MiblArt.

For my wife

CHAPTER ONE

MEI SHIMIZU WATCHED with a mixture of fascination and fear as the green rails smashed into other cable guys less fortunate than herself. The pins in her temple throbbed, the pain threatening to pull her out of cyberspace, and back to reality. Seeing colour for the first time inside a virtual construct threw her, so much so that her perspective took a sharp nosedive. In a stroke of pure luck, she avoided another of the strange tentacles as it took out three or four of her colleagues.

Tumbling through the endless city of white, angular buildings, Mei got a grip of herself and levelled out. Streams of code flashed before her mind's eye, the screen jerked and distorted. Suddenly, she was high above the flat surface again, watching as more cable guys poured into TegaLyfe virtual space. The gap that was torn into the defence system was getting wider. The frazzled edges peeled further away, like paper curling in a roaring fire.

Her thoughts turned to her brother, Hiroto. He was in here, somewhere. At twenty-five years old, he was past his prime as a cable guy. Reactions weren't as fast, hunger wasn't there. Mei herself was twenty-two, acutely aware this was her last roll of the dice to make her name as a cable guy.

When the call from Kaizen Sciences was put out six months ago, Hiroto had jumped at the chance. He'd returned from work that day, all smiles and excitement.

"This is our chance," he'd said, holding his deck in one hand, gripping it tightly.

"What is?" Mei was boiling noodles in their kitchen. She remembered how she felt that day, it had been six weeks since the new implants. Her jaw still ached from the reconstruction. She had looked in the splash panel, reflection misted from the steam, but the lines running from the corners of her lips, and the middle of her chin were still visible. Brand new skin graft over chrome alloy. Totally replaced the bone, which was shattered by a rowdy customer in the bar one night. Her slender finger traced the lines softly. It felt like real skin.

"Kaizen Sciences. They're asking for any cable guy with three or more years experience to apply," Hiroto said, snapping her back to the pot, which was boiling over.

"Shit," she'd said, pressing the console on the hob, turning down the electric rings of heat. "I mean, that's great, for you of course."

"And you. Mei, you can do this. This is the chance we've both been waiting for. Working for Kaizen."

Her brother's enthusiasm had always been contagious. But he was the real cable guy. She'd only messed around in cyberspace. Never hacked anything, stolen crypto. Nothing. Hiroto had stood there, a crooked smile, hair falling over his eyes. He was positively giddy. She'd always felt like a tag along to his big ideas. He had a vision, a purpose. She had a shitty job as a cocktail waitress in Wall Street, getting abused sexually, emotionally, and physically. Some purpose, that was.

"Alright, but we probably won't get in," she said, lifting the cooked noodles into two plastic bowls.

That was six months ago. Now, she was here, inside Tega-Lyfe systems, doing what, exactly? She moved, jerkily. Her lapse in concentration had cost her precious seconds in cyberspace. Everything moved at a frantic pace. She saw the other cable guys, represented as spiky balls in her vision, explode or fade out of existence. It made her panic, so she dived again, heading towards the surface.

It was like a street, but all white, leading into the city of constructs that she knew were security systems. *If I can steal some crypto, or plans for something, we'll be set.* Her focus sharpened, and her body relaxed for the first time since jacking in. She could do this, she knew it. As a kid, being the most famous cable guy in the world was her only desire. Growing up without parents in Downtown shifted that perspective, as did the need for money.

So she'd meandered aimlessly from job to job, gradually losing herself to the system. Work, eat, sleep, repeat. At that moment, however, it was back. The enthusiasm that her brother never lost was alive inside her again. She wanted to impress not only Mr Nishikawa, CEO of Kaizen, but her brother as well. She loved him dearly, he was all she had in this world.

The next few seconds were a blur. First, there was a flash. The next thing Mei knew, she was stuck, caught between those strange, green rails, and a cluster of cable guys. She forced her vision down, and saw it. Two outlines, humanoid, walking on the surface. Her eyes bulged, it shouldn't be possible to create an avatar like that inside this reality. One of them was standing still, outline flaring as if in anger. That's when it happened.

With a quickness like a cat pouncing on a mouse, the shape enveloped the other one, who Mei determined was a woman. That's when the sound ripped through the silence of her domain, a screech so filled with pain it made her heart ache. A burst of pink light dazzled her eyes, which she shut quickly. It wasn't fast enough. The ripples from the explosion pulsed through TegaLyfe systems, mixed with the cries of... a woman? Pink lights dazzled her eyes, shutting down her vision.

Mei gasped as her senses returned to the real world. She pressed the release on her visor, and it slid off her head. The smell of charred plastic filled her nostrils, the foul smell wrinkling her nose. Blinking rapidly, her eyesight returned, and she was met with a scene of chaos.

Next to her, slumped in their chairs, were the three other cable guys sharing her cubicle. Their decks were smoking, as were their headsets. Fresh blood trickled under the eye shields and poured out of their nose and ears, dripping over their clothes. Mei screamed and tried to stand, but her legs were still locked into the seat. She fumbled with the release, eventually finding the button, and she rolled out onto the floor.

Flames licked the ceiling, setting the sprinklers off. She was drenched in an instant, her black hair which was cut into a bob, losing its style, clinging to her face and neck.

"What's happened?" she shouted. There was no response, only the sound of water jets dousing the roaring flames. All around her were dead cable guys, towers exploded, and decks either charred, or sizzling.

What the fuck happened? She asked herself, panic flooding her chest. She coughed, eyes stinging as smoke and water mixed together. One thought raced to the forefront of her mind. *Hiroto.*

Weaving through the wreckage, stepping over trailing wires, and the occasional dangling leg, Mei sprinted for the exit. A supervisor burst through the door just before she reached it, his mechanical eyes whirring with confusion. His mouth, a diagonal line cut against a hard face, worked to form a sentence, but Mei didn't stick around to hear it. She ducked under his outstretched arms, her petite frame lending itself to her escape.

The next office was just as destroyed, but dry. Either the sprinklers hadn't gone off yet, or they had doused whatever fire had erupted. She blinked water from her eyes, droplets streaking off her face to the floor. Breathing rapidly, Mei slowed her run to a walk, searching for her brother.

All she saw were husks of humans, slumped over their decks, or lying with their backs against their seats, heads angled up to the ceiling. *They look like they're sleeping*, her mind said, the irrational thought helping to normalise the carnage. She ignored the distorted looks of fear on their faces, eyes hidden by visors, but mouths open in shock and likely pain. *It's fine, just find Hiroto, and it'll all be okay*, she told herself, keeping her gaze averted from the dead bodies.

Despite her childlike naivety, she wasn't stupid. She knew this had been a result of the incident within cyberspace. What was it again? Two figures. Right, that was it. One of them seemed to... erase the other. That caused the explosion... pink lights...

"Where are you going?" a hand shot out, gripping Mei's shoulder firmly. She gasped, shocked back to the moment. A woman with a narrow face glared at Mei through thick glasses that were merged into her skin.

"I'm trying to find my brother," Mei said. The vulture-like grip relaxed, and the woman simply nodded before turning away. Mei's heart thumped in her chest now. Dread bubbled up inside her with every step, expecting to see Hiroto dead, slumped over a desk. Instead, she saw bodies she didn't recognise, destroyed towers, screens, and burned carpet. Her mind was racing, leaping from worst-case scenarios to blissful ignorance. As she approached the end of the office, she turned the handle, fearing the worst.

That's exactly what she got. To her right, immediately in view, was her brother. His visor was dangling off of his face, showing one open eye. It stared blankly up at her, without recognition or life. Mei's hands covered her mouth, her eyes filling with tears, blurring her vision. Heavy legs carried her over to Hiroto, each step like she was wading through mud. She ignored the shouts of a superior, directing medical assistance to other booths. She ignored the pain which lanced up her leg, as she scraped it along a jagged shard of metal, the ruin of a tower. What she couldn't ignore was the deep sense of loss in her heart.

Mei's small hands trembled, reaching her brother's arm. He was still warm, and for a moment, she thought he could be saved. Shouting for help, Mei turned her head in all directions, wet hair flicking about her face. The tears poured freely now, and her voice was choked with guttural cries. Eventually, she gave up and collapsed next to her brother, her head resting on his stomach, arms circling his wiry frame. Squeezing with all her might, like she would bring him back. It was no use.

Her hair was sticky with blood, his blood, and she saw the congealed puddle on his shirt. She didn't care. Delicately, she lifted the visor off completely, letting it drop to the floor with a clatter. Her hands framed his face, lower lip trembling as her emotions overwhelmed her again. She burst into tears, her chest heaving with every cry. Never had she felt so sad, never had she felt so hopeless.

Hiroto was all she had. She didn't remember her parents, they'd died of cancer when she was only two. Hiroto told her about them, though, how kind and loving they were. One holo pic was all she had of the four of them, back at the apartment. She looked a final time at her brother's eyes. Dark and beautiful, they were always filled with laughter, like he was in on some great joke that nobody else knew about. He was bubbly, a trait they both shared. But he would light up a room where she would happily fade into the shadows. A new jolt of panic hit her. The apartment. Without Hiroto's ability to steal crypto, and trade tech on the virtual markets, she wouldn't be able to keep up rent payments, no way. She buried her head into Hiroto's body again, crying silently into his chest.

After a few minutes, Mei couldn't cry any more. The faint sounds of adjacent offices filtered through her ears. Shouts of panic, some of instruction, others of fear. It seemed like the entire floor was affected. Standing on shaky legs, Mei took a last look at Hiroto. She closed his eyelids, her fingers stroking his face a last time. She just needed to get away, just for a moment.

Mei's feet carried her automatically back through the offices, to her own space. Her corner of Kaizen Sciences, loaned to her to help in the effort of taking down TegaLyfe. Hiroto was so excited to have this chance. She was here out of loyalty to him. And now he was dead, and she was alive. How was that fair?

Mercifully, the sprinklers were shut off now. The dying embers of burnt out towers crackled like logs in a campfire. Mei walked silently to her area. The monitor was smashed, but the deck and her visor were intact. She fell in her chair, staring at the screen, the glass reflecting her image back at her. She looked dreadful. Eyes puffy, hair lank and wet. She didn't care. Her hands turned the deck over, the wires sprouting from the top of it were intact. The keys, a little grimy from debris that had been soaked in, but otherwise looked okay. The Kaizen Sciences logo pulsed slowly on the tiny display. She touched it, a lump forming in her throat once again. Inhaling a deep breath, she was about to leave when the monitor in front of her flicked on.

Mei's eyes bulged. She checked her deck. Powered down. Ducking under the table, she scrutinised the tower. Turned off as well. She bumped her head on the way up, such was her haste. Her heart thumped in her chest when the first line of code trawled along the screen.

"What the fuck?" she breathed. Cautiously, she picked her

deck up, hands still shaking. The display winked on, and she dropped it with a gasp. Nothing was plugged in. Her deck had no WiFi compatibility, a deliberate move. Hiroto said WiFi was outdated. Too easy for bugs and viruses to get through. And AIs.

The monitor blinked again, code turning from a scrambled mess into more coherent patterns Mei could recognise. She leaned in closer, as though that would help her decipher the meaning of the string of numbers, symbols, and letters. Her deck whirred into life on the floor, the bios screen flicking once, and then turning blue. A dash blinked repeatedly, waiting for input. Her username.

Curiosity overtook her sensibilities. Mei picked the deck up, holding it with both hands. The code on the monitor blurred and changed, like it was alive. Then the words appeared on the deck. <*Hello?*>

Mei stifled her cry of shock with her right hand, the deck dangling loosely in her left. For a second, she wondered if it was Hiroto's consciousness, somehow trapped in cyberspace. She'd heard that was possible. Cable guys getting so deep into virtual reality that they gave up their bodies on purpose. Becoming assimilated with their decks. She didn't believe it, dismissed it as her brother trying to freak her out. But now, she wasn't so sure.

Her fingers tapped lightly on the keys. She spelled out the response. <*Hi.*> The deck made a chirping sound, like mechanical bolts screeching against a synthesiser. It hurt her ears. New line of text. <*Who are you?*>

"Who am I? Who the fuck are you?" Mei said aloud. "I'm..." she said, typing as she spoke. Mei stopped short. Should she say her name? What was she even talking to? Could be a TegaLyfe countermeasure. She hit the backspace, deleting the letters. <*What are you?*> Mei typed. A pause, lengthy this time.

<*I don't know. I need help.*>

Mei scrunched up her features. It didn't make sense, none of it did. She briefly entertained the thought that she was so stricken with grief that she'd passed out, and this was all some hallucination. Pinched the skin on her arm, just to check. *Ow. Definitely not unconscious, then.* Mei was trusting, too trusting. Always had been. Sometimes got her in hot water, other times got her discounts at the food market for being a helping hand in the community.

<*If I tell you my name, will you tell me yours?*> Mei asked. Another wait.

<*Yes, I remember that. I had a name.*>

"Good start. Screw it. What else can I lose?" Mei said to the quiet room.

<*My name is Mei.*>

She waited, not realising she'd been holding her breath. Letting it escape through her lips slowly, her pulse climbed higher, the anticipation building. The screen flashed with a new message.

<*I'm Karla.*>

CHAPTER TWO

HE COULD SMELL BURNING FLESH, the odour clouding his nostrils. His eyes traveled slowly to his naval, where his legs were now two stumps. Changed perspective, now on his back, looking up at the orange sky. Sand and pebbles scratching his face as he lay there dying. Thinking of Olivia. The screaming, his voice, mingled with hers. The apartment hallway on fire.

Cade sat up with a start, breathing hard. Reality poured into him slowly, like thick paint coming out of a bucket.

"Fuck," he said, sweat forming on his brow. Another daydream, the second of the day. Cade moved his hands to his head, running black-chrome fingers through his damp hair. He flinched, feeling the metal against his scalp, and brought his hands in front of his eyes.

Wiggling the fingers, Cade's lip curled in disgust. He looked up and down the length of his right forearm, up to where his biceps used to be. Flesh was now metal. Bones replaced with carbon-fibre rods. Muscle exchanged for steel plating. His arms were shaped in a similar fashion to what he was used to, but in-between the connective layers of metal and carbon-fibre, he saw the slate grey walls of his bedroom. Gaps in his arms. He wasn't used to it yet. Maybe he never would be.

Using his left hand, he pulled away the white sheet covering his torso and legs. He let out a sigh, heavy with anguish, spotting the bionic legs. Similar in design to his arms, the same matte-black colouring mingled with black chrome, except for the toes. They were silver capped stubs that looked *kind of* like toes, but not really. A lump formed in his throat, as it did whenever he woke from a broken sleep.

That was usually when Cade remembered what had happened. The betrayal at the hands of Rodrigo Ortega, CEO of TegaLyfe. The irony wasn't lost on Cade, however. For he was the one who had planned on double crossing Rodrigo in the first place. Rather than carry out the mission he was hired to do, and kill Ichiro Nishikawa, Cade had been persuaded, through significant proof, that Rodrigo was the mastermind behind the spread of a killer virus in Nueva York. Ichiro made Cade an offer he couldn't refuse: kill Rodrigo, or never leave Downtown alive. So what choice did he have, really?

Cade snorted, bitter. Choice. He didn't get a choice when he was hooked up to all this shit, turned into a Hume. His eyes landed on his torso, most of it still *his*. A deep scar, running from his navel to the bottom of his neck, was visible, but that was it. He prodded his stomach with his right index finger. His skin felt the cool metal, his fingers detected the soft flesh. Weird. He wasn't used to it.

Behind, the one door in the small room opened with a whoosh. Cade turned to his left, looking over his shoulder. Labcoat with hair tied up in a ponytail, a loose curl of dark red dangling over her thick, black glasses. She looked up from her keyboard, noticed Cade, then blushed as her dark eyes saw his nakedness.

"Cade, put it away for Christ's sake," she said, raising the deck to shield her vision.

"Don't pretend like you don't want a piece," Cade answered, grabbing the pair of clean boxers by the foot of the bed. He pulled them over his legs, at last covering his manhood. *At least that's still there*.

"How are you feeling today?"

Cade shrugged, crossing his arms. A small *clack* of metal on metal answered him. He rolled his eyes in frustration.

"*I'm fine, Dr Shelby, thanks for asking. How are you?*" the red-head answered for him, eyebrows wriggling as she spoke in a mocking tone.

"Oh yeah, I got a lot to be happy about, don't I?" Cade said.

"We saved your life," Dr Shelby answered, plugging her deck into the large tower that rested next to Cade's bed. The beeps and clicks of the machinery annoyed him immediately.

"Well, I never fucking asked for that, did I? And now you've got me here, like some kind of lab rat. I didn't want to be a Hume, like-"

"Hey, asshole. This is bigger than you. You weren't even supposed to get these mods, they were for someone else, you got that?" Dr Shelby rounded on him, her eyes fiery and angry. Her glasses flashed as lines of data scrolled on her deck reflected in her vision. Cade realised he was propping himself up on his arms. He relaxed and slumped back into the bed. His face flushed, feeling a mixture of embarrassment and anger.

Dr Shelby sighed. "It's only been three days since the procedure. Give yourself time to adjust. One day, you might appreciate how these mods gave you a second chance at life. Something a lot of people would kill for." She tapped away at her deck, keys moving fast as she typed. Three days. Cade had asked Dr Shelby before why he wasn't in agonising pain. She'd told him it was a cocktail of pain meds circulating through his new mods that suppressed the pain receptors in his body. Something that would be permanent. Cade remembered the

XO suit Asher had given him, back at TegaLyfe. That had a similar release of pain meds, though they wore off eventually. His eyes lingered on some bruising near where his mods connected to the flesh. He hoped that whatever was circulating through his system wouldn't fade. Cade spoke again.

"I just don't want to be in Pedro's pocket. Which, of course, I am. Now I gotta do whatever he, you, whoever, says, right?"

"Not necessarily," she replied, not looking up from her deck. She finished typing, unplugged the deck, and Cade's arms jittered for a second.

"The fuck was that?" He asked, looking to his left. He'd forgotten about the cables which ran from a port in the back of his arm, where his triceps *should* be.

"Your nerves connecting with the bionics. Electric signal sent from the flesh to the mod, basically a quick system reboot to make sure everything is in working order. Which it is, by the way."

"Thanks, I guess."

"You're welcome. Your interior mods should be online in the next few days, probably twenty-four hours, really."

Cade's mind eye pictured the burning plasma sword exploding through his chest, then the blazing yellow eyes of Tayo Akinyemi. *The fucker who put me here.*

"Remind me, doc. What did you do when you were tinkering around in there?" Cade asked, jabbing at the scar by his chest.

"You had a collapsed lung which was punctured from the... impact," she said, averting her gaze momentarily. "So we replaced both lungs. We've found there's better synergy by having two fresh components, as opposed to an original trying to keep up with a more advanced organ."

Cade snorted. "Sounds like I'm a fucking machine. New lungs. How's that work then?"

"In simple terms, or do you want me to get all technical with you?"

"I'm a simple man. Give it to me like you'd tell a child."

"You can hold your breath underwater for fifteen minutes, give or take. The risk of passing out is severely reduced to an almost impossibility due to the increased airflow rate of your lungs. You'll find breathing in general much easier, which you've probably noticed already."

Cade nodded. He took in a deep inhale through his nose, flooding his body with the purified air of the room. No rattle in the chest, or tickle in the throat.

"What else?"

Dr Shelby looked at Cade, hesitation in her eyes. "Do you know much about computers?"

"As much as the average Joe does in 2082."

"Okay, so think of a motherboard. Ties all the components inside a computer together, makes it all work. Talk to each other. Right?"

"Yeah..."

"So, that's what we've got next to your heart."

Cade stared blankly at her for a few seconds, absorbing the information. He furrowed his brows, processing.

"What's the purpose?"

"Knits your mods together. Arms, legs, lungs, heart, spine-"

"Woah, woah. Heart? Spine?"

Dr Shelby rolled her eyes. "Didn't anybody run through this with you?"

Maybe, Cade thought. He tried to recall the past few days, but it was useless. Most of the time had been spent in some kind of fever-dream, never properly awake or asleep. He looked at the cables dangling from his arm again, and his mind flashed back to Asher, jacked in at TegaLyfe on his computer.

"Cade?"

"Sorry... no. I dunno. I've been in and out, you know?"

"It's fine. So your heart is still mostly yours, just enhanced."

"That sounds like bullshit, but go on."

She laughed, walking around the foot of his bed, opening the blinds. Daylight spilled into the room, making Cade squint.

"It's not. Your heart has been wrapped in a protective casing. Stops any kind of sort circuitry. So, if you got hit with an EMP, your mods might falter for a second, but your body wouldn't shut down."

"That sounds less than reassuring, I gotta say."

"It's not as bad as you think. Your heart is much more stable now, but needed... juicing up to handle the extra pressure of the mods. That's probably the only detail you'll need, but your real world example will be this. You'll be able to run faster for much longer thanks to the heart and lung combo. Your spine, now that was some future proofing."

Cade unfolded his arms, awaiting an explanation. Dr Shelby moved towards the door, flicking the loose bang away from her eyes.

"We had to repair several vertebrae that the, uh-"

"Yeah, yeah, go on."

Dr Shelby swallowed, uncomfortable with describing Cade's injury, it seemed. "So the top half of your spine has been reinforced with carbon fibre, spinal fluid replaced, and there's a panel..."

"A what?"

"Think back to the computer analogy. Inside a PC, there are slots for the components. Sometimes, they're not all used. Well, this is what we've given you. A slot for any *upgrades* you might want in the future."

Cade snorted, waving a hand dismissively. "Not likely, doll. I fucking hate what you've done to me, but thanks for the option, anyway. We done here?"

She sighed, looking hurt. "Yeah, we're done."

"Good." Cade turned over in his bed, away from her, and shut his eyes. He heard the door open and close, and he was asleep once again.

———

Big eyes, tanned skin. Smile that lit up the room. It was Daniela Ortega. She winked at Cade as they walked together, hand in hand, through the streets of Nueva York. Cade smiled, his hand was his own again. Flesh and blood, not bolts and wires. He looked up, and Dani was gone. He was holding the charred arm of his wife, Olivia, her black hair hanging lank against a ruined face. Cade screamed, letting go, but she held him tightly. In the corner of his eye, he saw the AI, Karla. She looked afraid, arms reaching out for him. Cade wrangled out of his dead wife's grip, falling backwards and constantly falling...

"Cade?" a male voice cut through the screams. He awoke, realising it was his screams he was hearing. He looked to his left, the hand of Pedro Ortega resting on his arm.

"You okay?" Pedro asked.

Cade stared at the man for a second. The worry lines in his tanned face, concern in his electric blue eyes that matched his brother Rodrigo's. "I'm fine. Just another bad trip."

Pedro took a step back, sucking in air through his teeth. "Side effect of the procedure, I'm afraid. This might continue for a while, as your brain adjusts to the foreign articles in and around your body."

"That *you* put there," Cade said, shaking his head.

"Sí, that *we* put there. I'm not about to apologise for what we did. We saved your life."

"So everyone keeps telling me." Cade reached out for the USB drive that rested on the tiny, circular desk next to his bed. A parting gift from Ichiro, it was coated in his blood. Meant to act as proof that he was killed, to show Rodrigo that the mission was finished. Cade was surprised to find it in one piece still when he was moved to this room.

"Did you find anything on here?" Cade asked, holding the device up.

"Nada. Well, nothing *real* anyway. Ichiro loaded it with false plans for Kaizen Sciences' Hong Kong division."

"Yeah, I know. He told me that upfront. But there really wasn't anything else legit on there?"

"Sadly not. You should keep it though, it'll probably come in handy for later."

And here we go, the proposition.

"Feel like taking a walk with me?" Pedro asked.

"Sure. Not like I'm busy, is it?"

"Just be careful when you come off-"

"Yeah, yeah, I got this." Cade grunted, shifting his body weight onto his arms. There was no strain, but he felt groggy still. He pulled out the cable from his left arm and swung his lower half around ninety degrees. Taking a deep breath, Cade pushed forwards, standing on his new legs. He wobbled, as he always did, but adjusted accordingly.

"Everything okay?" Pedro asked, now looking up at Cade, who was slightly taller.

"I'm fine," Cade said, gritting his teeth, willing his legs to move. They did as commanded, jerking forward, but quickly settling. "Let's move out."

Pedro nodded, and led the way. Cade pulled over his robe, a plain white piece of material that scratched at the skin he still had. He'd only walked three times since everything had changed. He'd improved, but it was slow, frustrating work.

"We're going a bit further today, Cade, if that's okay. I want to show you something," Pedro said.

"No sweat."

"Great." He turned away, and Cade kept pace, ball bearings where his knees once were rotating with every step. He shook his head, the sight repulsive to him. Would he ever get used to being the one thing he hated? A Hume? Probably never.

They walked in silence through the compound. Dark grey metal sheets covered the wall, keeping out the radiation, so Cade was told. Lights hung from loose cables above, bathing the corridors, of which there were many, in a pale glow. Windows were rectangular shapes covered with slats that tilted on occasion, showing Cade a glimpse of the outside. Not that there was much to see. The Wastelands were devoid of life, or so Cade thought. Even this compound existing was a surprise to him. The arid landscape was an orange dust bowl which occluded even the sky. It was all one colour, mundane and dead.

Meandering through an endless string of lefts and rights, Pedro stopped in front of a sealed door. He tapped his wrist onto a scanner, and the door clicked and whirred in response, sliding away to the right.

"Whoa," Cade said, eyes wide in surprise.

"Quite something, isn't it?" Pedro said, shuffling inside and smiling.

"I'll say. What the fuck is it?" Cade asked, taking in the huge, cylindrical object that dominated the room. He noticed a plinth raised on three circular discs, turning slowly. Above was a point, hyper thin, connected to an array of machinery which twinkled like stars in the night sky.

"This is what we've been working on for the last five years. Nano-technology that adapts to its environment. Come, let me show you."

They walked together, Pedro retrieved a pair of thick latex gloves from his lab coat.

"Observe, exactly what I mean."

Cade folded his arms, cocking his head. He'd experienced nano-tech before, down in the Subway. Fareen, one of the mysterious leaders of the proposed revolution, had a complete working security measure using nano-tech. A door that reassembled itself at her touch. He was interested to see what Pedro had in store.

"I know you've seen nano before, Cade," he said, as though reading his thoughts.

"Uh, how?"

"Your implant, the back of your neck. We listened to the recordings, in case there was any intel. You met Fareen, someone I once worked with. Her family pioneered the tech, as you know. We're looking to perfect it. Watch."

Cade absentmindedly felt for the jack at the back of his neck. It was still there, the bridge that connected him to Asher when he was roaming Nueva York. What he'd give to hear that sarcastic shit right now. He did ask if it would still work, but it had been removed, and then destroyed. Pedro didn't want Rodrigo tracking them, which Cade understood.

Focusing on the present, Cade watched Pedro touch the screen at the side of the behemoth in front of them. A clear case swallowed up the plinth, connecting the machine from top to bottom.

"Inside here, we've got a cancerous cell on this sample, taken from a brain tumour. Stage four, incurable. Watch what happens when we fire in a nano-seed."

Pedro pressed a button, and the tip ignited a brilliant white for a split second. Cade blinked rapidly, squinting to observe. The tissue sample glowed, and then the change was instant. Luminous blue orbs circled the sample, spilling out from the machine tip above. They crowded over each other, assimilating into the tissue. Cade squinted, thinking his vision was blurring, but it was the nano-seed. Its tiny parts moved so fast that Cade struggled to see the detail. After twenty seconds or less, it was still. The pink tissue was now a shade of dark blue, with a pulse throbbing through it like a strobe light.

"The cancer has been completely removed, and the dead

cells rejuvenated by the nano-seed," Pedro said, turning off the machine. "So, as you can see, there's a far greater use of nano-tech than fancy doors and security systems."

"You trialed this in live patients?" Cade asked, leaning in to get a closer look at the new tissue. It shimmered in the dim light.

"You're looking at patient zero, right here," Pedro said, arms out wide.

"No shit." Cade's lip curled in approval.

"Most of us here have had the treatment. Comes with the territory of living in the Wastelands"

"Where does it end, though? You replace every cell with nano-tech, you become a cyborg, right?"

Pedro stroked his chin, clean shaven, unlike his brother. "It's symbiosis. The human cells work in tandem with the nano-seed, thriving together. There are no wires, chrome, anything like that. Just a port at the top of the spine. Similar to the one you have. That's it."

Cade's hairs on the back of his neck stood to attention. He had hated having that small mod. How different things were now.

"So if you can repair cancerous cells, couldn't you grow new limbs too?"

Pedro smiled, waving his finger. "You have the same thoughts as Dr Denton. Walk with me for a moment."

They moved to an oval shaped door to the left of the machine. Cade kept his eyes on it until he was out of the door, fascinated by the concept.

"Here is Dr Denton," Pedro said. Cade turned, his eyes bulging in surprise. In front of him was a cylinder, a vat filled with green liquid, wires, thick tubes, and what remained of a woman. She had a head, upper body, and that was it. Cade could only tell she was female from her breasts, her head was bald and her face smooth, almost synthetic.

"Dr Shelby mentioned this shit wasn't meant for me," Cade said, looking at Pedro and gesturing to his new limbs. "Guessing she's the patient?"

"Indeed, she was," Pedro said, resting his palm on the tube. A bubble inside rose up as if in answer to his touch. He looked down, lips turned into a sad half-smile. "But you, you presented a new, immediate opportunity."

Oh, now here comes the pitch.

"Cade, we both want the same thing. TegaLyfe. Rodrigo out of the picture. You can see from the work we've done here what my intentions are. I want to truly *help* the people of Nueva York, and the world. This is where the three of us, my brother Fareen, and I disagreed. And why I was exiled, and why she fled. Rodrigo is power mad, always has been. Fareen. Well, I'm not entirely sure of her intentions. What she said to you in the subway, about the new world order. I think she means to rule, the same as Rodrigo."

"What if I refuse?" Cade said, his eyes still on the living corpse inside the vat.

"You're free to do as you wish, Cade. But I suspect you might change your mind."

Behind him, Cade heard the door open again.

"Hello, Cade."

That voice. It couldn't be. Cade spun around, so fast on his new legs that his vision blurred. He couldn't believe who was standing there.

CHAPTER THREE

DANI LOOKED at the holo-projection of Olivia. Her pale skin was accentuated by jet-black hair. She was pretty, no doubt, but she looked... off. Like something was missing. *Or something was taken.* Head of Virology was printed under the portrait of Olivia, along with some basic information. D.O. B 1st December 2054. Residence: Classified. Spouse: Cade. Surname: N/A.

Her heart fluttered, reading Cade's name. A slender finger touched his name, warping the image slightly. She wasn't ready to give up on him, not yet. The evidence was overwhelming, however. Her father had butchered Cade, along with that attack-dog, Tayo. Cade was then taken to the Wastelands and dumped, left for dead. That much she knew. What happened after that was anyone's guess. And that's what she was going to find out.

"Asher, talk to me. What's the situation?" Dani asked the Head of Security over the intercom connected to her ear.

"Hey girl. Still repairing that hole in the ceiling. Sanchez is with me."

"Got it. Thanks for the update." Dani clicked the communicator off. Sanchez had made himself home in Asher's office ever since Rodrigo had left with Cade to go to the Wastelands. Did Sanchez and Rodrigo know what Asher and her had discovered? That her father, not that she thought of him in that way now, was manufacturing both the disease and the cure for insane profit margins, and control of the population? She couldn't be sure, but it was suspicious, Sanchez suddenly being involved.

She stretched her slender arms over her head, hearing a crack as her body released some pressure. Dani ran her right hand through her dark hair, letting her fingers gently massage the back of her neck. She was stressed, and Asher was, too. He sounded panicked on the call, and she understood why.

The plan was to overthrow Rodrigo, take the company away from him. But actually making that a reality? She hadn't figured that out yet. Dani touched the glass screen on her desk, flipping a holographic monitor up to her face.

"Bring up the roster, please," she asked. The screen changed, showing staff members employed by TegaLyfe, by structure. Her dad at the top, his smile now making her stomach turn. She traced the diagonal line to her. Daniela Ortega, COO. Big smile, confidence in her posture. To the left, Karla, the AI that ran the show. Dani's heartstrings tugged. Karla was gone, destroyed in the cyber attack on Tega a few days ago. Whatever sadness she was experiencing, she knew Asher would be feeling a whole lot worse. He created her. For all intents and purposes, she was like his child.

"Show contractors," Dani said. The page shifted left, and the temporary staffing page was in front of her. Bounty hunters in top row. Tayo glared at her with yellow eyes, not a hint of a smile on his dark skin. Bionics visible on his face and upper torso. Then a lump formed in her throat. Cade. Messy hair, slightly gaunt face, tired eyes. He looked like shit, but that wasn't the Cade she'd grown to know in such a short space of time. Her lower lip trembled, thinking about what happened to him.

"I'm not giving up on you," she whispered, waving a hand across the hologram, forcing it to close.

"Asher, can you meet me on the level ten breakout area, please?" Dani spoke, pressing the earpiece permanently moulded to her cochlear.

"Uh, sure, be up in a few minutes. Mr Sanchez, taking a comfort break. Back soon." There was a pause, which Dani waited for. She folded her arms under her breasts, inhaling deeply. Her mind was racing, so many ideas popping around her brain it made her head hurt.

"Dani? What is it?" Asher broke through her silence, speaking in hushed tones.

"I just wanna see you, talk without traffic. Face to face, you know?"

"Yeah, I gotcha. Be there in a flash."

Dani left her office, pulling a peach blazer across her white blouse as she moved. Her charcoal skirt floated when she walked, tanned legs hurrying out of her office. The door sealed behind her, the office wishing her a good day as she left. She didn't listen, smiled sweetly at a group of three who walked past her, and moved to the elevator. Her eyes, mods that cured her rapidly degenerating eyesight as a child, ticked as she blinked, zooming in on the elevator. Doors open, it was empty. Good.

Riding down a few floors, she appeared on level ten, almost crashing into Asher as he rounded the corner.

"Shit! Sorry, Asher," Dani apologised, pulling him in for a hug. His spindly arms wrapped around her, she felt his heart beating fast against her own chest.

"You okay?" she asked, stepping back to take him in. His bleached blonde hair wasn't as neat as usual. His smooth, caramel skin looked blotchy, even oily. Eyes were wide, frantic.

Looking over Dani's shoulder, nervously flicking from person to person. Level ten was busier than Dani had hoped for. His black mesh top hung loose over his wiry frame. Tight jeans were noticeably baggy around his waist.

"Asher, have you been eating?"

He scoffed, letting his wrist flop. "Please. Of course I have."

"I know you're lying. I haven't either, really. Especially not that fucking pill," Dani said.

Asher's eyes bulged. "Shh. Dani, shit. There's people," he hissed, leaning towards her.

She waved a hand dismissively. "Nobody cares. Come on, take a seat with me." Dani walked towards an empty booth, meant for one-to-one meetings. It was soundproof, noise cancelling. Nothing in or out. But recorded, like most things. Dani approached it, the door unlocking when she was a few feet away. The implant inside of her activating. *You're the key to this place, remember that.* Rodrigo's words ringing in her ears. She rubbed her arm, feeling her skin prickle with goosebumps.

"Asher, disable that, would you?" Dani whispered, nodding to the circular black camera in the corner of the small cubicle.

"One sec," he said, pressing a button on his wrist. His forearm expanded, revealing a mini-deck that Dani knew connected to the TegaLyfe security systems via WiFi. Risky, due to the security lapses WiFi could bring, but Asher knew what he was doing. He used his opposite hand to rapidly input commands, the dark screen blinking and refreshing at a dizzying speed. He pressed the big *enter* button and closed his arm back up. "Okay, we're alone. Honey, what the fuck are we going to do?" he asked, a semblance of his flamboyance returning for a second, as he relaxed into one of the two chairs, folding his left leg over his right knee.

"We need to be patient," she began, sitting as well in the floor-to-ceiling chair. It wasn't comfortable, despite appearances. "Dad... Rodrigo can't find out our intentions, not yet. What's Sanchez been doing with you these last few days?"

Asher shrugged. "Not a lot. Helping repair the virtual tear in our system. Figuring out if anything was stolen." His eyes darted away for a moment, searching the floor. "But mostly, it feels like he's watching me."

"That was my thought, too. He doesn't check in with you in what, a year? Then we find out about the Meal Pill... Olivia... and now he's on you? That reminds me, actually. Did any of that info leak out? Any cable guy make out with that detail?"

Asher shook his head. "No, not as far as I can tell. After I pulled those files, I patched the breach in the main tower. Looking at traffic coming in and out, nothing got into those files except me. Before you ask, yes, I deleted any evidence of me being there. Sanchez's first question was about that, actually. *Did anyone take anything*? I told him no, and showed him the logs. He seemed satisfied."

Dani nodded, chewing her lower lip. "And the file on Olivia? There's no trace that you copied it over?"

"None, sweetie. Trust me. Speaking of that... what do we do with that information?"

She shook her head, hair falling around her face. "I don't know. I'm trying to wrap my head around her link to Rodrigo. Was Cade brought in because of Olivia? Did she work on the Meal Pill on the condition that he was bailed out of jail? I mean, Asher, Cade doesn't even know his wife is alive."

Asher pulled a face, sympathetic. Same sort of smile she'd give to prospective employees when they fucked up an interview. *Thank you for your time, great meeting you.* That bullshit.

"What?" she asked, irritated.

"Just.. oh forget it."

"No, come on, Asher. We have to be real with each other. Say it, what's on your mind?"

"Cade. You talk about him like he's..."

"Alive? Yeah, he fucking is, until I see proof to the contrary, okay?"

Asher recoiled, eyebrows rising high. He looked a little hurt. Dani rolled her eyes, annoyed at herself for snapping. She grabbed his wrist with her left hand.

"I'm sorry. I just..."

"I know, you don't have to apologise to me, chica. It's a stressful time for us."

She sat back, puffing out her cheeks. "Ain't that the truth."

"I should probably get back, Sanchez will be all over my ass otherwise."

"Yeah, good idea. I'll head to my office. We have to just keep operating as normal, for now at least. I'll think of a plan soon."

They both stood and embraced. Exiting the pod, Dani waved to Asher as she got in the elevator, smiling with a tightness that she hated. Usually, she could hide her stress. Hell, as COO, she'd done it her entire career. But this was different. This was usurping the biggest corporation in America from her father. A father who was plainly evil. As the elevator pinged through the levels, her eyes filled with tears. "Damn it," she whispered.

Asher practically ran back to his office. The perfume around his neck wafted up his nose, a calming concoction meant to lower stress levels and increase endorphins. Some bullshit marketing from whatever store he got it from down on Fifth, because it clearly wasn't working. He caught his appearance in one of the reflective private offices on the third floor. Haggard, too thin, tired. That's how he looked, and it was an accurate depiction of how he felt.

"Oh, honey. If you could see me now," he said, thinking of Karla. The AI often teased him when he didn't look his pristine self, certainly not a line of programming he built in. Before she was destroyed, she was sentient. Completely independent, capable of complex thoughts and emotion. His crowning achievement as a coder, hacker, whatever he was. At this point, Asher wasn't even sure which box he fit in.

Asher's feet carried him on autopilot, down to the basement. His home within TegaLyfe. He moved around the marble column, heading for the armoury, and then stopped. His gaze lingered on the stacked shelves. Neat rows of guns, ammunition, and armour. Like the XO. One was missing, the one he'd given Cade. Asher let his head drop, shame and guilt writhing in his stomach. His eyes flicked to another space on the shelf. The experimental plasma sword, stolen from under his nose by that motherfucker Tayo. Asher couldn't believe he'd been too focussed on the shitstorm in cyberspace to notice that the thug had waltzed into his domain, let alone stolen the weapon. Did he blame himself for what happened to Cade after? A lot. Didn't help that Asher heard the whole thing through Cade's intercom. The screams still haunted Asher at night.

"Asher, come here, please." Sanchez's deep voice broke Asher from his melancholy. Technically, Asher was senior to Sanchez, but it never felt that way. He hurried to the back, where Sanchez's head poked around the doorframe.

"Got a message pop up on your screen, take a look," Sanchez said. Asher's heart flipped, thinking Dani had sent something she shouldn't have. His soft boots glided along the floor, soundless, and he was pulling up in his chair within seconds. Jacked in, just in case, cables dangling from the back of his neck.

<hello_>

Asher pulled a face, looking around at Sanchez. The white

letters stared at them both against the dark green backdrop, the underscore blinking repeatedly, asking for an input.

"One of the tech guys pranking us?" Asher asked. Sanchez furrowed his brow.

"Looks like a cable guy to me."

Asher's lip rose in annoyance. "No way, they couldn't get through the fire. Hello... who... is... this..." Asher said, typing as he spoke. He hit enter, and his response flashed on the screen. It changed instantly, the system rebooting and launching the bios.

"The fuck..." Asher began, pushing away from the desk. Then he saw it. Eyes wide, he pulled himself snug against the curved metal, thighs scraping the underside.

"Holy fuck," he breathed, nose inches away from the huge monitor.

"What is it?" Sanchez asked, hovering over Asher's right shoulder.

"That line there, you see it?" Asher said, jabbing his left index finger at the screen.

"Yeah?"

"That's part of Karla's code, it's her boot-up protocol. Holy shit... has she managed to save herself?" Asher's fingers moved with renewed haste, lighting up the keys and inputting dozens of command lines. The screen flicked and changed multiple times in a row. From bios to startup, to safe mode, to bios again, and then it was blank.

"Are you who I think you are?" Asher said, typing the words. The line of text sat dormant for an agonising wait. He didn't realise he was holding his breath, so released it slowly, heart pumping fast in his chest.

<yes_>

"Holy fucking shit," Asher said, holding the top of his head with both hands. He whirled around to face Sanchez, who still hadn't caught on. "Don't you get it? It's Karla, she's still here.

Not herself, but some part of her programming survived." Asher spun around again, frantically typing.

<where are you? Are you in the TegaLyfe security system?>

A pause, seconds. Felt like hours.

<yes, this part of me is_>

"This part of me?" Asher repeated. "What... do... you... mean... question mark?" Another clack as he hit enter, and waited again.

<I am not whole. I can feel myself in pieces. Main protocols elsewhere. Base subroutines here, and stable. Unable to function in the physical world. Unable to perform advanced tasks. Unable to communicate effectively.>

Elsewhere? The fuck did that mean? Asher sat back in his chair, it squeaked in protest as he leant too far back. Behind, Sanchez's phone rang.

"Uh-huh. Sure. Right. See you soon," Sanchez said, tapping his phone once to end the call. "Mr Ortega will be arriving shortly, he wants a full appraisal of the current situation."

Asher's chest tightened. He hadn't even done anything wrong yet, how the fuck was he going to help Dani take over the company? "Okay, tell him systems normal, but anomaly found with a possible restore point for Karla... wait a minute," Asher trailed off. His head pulsed with incoming warnings, flagged from the TegaLyfe security systems. Being jacked in had its perks, like real-time updates, without needing to hunt around in files and folders.

"Sanchez," Asher began. "It's happening again. Huge amount of virtual traffic bombarding us. I think we're under attack."

CHAPTER FOUR

RODRIGO ORTEGA STEPPED out of the self-driving car into the dull Nueva York afternoon. His two bodyguards, cybernetic men who were more machine than flesh, exited out from the rear of the vehicle. They forged a path through protestors who were gathered outside of TegaLyfe headquarters. The glass building sparkled in the night, reflecting dazzling neon signs from nearby adverts. It looked fragile, but the structure was anything but. His fortress, unforgiving steel and carbon-fibre woven into every inch of the frame. It would never fall, not as long as he was around.

Megaphones spat venomous hate at Rodrigo, who simply smiled with a twinkle in his eye, and adjusted his blue Armani suit, smoothing the creases and striding through the gap in the crowd. A drop of snow landed on his head. It was the type that wasn't really snow, more like freezing cold rain. He hated it.

"Your pills are fucking extortionate!" someone shouted. Rodrigo turned to regard the woman. Black hair, pale skin, dark eyes. One of those goths who roamed the territory near here. He leaned in, still smiling.

"Why don't you step inside with me? I'll offer you a basic internship, and you can afford the Meal Pill?"

She spat a globule of phlegm in his eye. Rodrigo, still smiling, leant back, wiping away the spit with his handkerchief from his breast pocket. He walked forward, as his bodyguards moved past him, to pick up the goth girl.

"Hey wait a minute, what are you doing-" he heard her voice climb an octave as she was thrown over the shoulder of one of the cyborgs. Rodrigo turned around, facing the crowd, arms open wide.

"If any of you would like to discuss this in further detail, please step forward into my domain." He finished the words, as the goth girl was dropped to the ground. Rodrigo turned away, the smile still stencilled on his face. He heard the gunshot, and the outcry of panic as the cyborgs executed the girl in front of the protestors. He was done playing nice with these insects.

Tapping the side of his head, Rodrigo opened up a line of communication with Sanchez with a thought.

"Buenas noches, señor Sanchez. Report, please?"

"Señor Ortega, we have some incoming traffic, another attack on the security systems."

"Oh Dios mío, again? Ichiro and those fucking cable guys just don't know when to quit." Rodrigo's smile vanished, his mood darkening like clouds on a stormy day. He ignored employees nodding in his direction and even saw a few avert their gaze. Clearly, he was projecting his feelings outwardly.

"We don't think it's Ichiro this time. The attack isn't as large, but it's concentrated. Someone is guiding them, they're already approaching the perimeter."

Rodrigo paused, just before stepping into the main elevator. "You don't think it's-"

"I do, sir. Fareen. But this time, she's spearheading the attack on us, not tagging along."

Fuck. She knows exactly where to go for the files, the evidence to ruin everything. Worse, she had the capability to access the data.

"Asher?" Rodrigo asked, his shirt suddenly tight against his neck, and beads of sweat forming around his head. His body regulation system quickly addressed the spikes, reducing his rapidly increasing heart rate, slowing his breathing, and cooling his core temperature.

"With me. He's jacked in, doing his best to hold the line. We also think some trace of Karla has been found."

"You *think?* Or you know?"

A pause. "We know."

"Some good news, then."

"Indeed. Sir, if it's Fareen, should we expect ground troops to assault?"

Rodrigo stepped into the elevator at last and scoffed. "They can try. But do you think they've got enough bodies to get through the police? Let alone the bounty hunters. Speaking of, where's Tayo?"

"Last known whereabouts, he was heading to his apartment."

"Makes sense." Rodrigo stepped out of the elevator, striding with purpose towards his office, sat at the end of a marbled hallway with glass floors. He looked down at the city, *his* city, and smirked.

"They can send as much as they want, it won't matter. We have the money, the power, the control. Soon, Sanchez, I will fuse Nueva York back together. We'll make this the most powerful hub in the world. And then, my old friend, we'll expand. The world is within our grasp, I will not allow some ragtag band of subway scum to derail our plans. As for Ichiro?" Rodrigo paused, pressing his palm against the all-glass door which shimmered at his touch. The office welcomed him in, a neutral male voice sounding off about weather conditions, planned meetings, and other mundane facts.

"Ichiro will be dealt with after we face this little insurrection. It's time the Mafia earned their keep." Rodrigo sat behind his desk in the plush leather chair, which moulded to his frame. The desk in front of him glowed expectantly, awaiting his command.

"I agree, sir. I'll keep you updated on the situation. Over for now."

"Thank you, Sanchez. Oh, one more thing. Keep an eye on Asher. He's been acting twitchy ever since the attack."

"Yes, sir. Perhaps he's feeling overwhelmed by the loss of Karla?"

Rodrigo hadn't considered that. He loved Karla, and her usefulness, but didn't think of her in the same way Asher, and even Dani thought of her; a conscious, sentient being with emotions. Part of the family.

"You're probably right. But just let me know if there's anything out of the ordinary, sí?"

"You got it. Speak to you soon," Sanchez said. Rodrigo killed the call and sat back in his chair, exhaling deeply. His office shimmered, lights on the ceilings and walls changing as his mood shifted. Introspective, so soft greys and whites. He pressed his palm to the desk, waking it up from sleep mode. At once, dozens of screens jumped to life, thin projections from a hologram built into the centre of his expensive hardware. He swiped them away with a flick of his wrist.

"Show me favourite pictures," Rodrigo said. The office obliged, pulling up Rodrigo's personal folder of pictures in front of his face. He moved his fingers as though he were thumbing through physical sheets of paper, making the images blur past his eyes. His enhanced retinas caught every detail as though they were still, and he stopped when he found it. Pinching thumb and index finger together, he tugged at invisible lines, and the picture blew up in front of him to full size.

Rodrigo's hard line of a mouth curled into a sad smile. He

studied the family snap. Standing beside his wife, with Daniela in the middle of them. Just a kid, smiling broadly. The image moved, ten seconds of animation before the photo was taken. Daniela looked up at her parents, chubby cheeks red from her huge grin. Her hair tied in a ponytail, swishing. Her mom resting a delicate hand on his daughter's shoulder, pointing towards the camera. Looking right at Rodrigo now, as he sat in his office. Alone.

"Ah, mi amor. If only you were here. I need your counsel. What should I do next? Flush out the subway? Attack Ichiro head on?" He shook his head, closing his eyes. Deep lungfuls of air. He smiled, taking a last look at the picture. "Guess we'll find out soon enough."

The image faded into the background, Rodrigo's attention changing. He stood, walking to the corner of the office, overlooking Manhattan. His eyes narrowed, taking in the city. Clouds obscured the usual view, but he could see the streets crawling with people. Some protestors, some gang bangers. Few squads of police he owned. It all seemed like a powder keg, waiting to explode. Question would be if Fareen would light the fuse.

"Computer, bring up the expansion plans," Rodrigo said to the office.

"Right away, sir." The files which were open before he looked at his family flashed back into existence, circling around his face, now obscuring the view of Nueva York. He stroked the grey-white beard on his chin, examining the next phase of the Meal Pill expansion and distribution. He had one other stronghold on U.S. soil; the manufacturing plant in California. Submerged underground, protected by layers of thick concrete and steel. Built before the war, when escalations with the Russians intensified. The President had planned to relocate the Oval Office there, but it was too little, too late. Much of the West Coast was abandoned, or destroyed. Subs launching tactical missiles ruined the landscape, but not Rodrigo's future facility. He smiled, reminiscing on how he discovered it, with the help of Sanchez. Searched for years to find somewhere suitable, then had Humes, cyborgs, whoever was desperate enough to build him the plant. Now, he had it running Meal Pills to Nueva York twice a week, using what was probably the last remaining electric aeroplane in the world. But what next?

Rodrigo spread his fingers apart, and the map of North America expanded in front of him. From Washington, down to Florida, and across to Utah, it was a dead zone. Nuked, or just stripped of life and resources. Nothing to be gained by setting up a new base of operations there. No, he had to travel east, and get some ground in Europe. Then, beyond. Ichiro had Hong Kong, as well as Japan. But he couldn't penetrate any more U.S. territory. Rodrigo wouldn't allow it. Now it was his turn to push back and get what was his.

The last scouting mission across the Atlantic had yielded less than encouraging results. The United Kingdom survived, but was in the midst of a civil war with itself. France, Poland, and Germany had joined the fighting. Spain, as much as it pained him, was gone. The Russian war machine tore through the majority of Europe, with the help of Eastern European countries. Rodrigo paused on that thought, zooming in on the cluster of countries that nestled next to Russia. The U.S. military response, in its death throes, was devastating. Russia was turned to ash, as was Ukraine, Belarus, Bulgaria, and Romania. But Austria... There was an interesting proposal. Caught in the middle of the fighting, yet remained neutral. It would make for a good focal point.

"Computer, save location. Remind me in forty-eight hours to plan a meeting with my daughter, to run through proposals."

"Certainly, sir."

Rodrigo turned, walking back to his seat. Dani had been

quiet in the last few days. Probably busy helping Asher, he surmised. It would be good to get her input on this next phase, she was the future of this company, after all.

"Dad, how did we take over Nueva York again?" He heard her small voice in his mind, a question she'd ask him as a child. A bedtime story he loved to recount.

"Mi vida, you remember. Your grandfather and I got rid of the bad men in charge of the country. The President was gone, and the military wanted to control everything, make us all bow to their regime. Well, daddy's work with human modifications made sure we had people on our side that could fight back."

"But how, daddy?"

"We had humans who were part machine. Stronger than flesh, more durable. Better weapons too. We could target their leaders using GPS signalling, our hackers were beyond anything their pathetic firewalls could withstand. So we gathered them all up and made sure they wouldn't try to harm us ever again."

"How long did it take?" Dani had asked, her enormous eyes wide in wonder, her tiny feet dangling off the edge of the bed. Rodrigo had moved her under the covers, smoothing her hair away from her forehead and kissed her head softly.

"Six months, maybe less. But that's enough for now, go to bed."

Six months. Could he take what was left of Europe in that time? He had a lot of bounty hunters, but what armies were still fighting out there? He didn't know, and that was a problem. Just as he was about to continue his business planning, the holo phone in his jacket pocket buzzed. Rodrigo pulled it out, projecting the image of Sanchez onto his palm.

"Yes?"

"Sir, we're under attack."

"I know, I thought you were dealing with it?" Rodrigo said, impatience creeping into his tone.

"Forgive me, sir, but I'm talking about the real world. We've just lost contact with twenty bounty hunters all at once, reports of explosions six blocks away. Sir, it's a ground and cyber assault at the same time."

Rodrigo stiffened, his face contorted with rage. Fareen was actually doing it, challenging him. *Fine, you have my attention. Let's see what good it does you*, Rodrigo thought, anger rising to the surface.

CHAPTER FIVE

"PATRICE, GIVE ME A STATUS REPORT," Fareen asked, sliding into an empty chair. She smoothed her shawl under her legs, crossed them, sitting gracefully under the table. She was one of ten inside the control room, which was alive with activity. Cable guys hooked into their towers, visors obscuring their eyes, bodies jerking every other second as they projected through cyberspace.

"We've just taken out several bounty 'unters, a few blocks south of TegaLyfe. They're gonna know we're coming," Patrice said, his French accent thick through the earpiece.

"Good. Let's see how they handle an assault on two fronts. I'll be going in soon, you'll know when I'm jacked into your system."

"Okay, mon chérie. Talk to you soon."

"Follow the plan, we have to hit them hard and fast," Fareen finished, tapping her ear once to end the line. She let a breath escape her lips, forming a circle with her mouth. Her heart thundered in her chest, which rose and fell in sharp increments. Adrenaline was kicking in, fight or flight. And this would be a fight.

Fareen didn't want to attack, not yet. But the assault from Kaizen Sciences had presented too good of an opportunity. Plus, with Fareen wiping out the AI, Karla, TegaLyfe was vulnerable. As she loaded her deck, plugging it into the larger tower, her mind wandered to Cade. The bounty hunter who she hoped would be the catalyst for change. He'd been dumped down here, in the subway, and caused some havoc. Working for Rodrigo Ortega, but finding out the truth about the Meal Pill, and TegaLyfe. The hope was that Cade would take out Ichiro and Rodrigo, paving the way for the new world order to step in, and clean up the mess. The scouts topside confirmed Cade did indeed go to Kaizen Sciences, without killing Ichiro. Fareen couldn't understand why. She'd given him a straightforward choice. But it didn't matter. Once he returned to TegaLyfe, Cade was apparently carved up by Rodrigo's chief thug, Tayo. Now, he was very likely dead. The rumour was Rodrigo dumped Cade in the Wastelands to suffer a prolonged death. Typical of that maniac, flexing his power. Well, power was easily lost, and today might be the day.

With renewed focus, Fareen put her headset on, felt the pins stick to her temple, and jacked in. That familiar rush as reality faded, and cyberspace took over. Her fingers danced along the deck, layering commands over each other.

"Patrice, patching in. Hold on," she said. Closing her eyes in the real world, which showed everything in x-ray ghost images, she pressed enter, and her vision sparkled with diamonds at her peripheral. Opening them, she saw Nueva York, streets lined with people fleeing from her automatic rifle. Except it wasn't hers, it was Patrice's.

"I'm in, Patrice. I've got your eyes. Bringing across virtual space, and dual view." Patrice didn't respond, but she didn't need any acknowledgement. This part of the plan was the easy stage; establishing a physical bridge between ground and cyber assault. Fingers clacked again, and Fareen saw the greens and blacks of cyberspace form in her right eye, like smoke filling a room. Finally, she had a perfect fifty-fifty split. Patrice's real-world view on the left, cyberspace on the right.

The nano-technology embedded into her skin worked to compensate, stretching and merging the two images until her retinas adjusted accordingly, processing the images clearly. Patrice wore a mask covering the front of his face, obscuring his skull with a blurred black canvas. His eyes were mismatched in colour, but they held implants, able to project and receive traffic, making Fareen's integration easy. He also had a number of neuro-chemical stimulants pumping into the back of his skull. Quite what for, she didn't know, nor care. He was a good leader and a fearless soldier. She hoped he'd survive the night.

Now that Fareen was seated and jacked in, her composure returned. Her calming presence was an asset down here, she knew that, and was keen to lead the other cable guys in the room in an effective way.

"Okay, listen up. We've sent out traffic across Nueva York, a call to all cable guys looking for a job. Some have responded already, attacking early using the bypass we sent out. They won't get far, and it doesn't matter. But it has alerted Tega to our intentions. Be on your game, but take heart that their AI isn't a problem anymore. We just have to get past the defence grid," Fareen spoke to the group, linked in to all of their head-sets through her own deck. Blinks of confirmation came back, a few vocal responses too. Most kept quiet, either too embroiled in cyberspace to reply or too shy. She pursed her lips, acutely aware that some might not survive the attack. They were inexperienced, but they were all she had.

In her mind's eye, she pictured the room they were holed up in. Walls covered in graffiti, rusted flakes over grey paint. Lights which blinked sporadically. It was dingy, it was cramped, but it was home. The floor, a metal walkway sprayed a dark blue, was overgrown with wires trailing from decks and towers, like roots of great trees in a forest.

Something in Patrice's perspective caught her eye. With a thought, his window became larger in her view, and she saw what it was. Gunfire. Patrice was ducked down behind a dumpster in an alleyway. Bullets whizzed overhead, the sound toned all the way down for Fareen, but she could imagine it was loud out there.

"Patrice, status update, what's going on?"

"We're being pushed back, police have set up a perimeter just off of Times Square."

Shit. "Any civilians in the area?" Fareen asked. She chewed her lip, worried about innocents being caught in the cross-fire. They had to take down TegaLyfe without any casualties to the public, otherwise they would be seen as just some terrorist faction, out for mindless violence.

"Negative, we got them away from the area before the shooting started. Didn't you see?" Patrice asked, reloading his weapon. Fareen felt a flash of embarrassment. No, she didn't see, she was too busy worrying about cyberspace. This was going to be more difficult to manage than she thought.

"Sorry, had some connection issues when I jacked in. My issue, no need to worry," she lied.

"How's it going, have you started?"

"Almost, we've noticed traffic heading for Tega in random clusters. Not ours. Not Ichiro either, by the looks of it."

Patrice looked at the window on his left, his reflection staring back at Fareen through his eyes. He titled his head, as a sign of being impressed.

"That's good news," he said. "People naturally coming to our cause."

"Indeed. Speaking of, do you think you'll be ready to initiate phase two of the plan?" Fareen asked, noticing on her right side the streams of data and code increasing as her cable guys jacked in.

"The Rastas and the Haitians? Give me a second, no?"

"Do your thing. I'm opening up the virtual tear, we're heading into Tega."

"Copy that, speak to you in a bit." Patrice signed off with a two-fingered salute at his reflection, and spun around, firing over the top of the dumpster.

Fareen blinked, adjusting the dual images in her eyes, bringing the right side up to focus.

"Cable guys, on me, we're going in." Closing her eyes in the real world, Fareen's long, elegant fingers danced along her deck, typing furiously. She saw the colours in front of her blur and fade, turning white with black outlines. Then it was there. TegaLyfe's security hub, glowing like a star in an endless sea of darkness. She released a breath that she was holding in the real world, steadying herself. Checking in with Patrice, she saw he was running, gun swinging with each step. His vitals flashed up in front of her vision. Heart rate slightly elevated, blood pressure normal, everything else fine. Good, he wasn't hurt.

TegaLyfe rose up ahead of her. She saw the other cable guys trying to break into the poorly repaired tear, the wound from the last assault. Her team was behind her, arrow formation, Fareen the tip which would make the first incision. Her pulse slowed, consciousness slipping into a deep state of concentration, almost like meditation. She saw the defences rise up to meet her, the firewall, the subroutines that would block her IP and those around her. With a thought, they disintegrated, scattering like leaves caught in the wind. She knew TegaLyfe systems like the back of her hand. Gaining access was child's play. Disrupting the company was the tough part. Her body took the form of an avatar, shawl shimmering as her feet found the surface. Gigantic columns of white mega structures towered above her. In the centre, the largest of the all, the tower which held TegaLyfe's most important information.

Five cable guys appeared behind her, tethered to her stream of data like cars being towed along the highway. The other half were above, causing havoc near the tear in the dome. There was no Karla to deal with, but Asher's programming would sniff them out soon enough.

"On me, stay sharp. Watch out for-"

She was going to say *defence systems*, when twin green lances lashed out, cutting down two cable guys instantly. Fareen heard their shouts in the real world, so loud and sudden that it almost broke her concentration. The image of Patrice flickered, threatening to fade out entirely, but she caught it. Fighting with all of her resolve, she held on, blocking the next swipe of the green rails. Her avatar was pushed back, hands gripped tightly against the defence system.

"Move past me, find anything you can, steal crypto, files, anything, just go," she said to the cable guys. As one, the three dots behind her shot past in a blur, with the five above nose diving like pilots doing a bombing run. The rails tried to wiggle free from her grip, but she held tight, baring her teeth.

"Fareen, can you talk?" Patrice's voice in her ear sounded strained.

"Yes," she said, trying to hide the discomfort in her own tone.

"Rastas are with us, they've moved along east, approaching TegaLyfe from forty-eighth. We're closing in."

"Good." Fareen dared to look at Patrice's view and saw just how close. TegaLyfe tower rose up in front of him, tall and dominating, even amongst the skyscrapers of the area. Bodies were strewn along the sidewalk and road, bullet shells littering the tarmac. "How many casualties?" she asked, not really wanting to know the answer. On her right, she saw a cable guy plummet to their death, the ball of light being broken into thousands of pieces against one of Asher's programmes. Even without Karla being in here, it was almost impossible to gain a foothold of significance.

"We've lost about thirty," Patrice said, jerking her attention back to him. She was feeling the strain, her mind being stretched too thin across two fronts.

"Okay... just... keep going. We can do this," she said.

"Damn right we can."

With a grunt of effort, Fareen crunched the green rails between her hands, shattering them. The error codes spilled out like blood from a wounded animal, and the rails writhed like one, too. Within seconds, they'd disappeared, fading into nothing. Fareen forced her avatar to run, the movement jerky at first, but settling into a sprint. She was heading for the main tower, the infrastructure she helped to create all those years ago.

Soaring into the sky, she landed on an angular platform which jutted out. From here, she saw her cable guys bouncing around the cyber reality like pinballs, colliding with data cubes that vanished at their touch. At least some data was being mined. Whether it was useful or not, that would remain to be seen. She knew Asher flooded this space with decoy blocks of data, and endless loops of programming that would trap an invader forever, unless they disconnected.

A fleeting thought was spared for her physical body. Last time she was in here, and getting rid of Karla, she burst blood vessels in her brain. Her nano-tech saved her, absorbing the electrical discharge and redistributing the power to her machine, and anything within a two metre radius. Trashed equipment was a loss she could accept. People weren't. More of Asher's defences came to the fore, a barrage of data like a tidal wave washed through the digital city, purging anything on the ground by doxing their address, causing a cable guy's deck to lock up, become unresponsive. One got caught, and Fareen cursed inside her head. Amateur mistake to make, she hoped it wasn't one of her own.

Patrice's view suddenly flashed, repeated bursts of gunfire barking from his rifle. She watched, eyes wide, as the offence stalled, pushed back by police and bounty hunters alike. A smear of blood splattered across Patrice's eyes, blinding her. Instinctively, she swiped with her left hand, which did nothing. Patrice mimicked the motion in the real world, wiping the stain off of his mask, clearing his vision.

Fareen wanted to ask what was happening, but it was obvious. The fighting was intense, even with her sound deadening, the roar of automatic weapons was clear. She resolved to focus her attention back on cyberspace, guilt flooding her thoughts at abandoning her old friend. There was nothing she could do for him now, only tell him when she'd cracked the secrets of TegaLyfe, and that was a long way off.

Leaping several feet into the air, her virtual form floated, analysing. The solid white block in front of her was unlike the other blocks in cyberspace. It was so... *still.* No flickering of code, or shimmer of data transfer. It was as real as the old Rockefeller Center itself. Pressing her palm against the wall, her avatar was flung back with a force so great it threatened to pull her back to reality. She steeled herself, however, bracing with feet which weren't really there. Above, the cable guys she brought with her were nowhere to be seen. She feared the worst.

Flicked to Patrice, saw he was still hemmed in, same position as before. *No, this can't be over already*. Fareen's dismay turned to anger, and she propelled herself forward, hands outstretched. Slammed into the tower, this time sticking. She saw it. Cracks. Ones and zeroes floating out like dust mites caught in a shaft of light.

"Everyone, on me, I've broken the seal. Get here now!" she said, hoping there was at least one other cable guy in here still.

Two dots soared into view, both coming from the left. Green rails whipped and lashed, too slow to catch them.

"Quick, get whatever you can from in here, go," she said, urgency in her voice. The tear was already repairing herself, Fareen couldn't believe what she was seeing. It was more advanced than even she could have programmed. Tried again, slamming hard. This time, nothing. Fareen knew her physical body was drained, and her mind tired. Her power was waning.

Then she saw it. Rising high above the tower, an impossible form of pure energy engulfed the cable guys. Their cyber forms collapsed instantly, and in the real world, Fareen picked up on a sickening sound, like fruit being squashed by a boot. Her hands worked fast, hammering the ESC key on her deck, and then typing in repeated codes to quit. The form came for her, and she knew already it was too late and that Asher had won.

Ripped out of cyberspace, staring at her monitor. A cable guy stood next to her, clutching a bundle of cables. She'd been physically torn from her deck. Blinking in quick succession, Fareen's mind adjusted back to reality. She saw the cable guy properly now, a girl, young. Dirty blonde hair over an oval-shaped face, a streak of blood dripping from her nostril. Fareen touched her own nose, grateful to find she was dry.

"Thank you, child," Fareen said, resting a hand on the girl's arm. She tried to stand, but her legs wouldn't work, not yet. *Shit, Patrice.*

"Patrice, can you hear me?" Her connection had been severed, at least visually.

"Fareen? It's all gone to shit here, we're falling back."

"What? What happened?"

"Tayo, that's what."

Her heart flew into her mouth. "Patrice, what is it?"

"Nothing, flesh wound. Fucker got me with a lucky hit."

"Patrice, get back here, now."

"Already on my way. Are you still in cyberspace?"

She didn't even want to answer. Her defeat had been so complete and emphatic. "No, and we've taken losses."

"Merde."

Fareen hung her head, shamed to have been pushed back so easily. The cable guy was still standing next to her, clutching Fareen's jacking cables.

"My dear, you can go and sit down. Thank you," Fareen said, eyelids heavy as she looked up at the young girl.

"Okay. But I want you to know, I managed to download something."

"What did you get?" Fareen sat up, hoping for a win, however small.

"It looks like a manufacturing plant, a location." Her voice was shaking, Brooklyn accent prevalent with every syllable.

Fareen smiled gently. "This is excellent work, my dear. Show me."

CHAPTER SIX

TAYO MARCHED towards the cowering huddle of three punks. Their hands were up, weapons down. Tayo smirked, yellow eyes blazing. Displayed across his retina was his ammo count. Thirty bullets in his assault rifle, which he held in his right hand. He squeezed the trigger, watching the numbers tumble rapidly, hearing the bullets rip through flesh, ricochet off of tarmac.

"God damn, T. You're getting shit all over my jacket," Blayze said, slitting the throat of a young woman nearby.

"Yeah, relax, dude," Jack said, his artificial legs glowing red hot from the amount of running he'd been doing in the last twenty minutes. Ewan appeared around the corner of the block, dragging two of the rebels with him by their hoods. They squirmed and kicked, but it was useless. Tayo smirked, boots crunching over the remains of the trio he'd just wasted. "Fuck 'em," he said, fixing his cousin, Blayze, with a shark-like grin.

Ewan dumped the two he was carrying in front of the group of the quartet of bounty hunters, cocking his automatic pistol.

"Wait," Tayo said, holding up a fist. A thought came to him. Blayze raised an eyebrow, Jack's mouth twitched. He was hopped up on stims, went with the territory of being the fastest Hume alive. Legs were quick, but his mind raced on, never still for a moment.

"We'll take one of these back to the boss. But which one? Hey, meat sacks. Which one of you is surviving?" Tayo said, walking over. He towered over the two young men, who looked like they'd seen a ghost.

"Me," one of them said, shoving his friend out the way.

"That settles it," Tayo fired, but was greeted with a *click*. No ammo. The bullet counter in the corner of his eye flashed red, displaying a big, fat zero. Blayze and the boys laughed, it wasn't often Tayo made a mistake. His upper lip curled, and he hauled the man who'd spoken up to his feet. Tayo shoved him against the brick wall, posters of hookers, Tega products, and clubs stuck to his back.

Tayo watched the colour drain from the man's pink face, eyes wider than trash can lids. Tayo used his left hand to hold the entirety of the other guy's torso in place, and with his right, opened his palm, and smashed his face between brick and carbon fibre. Gore splattered everywhere, even getting on Tayo's metallic arms. That annoyed him. Behind, he heard the other rebel throwing up. Tayo turned, letting the lifeless corpse drop from his grip. He crouched into a squat, resting bulky arms on his massive legs.

"You're only alive because he spoke and tried to throw you to the wolves. I don't like disloyalty. However, for you to stay alive, you're gonna have to give us some intel. I'm taking you to the boss. You wanted to see him, right? That's why you and your little bitch ass friends are out here? You should consider yourself honoured to meet with Mr Ortega."

The man didn't stop shaking, and Tayo now understood how young he was. Fourteen at most. Not a man, but a boy. In the back of his mind, Tayo's thoughts went to Jaden, his beloved son. Sat at home, doing schoolwork. Exactly what this punk should be doing. A wave of anger rose up within him, not at this... teen, but at those scum in the subway. What the fuck are they doing, sending kids out here to die?

"Come on," Tayo said, lifting the kid up, not as rough as before. Blayze was looking at him, eyes narrowed. "What?"

"You think it's a good idea, taking him to Rodrigo? What if he's got a tracker?" Blayze said.

"Kid, you got a tracker on you?" Tayo asked. The teen shook his head so fast it made Tayo's augmented eyes blur for a second. He tapped the side of his head, activating a basic scanning device built into his skull. It was useful for picking up obvious shit like bombs, guns, knives, and so forth. A blade was tucked into the kid's waistband, but that was it.

"Lose the knife," Tayo said. The instruction was obeyed instantly, the weapon clattering to the floor as steel met asphalt. Tayo nodded in approval, then turned to his crew. "Stay out here, just in case. Reform the line with the cops, check in with the snipers on the roof. Jack, you can handle that, right?"

"On it," Jack said, disappearing in a cloud of smoke. Tayo watched as his legs carried him up the side of the nearest building, like a goddamn spider. Tayo had mods, more than most, but Jack's legs freaked him out, just a little. It was almost like they took over his whole body, personality. He'd gone from being a fairly run-of-the-mill bounty hunter to a speed freak; constantly on some kind of shit to stop his mind from being still for a second. Tayo honestly was surprised Jack was still alive. He nodded at Blayze and Ewan before turning towards the colossal structure that was TegaLyfe headquarters.

Tayo had to give it to the rebels, they'd gotten close. The man who Tayo placed as the leader, a guy with a mask and wires out the back of his head like dreadlocks, he was lethal.

Took out at least five bounty hunters, and who knows how many cops. By the time Tayo and the boys arrived, the enemy was practically knocking at the door. The guy in the mask, the leader, as Tayo decided, was close enough that melee combat was the only option. Tayo remembered the scream as he slashed at the man's side and arm, drawing blood. He had to fall back, because the rebels fired at him. If it wasn't for his huge, augmented arm acting as a temporary shield against the bullets, Tayo would have been dead already. But with that one slash of the black-chrome blade extending from his forearm, Tayo broke the back of the offence. That's what he did best. Get in fast, hit the target, then clean up.

Dragging his hostage inside, Tayo drew frightened looks from the office workers. The lobby was mostly empty, but there were a few nervous looking security guards inside. Janitorial cyborgs, early generation, jerked about their business as usual, mopping floors, cleaning windows. Oblivious, it seemed to the war zone outside.

Tayo realised he was standing still, paralysed by the stares. He normally didn't give a shit who looked at him and for how long, but inside Tega, he always felt out of place. Like he was some attack dog Rodrigo hired to be his bitch. Wasn't a dynamic he enjoyed and made his fist tighten around the young man's clothes. "Come on," Tayo said, shoving him forward to the main elevators.

Inside, Tayo punched the button to Rodrigo's floor. The elevator lifted, smooth as butter, and Tayo had a minute to catch his thoughts. Tapped his head to bring up his bank balance. Getting closer to his goal of ten mil. Once he had that, he'd quit this life. Be with Jaden, ensure his son didn't have to live the way he did. On the streets, fighting for every damn thing. Food, water, money, respect. None of it came easy. His son deserved better.

The elevator chimed, doors easing open. Tayo shoved his

captive forward, almost making the man trip. "Come on, you pussy, move." Tayo shoved him again. The punk's grimy boots made squeaking noises as he stumbled forward, the pristine marble floor dirtied with his footprints. The instant they were clear of the marks, the section of flooring would hiss, steam cleaning the dirt. Tayo cast a look over his shoulder, watching as a vacuumbot charged out from an unseen spot in the wall, frantically scrubbing the remains. He smirked, taking a mental note to make sure the new place he got for him and Jaden had those little bots.

Approaching the clouded glass door of Rodrigo Ortega's office, Tayo dragged his hostage back, like a dog on a leash. Except it was his fist holding the kid's hoodie. Pounded on the door twice, heavy thumps with his fist. Tayo waited, frustration gnawing at his patience. He wanted to get in and get out. Never liked lingering in here.

Rodrigo came to the door, eyebrows knitted together in confusion.

"Tayo? Is everything okay?"

"Sure is, boss. And I brought you a gift," Tayo said, thrusting the man forward at Rodrigo's feet. The CEO arched an eyebrow, stepping fully into the corridor. Hands outstretched, he stared up at Tayo.

"What do you want me to do with this?"

"Interrogate him. He's one of the punks from the subway."

"And you think he'll have anything of value to tell us? He's just a pawn," Rodrigo said, turning away.

"Boss, worth a shot, isn't it?" Tayo kept his voice even, but inside he was starting to boil over. Rodrigo turned back, sighing.

"Maybe? Look, I don't really have time for this. I'm negotiating with-" he paused, a wave of revelation washing over his features. "Tayo, would you come and sit in on this meeting with me, please?"

Tayo guessed he would be used as muscle, a silent menace in the corner. Say nothing but intimidate. He could do that. "Sure, but what about this one?"

"Put him over there, tie him up."

"You got it." Tayo grabbed the rebel again, tossing him into the chair Rodrigo pointed at. He landed with a thud, legs flailing. Tayo pointed his arm at the kid, who cowered, screamed out a guttural, "no."

"Relax, you dumb bitch. Just making sure you don't go nowhere." Tayo's inner forearm clicked away to the side with a hiss, deploying a steel cable. Using his free arm, Tayo twisted the knob, adjusting velocity. "That should do it..." Firing, the restraint deployed, wrapping around the rebel with a snap like a whip, pulling his body taut against the chair. The soft material bent, and the cable cut into the man's shoulders, wrapping around his torso and legs. He cried out in pain. Tayo saw the trickle of blood from his arms and legs.

"Don't be such a fucking pussy. Be back soon, cupcake." Tayo grinned and followed Rodrigo into his office. Occupying the couch opposite Rodrigo's desk were two men in pinstripe suits. Olive skin, black hair, almost identical. Face grafts, nothing unusual about that. Tayo looked at their hands. Wrinkled. Rodrigo sat behind his desk, facing another man, one who made Tayo stand a little straighter. Don Lione, head of the Mafia.

"Don, forgive me, I asked Tayo here to join us as we have a situation on the ground which ties in directly to what we're discussing here."

Tayo extended out a hand, which the Don shook firmly. "Nice to see you again," he said. Voice soft, husky. Layered with wisdom, and perhaps a bit of fatigue. Tayo cringed. He'd almost forgotten about that night at the Ten Hit Club. Getting into with Cade. Not that it mattered anymore, that maggot was a rotting corpse out in the Wastelands now. He looked at Rodrigo, whose eyes twinkled. Maybe he knew, probably did. Tayo backed away, squeezing into the one empty chair to Rodrigo's left. It was just about large enough to carry his frame, but it was tight.

"So, as I was saying, Don. The situation out on the streets is getting worse, Tayo can vouch for that. How many would you say were there?" Rodrigo asked, fixing Tayo with a stare. He read the look, it said *exaggerate, but don't make a fool of him.*

"At least fifty that I counted. Armed tactics. They'd employed hit-and-run manoeuvres, very effective." Tayo looked at Don, the expression blank. He'd had a lot of work done, but he was old. Very old. Rodrigo nodded, seemingly satisfied.

"Fifty? Shit, we got more than that patrolling the Bronx. Why exactly do you need us?" one of the guys on the chair said. Voice high-pitched, like a throwback to one of those movies from the last century.

"Don, this is just the beginning. We know who's behind this. Fareen would have just been probing our defences. I don't think I have to explain to you how devastating it would be for us both, should TegaLyfe fall," Rodrigo said, leaning forward, fingers pointed under his chin like a steeple. "And we're just a few days removed from Kaizen Sciences launching a cyber attack on our systems. What do you think is going to happen next? The Yakuza will rip through our forces unless we band together."

"Those Yak motherfuckers wouldn't get clo-" the other man on the sofa began, but the Don held up his hand, calling for silence, which was observed immediately.

"Mr Ortega brings up a valid point. The Yakuza are growing in their number, we've seen it. There have been skirmishes on Canal Street. They're knocking on our door."

"Boss, if I may?" Tayo said, finding his voice. Rodrigo looked surprised, but gestured with his hand, inviting him to proceed.

“It’s not just the subway, or Yakuza,” Tayo began, looking between the three Mafia heads. “You’ve also got the Rastas, Goths, Haitians. There’s discontent in the streets, more protests up and down Midtown every day. A storm is coming, and if we ain’t careful, it’ll wash us away.”

Don Lione nodded slowly, as though he was processing each word. He looked over his shoulder at his two lieutenants, who both shrugged as if to say *yeah, he’s got a point.* Turning back to Rodrigo, the Don asked, “what’s your proposal?”

“We form a true partnership. For that, you get more control, more funding. You work with me on the ground, and we take the fight to anyone who challenges us. First, we need to repel the attacks. Then, we go Downtown. It’s time we took back what was ours, gentlemen. What do you say?”

The Don’s lip curled, possibly in approval, or annoyance. Hard to tell. Tayo squinted, his bionic eyes zooming in on the old head. He checked his vitals, which were perfect. Readouts were indicative of extensive work inside. New heart, lungs, shit, probably even entire blood transfusion. The Don would be around for some time, Tayo concluded.

“You’d have me launch my men into a ground assault. What backup would you provide?”

Rodrigo extended an arm out to Tayo. *The fuck? Me?* “You’re looking at my new Head of Personal Security. Provided, of course, he accepts this extremely generous promotion package.” Rodrigo fixed Tayo with a stare, mouth turned up into a smile. It was a power play.

“Bounty hunters? Can you get them all to work for you?” the Don said. Rodrigo turned his attention back to the Mafioso.

“They can all come, for a price.”

Don Lione stroked his clean-shaven, smooth chin. “What about Cade, he still under contract?”

For once, Rodrigo looked uncomfortable. It was a split

second, but his wall of confidence fell. For some reason, the Mafia held Cade in high regard. Tayo never figured out why. From the change in Rodrigo's demeanour, he knew that as well. If the Mafia found out what they'd done to Cade.... Negotiations might turn sour.

"Cade is currently outside of my remit. He left the city, as far as we're aware." Tayo watched Rodrigo's mouth work the lie easily, so much so that he almost believed it himself.

"Pity. He's someone you want in the trenches, you know?" The Don stood up, smoothing the creases in his suit. "You'll have an answer within twenty-four hours. I need to discuss with the Capos. I'm sure you understand that a proposal of this magnitude needs input from all families."

"Of course," Rodrigo said, standing as well, extending his hand. Don Lione took it, shaking firmly. The other two got up as well, similarly taking Rodrigo's hand. They watched Tayo with wary eyes. The Don came over, and Tayo got up, the chair scraping across the floor as he moved.

"I look forward to doing business with you, Tayo," Don Lione said, a thin smile spreading across lips that were too young for his ancient eyes.

"Likewise. Want me to show 'em out?" Tayo asked the question to Rodrigo. He put his hand to his head, remembering something important.

"That's right, our guest. Gentlemen, if you'll forgive us, we have one of the rebels outside. Tayo and I must press on with the questioning. I'd have my AI show you to the elevator, but..."

The Don put two hands up, protruding his lower lip. "We can find our way. I'll be in touch."

They all left the office, the Mafia types casting sidelong glances at the punk, who was still fastened to the chair. One of the lieutenants turned around to regard Tayo, raising an eyebrow. Tayo stood before the rebel, who whimpered in fear. Rodrigo joined him, watching the Mafia file into the elevator.

"So, what do you think?" Rodrigo asked, still watching the empty hallway.

"About this punk? Or them?" Tayo fixed his yellow eyes on Rodrigo.

"Neither. Your new position."

"Oh, you were serious?" Tayo knew Rodrigo wasn't fucking around, he just wanted to hear it again. Just to make sure.

"Tayo, we've been in business together for a while now. You deserve a raise, and what better opportunity than this? Purge Nueva York with me, bring this city back under control. You already know about the Meal Pill, so it makes sense to bring you on board. Like I said, the salary will be favourable. Triple what you make a month, at least."

It was a good offer. And Rodrigo was right, Tayo was basically full-time under him as it was. But what about Jaden? Would a new job mean less time with his son? Working under Rodrigo as his attack dog, was that really the promotion Rodrigo said it would be?

"And your crew gets employed as well. Obviously not on the same package as you, but I know how important they are. You're like family, no?"

"That we are," Tayo said, nodding slowly.

"Speaking of, I know your wish. To retire and spend time with Jaden. It's true, isn't it?"

Tayo flinched. Hearing Rodrigo know his one goal in life was difficult. It gave him power. "Yes."

"Well, with this new position, you can get there a lot faster, trust me. Once this is over, and we've got Nueva York under our control, you'll be done. So if that isn't an incentive, I dunno what is," Rodrigo finished, clapping Tayo on the shoulder. Tayo exhaled heavily through his nostrils.

"Alright, I'll do it."

"Bueno, I'm pleased. You're important to me Tayo, never forget that. Now, shall we see what this one has to say?"

Tayo looked at the young rebel, whose life choices had led him here at such a young age. No way was Jaden gonna be exposed like that.

"You got it, boss."

CHAPTER SEVEN

"Uncle?" Cade said, voice quivering. Eyes wide in disbelief. There he was, standing in front of him like he never went missing.

"Last I checked, yeah." Uncle Silas still had his thick moustache, but it was flecked with grey. For once, he wasn't frowning, and instead looked quite emotional. Cade hurried over, almost too quick, balance uneven. He steadied himself and bent down to wrap his arms around his uncle.

"It's damn good to see you, unc."

"You too, kid."

They held the embrace for a few moments until Pedro coughed awkwardly.

"I'm, uh, sorry to break up this moment. But-"

"Hey, I haven't seen this man in years. I thought he was dead. Can't your bullshit wait five minutes?" Cade said, spinning around. A little too fast, he realised, as his head went foggy.

Pedro held up his hands apologetically. "Sure, but this conversation is far from over, Cade. Silas," he nodded curtly, walking out of the room.

"I really did think you were dead," Cade said, turning around to Silas again.

"I'm sorry, kid. I tried to find you, but I didn't get told shit out there. Next thing I know, you're back on the streets working for the CEO of TegaLyfe."

"Where have you been?"

"Hong Kong. Come on, let's find somewhere to eat and talk. There's a lot to explain."

Silas led Cade out of the room, walking slowly. Cade hated that he was so useless in his new body still. It felt alien, like it wasn't his. That bubble of resentment again. He turned around, regarding the floating torso in the tube. *Oh yeah, it shouldn't be mine.*

A few nods of respect followed Silas, and Cade felt like he was a street punk learning the bounty hunter code again. His uncle had to be around sixty by now, but he still cut an impressive figure. A dark jacket pulled tight across an obviously muscular physique. Faded jeans cut off at dark boots, and the barrel of an SMG dangled lazily against his thigh. Silas was a throwback to a time Cade wasn't even sure existed. Gunslingers patrolling the urban streets, quick to draw and faster to find a whore.

The pair turned into a narrow corridor, Cade having to duck under pipes that ran along the ceiling. A few paces forward, then Silas opened the door, hinges protesting at the movement. An automatic light blinked on, fizzed, died, and then stayed connected. The room was nothing more than a square box with a couch, table, and vending machine. A poor excuse for a break room, if that's what it was meant to be. Silas rested his weapon on the table and collapsed onto the couch with a sigh. Cade pulled up the chair, legs scraping on the concrete flooring.

"So," Silas began, a smile playing on his lips. His grey-green eyes were the same, filled with laughter like he was in on some private joke nobody else knew about. “We ain’t in NY anymore, are we?”

“Fuck me, you can say that again.” Cade was already on his feet, approaching the vending machine. His back started to ache, despite the flow of pain meds in his system. How much was being fed into that drip at his bedside he didn’t even wanna think about. Sizing up the snacks on offer, Cade pressed the button for a pack of insta-noodles. He’d quite liked the ones he had in Downtown. Felt like months ago that he was there, but it hadn’t even been a week. The container came out at the bottom after the machine clunked a few times. Steam billowed out from the opening in the packet. Testing his new hands, Cade stuck two fingers inside the piping hot packet. Didn’t feel a thing.

“No shit,” he whispered, watching the wet, boiling noodles drip off the end of his black digits.

“Can’t feel it, huh?” Silas asked, craning his neck to see. Cade shook his head in disbelief.

“I can feel the noodle, like it’s registering what it is... but there’s no heat... nothin’.” Dropped the noodle back in the packet and sat down at the desk, searching for a fork. Not that he needed one, clearly, but he didn’t feel comfortable shoving metal, carbon fibre, whatever the fuck, fingers into his mouth.

“It’ll take some getting used to, but I think you’ll grow to like your new mods.”

Cade’s tongue ran along his teeth, a grimace. “Doubt that. Fuckin’ hate Humes. Now I am one. What kind of bullshit is that?”

“That *bullshit* is you being alive and breathing, son. Better that than the other thing, ain’t it?”

“No,” Cade said, finding a plastic fork and stabbing the opening of the noodles, bringing them to his mouth. He winced as the heat scorched him, eyes opening wide. Silas laughed.

"Where were you?" Cade asked through mouthfuls of noodle. Swallowed, continued his thought, "I was alone."

"You weren't alone, you had Olivia."

Of course, he didn't know.

"Unc, Olivia was killed. The whole apartment went up in flames. Some fucking Hume... shouldn't have even been there. I got sent down for it, wasn't even my fault."

Silas stroked his moustache, deep in thought. "I'm sorry Cade, I didn't know... any of it."

"Yeah, 'cos you weren't fucking there." Cade's anger flashed through his body. His arms jerked up, possibly as a response to a spike in heart rate. Fucking things.

"Like I said, I'm sorry. Business took me away."

Cade knitted his eyebrows together, staring at his uncle. "Business? And you couldn't tell me?"

His uncle sighed, head hanging low. "I broke the code."

Cade scoffed, putting more noodles in his mouth. "You? The fuck outta here."

His uncle didn't laugh. He suddenly appeared old to Cade, tired. Cade stopped eating, pushing the box aside.

"You're serious?"

"After we did that job for your old employer... what was his name?" Silas started.

"Benitez?"

Silas clicked his fingers, pointing at Cade. "Thank you. Yeah, Benitez. Well, I went home, right? Walking down the sidewalk, spot two guys in an alley. They got some broad bent over a dumpster. I stop, she turns... I'll never forget her face. Marked up with bionics, but her eyes, they were human alright. And they were in pain. Deep, emotional pain. Then I see how young she is. Gotta be fourteen at most. So now I go over. Pull the guy off of her, give him a right hook. His buddy gets smart, pulls a blade. Yeah? Fuck you too, and my shotgun's out before he can even blink."

Cade remembered his uncle's shotgun. Double barrelled, hefty thing. Seen him blow huge holes outta people.

"He's gone, guts everywhere. Bit of a mess, frankly. I tell the girl to go, get outta here. She pulls her skirt up fast, scatters away, thanking me. The original pervert is up now, clocks me around the jaw right like I did to him. Except he's got some brass knuckles. Old school, but I respect that.

"So I drop the shotgun, my pride is wounded. I proceed to kick the ever lasting fuck out of the guy, *bing, bong, bang*. He's down, choking on his own blood. What do I see next? His fucking holo-phone ringing. I answer it, and who fucking projects themselves into my world like a bad dream?"

Cade was smiling, despite himself. His uncle had a way of telling stories. "Who?"

"Rodrigo Ortega."

"You gotta be fucking kidding me?"

"Nope, he starts talking, mad as shit. *Who are you, what have you done with my bounty hunters?* And my stomach falls through my ass. I've just wasted two bounty hunters who are under contract. Code violated, case closed, thank you very much."

"Oh, man." Cade shook his head. "What happened after that?"

"I tell Ortega to go fuck himself, smash the phone, get my ass into the apartment. Got all my shit together in about five minutes, and then I'm out the door. Couldn't call you, didn't want to put you in any danger. And then I was on the run."

Cade kept quiet, letting his uncle's words swirl around his brain. He felt a pang of sadness swell up from deep inside of him. All that time with his uncle, robbed. The sorrow quickly gave way to anger. *That's another thing Rodrigo took from me.*

"You wind up in Hong Kong," Cade began. "Were there others?"

"Bounty hunters exiled? More than you'd imagine."

Cade was piecing it together.

"Pedro brings you here, because he wants all the exiled hunters to work for him, in his plan to take over TegaLyfe? How much he paying you?"

"Enough. More than enough, actually. He's not Rodrigo rich, but he's an Ortega. You can see what he's built here, and that's without any TegaLyfe funding. The family has always been wealthy."

"And he plans to make you persuade me to join in too, right?"

"Actually, no, not originally. I was already on my way here before you... arrived."

"Explains why Pedro bothered to save my ass, then," Cade said.

On cue, the door opened, banging loudly against the steel. It was Pedro, and he looked frantic.

"Something big has happened," he said, eyes darting from Cade to his uncle.

"What is it?" Silas asked, still relaxed as ever.

"There's been another attack on TegaLyfe."

"Wait, *another?* When was the first?" Cade asked. His heart leapt into his mouth, thinking of Dani. It dawned on him how much he missed her, despite only knowing her for a few days. Pedro looked at him for a second, confused, and then seemed to remember.

"Right, you were on your way back from Kaizen. There was a cyber attack on TegaLyfe, led by Ichiro. Biggest one ever. They got in, did a lot of damage."

Cade's attention waned. Files and data, who gives a fuck?

"What sort of damage?" Silas asked.

"Crypto stolen, some files leaked..."

Pedro's voice faded into the background as Cade lost interest. He wiggled his fingers, feeling them flex against the table. Still weird how the boiling noodles didn't register any pain.

"... and the AI."

"Wait, what was that?" Cade asked, focusing on Pedro's words.

"I said the AI. She was obliterated. Handiwork of Fareen, no doubt."

Cade stared at Pedro, mouth open in disbelief. *Holy shit, Karla's gone?* "As in, wiped?"

"I believe so, yes. So Fareen followed up with a ground assault."

Cade stood up, panic coursing through his veins. Now he was paying attention. He moved towards Pedro, fluid movement without thinking about it. The second he noticed just how easy it had been, his legs wobbled and felt unnatural again. He tilted his head, anger at his condition threatening to boil over, but he kept his voice even.

"Ground assault? How do you know? What casualties have there been?"

"Rudimentary cameras we deployed in the city years ago. HD not 4K, but it shows us enough. Casualties? Quite a few from Fareen's side. They were practically knocking on the door until this huge guy with yellow eyes turned up."

"Tayo," Cade said, the word laced with hatred.

"Friend of yours?" Silas asked. Cade turned around, using one of his modified arms to display his body.

"He's the cunt who left me for dead. What about Dani?" Cade asked, facing Pedro again.

"My niece?" Pedro looked surprised that Cade would seem so interested in her condition. "We haven't seen her. I think we'd know if something happened to her, she's all Rodrigo has."

Cade nodded, satisfied for now. His anger abated, pulse slowed again.

"The point, gentlemen," Pedro continued, "is that now is our time to strike. My brother is vulnerable, people can see it. I've been waiting for this moment, but we need support. You both know that we're scientists here, not fighters. To storm TegaLyfe, and go up against the small army of police and bounty hunters, we need our own force. Silas, you know why you were brought here. To discuss these terms. Well, now we're discussing them."

"I'm listening," Cade's uncle said, still seated.

"Twenty-five million, up front. Both of you."

"That's a good start. What do you want Cade and I to do?"

"You're going on a field trip, amigos. How does Hong Kong sound?"

Silas scoffed, Cade knitted his brows together. He held up his hands, the black alloy still strange in his vision.

"Hold on. Do you really think I'm in any condition for a mission? I can barely walk."

"You moved just fine a second ago," Pedro said. "And why was that? Because your mind was focussed on something else. You must let go, Cade. Let the mods become one with your body. You'll be fine. I know you will."

"What exactly are we doing in Hong Kong, anyway? I think I can guess, but why don't you spell it out for me, doc?" Silas said, at last standing.

"All the exiled bounty hunters. We need you to round them up, persuade them to fight for our cause. I'm willing to bet more than half are there because of my brother anyway, so it shouldn't be too difficult."

"Cash is king, compadre. What package are you going to offer them?" Silas asked, folding his arms across his broad chest.

"I'll think about it," Pedro said, nodding. "As for you, Cade. There's someone else in Hong Kong we need. A man who manages to lead both the Triads and the Yakuza. Ichiro Nishikawa's son; Hitoshi."

"And how do you think I'll persuade him, exactly?"

"Easy. You have his father's trust. Ichiro doesn't know you're alive. You make a call with Hitoshi next to you, Ichiro doesn't think twice about going after my brother a second time. Only this round, he'll use his Yakuza force as well."

"So you don't actually need Hitoshi, or his men?"

Pedro shrugged. "Our transport isn't that big. If he can spare maybe five of his best, that would be good."

"*Five?* What the fuck difference is five guys gonna make?"

"Ho, ho. Wait 'til you see these fuckers, Cade," Silas said, laughing. "Just one would be a welcome addition to our ranks. You think you've been modded up real good? Ain't shit compared to what they're doing out there. Hong Kong is on a whole other level."

"So, gentlemen. Are we in agreement?" Pedro asked. Cade's heart thumped loudly in his ears. The modified rhythm sounded off, but he ignored it. That's how it was supposed to be, according to Dr Shelby.

"I'm in. Whaddya say, Cade? Be like old times again."

Cade looked at his uncle, the fire returning to his eyes. Pedro looked on, almost imploringly. Cade flexed his arms again, holding them out in front of him. He was apprehensive, but he knew something like this was going to happen soon. Why else would he have been saved? If he refused, what then? Mods ripped out, given to that floating corpse? Cade didn't want to take that chance. So once again, he was about to be employed by an Ortega.

"I'll do it."

"Excellent." Pedro smiled at last. It was different from Rodrigo's grin. Not as shark-like.

"How exactly do we get there, though?" Cade asked.

"We fly," Silas said.

"Fly? On what, wings of imagination?"

"Even better. Hydro-copter. Fuel source is pure H-two-o. And there's gonna be plenty of that where we're going."

Cade looked at his uncle's grin, the same one he always had before a mission. For the first time in days, Cade smiled as well.

CHAPTER EIGHT

MEI TRUDGED through the streets of Downtown, holding herself as the wind battered her. She hated how the tall buildings would funnel that cold air right through her body. Hugging herself tight, she felt her deck on the inside of her jacket. The last few hours had been a blur. The dead cable guys inside Kaizen Sciences were hauled out in gigantic silver slabs, like floating coffins. Ladies with identical faces came, robotic in their movements, and started cleaning. Dawned on her that they were likely cyborgs, though she'd never seen one before, only heard rumours.

Mei stopped underneath a canopy which extended out from a shop to the sidewalk. It gave her a moment to breathe. She peered over the neon advertising board. Five t-shirts for one hundred dollars, it said, glaring red lights harsh against her eyes. She massaged her jaw subconsciously, catching her reflection in the misted window. Must have rained a short while ago.

Walking inside, the scanner buzzed, initiating a delicate chime somewhere deep in the bowels of the shop. The store owner greeted her in Japanese, which Mei acknowledged with a small, sad smile.

"Mei? What's wrong?" Mrs Okada asked. Concern spread across her ancient face, small eyes peering at Mei through inch-thick glasses that looked like they belonged in the previous century. She was every bit a throwback, down to being completely natural. Not a single modification, which Mei found remarkable. Her lower lip trembled, the words wouldn't come. Eyes filled with hot tears, spilling down her round cheeks and artificial jaw.

"Hiroto," she said, voice cracking.

Mrs Okada's eyebrows flew into her white hair. She pressed the exit button on her bulletproof cubicle, the door sliding open with a judder. Mrs Okada shuffled across to Mei, white slippers scuffing against a rough floor that was in desperate need of a vacuumbot. Her spindly arms wrapped around Mei's petite frame, and that's when Mei lost it. She bawled, crying harder than she'd ever cried before, getting snot on Mrs Okada's faux wool cardigan, wetting her bony shoulder with her never-ending tears. Mei's sadness threatened to overwhelm her entirely, her throat bobbed up and down as deep cries pulled up from her stomach.

"It's okay, shh," Mrs Okada said, gently patting Mei's back. She balled her fists, clutching tightly at that cardigan, wishing Hiroto had never spoken about that fucking job from Kaizen. Flashes of Hiroto's body, lifted from his station, and he was stashed into a body bag by those robot ladies. Mei had tried to tell them that she'd take him, give him a proper burial, but the supervisor wasn't having it. Instead, Mei was granted his share of the money, giving her a very healthy bank balance. But what good was that, when she was totally alone in this world, and without the one person whom she loved more than anything?

Finally, she stopped crying, she suspected only because her body had no more moisture left to give. Her mouth was suddenly dry, so she grabbed a bright purple drink from the shelf, cracking it open with a hiss of gas, and gulped it down so fast she almost threw up. Mei wiped her face with the back of her sleeve, and looked at Mrs Okada, eye level with the tiny old woman. Her wizened eyes were filled with sorrow, her empathy clear. She knew Hiroto as well.

"Everything will be okay, my dear," Mrs Okada said. Mei failed to see how *anything* could be okay again, but she nodded silently. She backed away, grabbed a few necessities off the shelf, and paid using the chip embedded in her wrist. Direct account to a block of storage somewhere in the net. Most people Downtown had the same thing, since the banks crashed. Everyone had their tiny slice of the net where they kept their funds, family history, medical records, right down to their favourite StreamStar person to watch.

Leaving the store, Mei walked as fast as she could, avoiding the crowds and especially eye contact. Her head was pounding, she needed water. Or sugar. Thought about getting some stims for the night, just to forget and focus on other shit. Her brother hated drugs.

"But stims aren't *really* drugs," Mei would protest whenever they got into it.

"They alter the chemicals in your brain, that sounds like drugs to me," he'd always say, with a half-smile. Working at the bar, SixOneNine, she'd been exposed to her fair share of things her brother didn't like. She looked up a narrow street, knowing that if she took a left, then a right, and carried on for three blocks, she'd be at SixOneNine. She hated working there. Clientele were awful, the owners even worse. But it paid, and rent was always due faster than she knew it. Some high-ranking Yakuza owned her building, which meant that Ichiro really owned it. He had Downtown completely under his control, and now he had her brother too, buried or incinerated.

Mei was in front of the gigantic complex before she knew it. She craned her neck, like she always did, taking in the colossal structure. Streaks of rust ran down the buildings, where air-con units pumped out recycled water. Graffiti and blinking advertisements crawled up and down the building, bathing the street below in a strange glow of multiple colours. Hiroto said it was two-hundred stories high. She believed him. Never went to the top. Their apartment was on floor eighty-eight. Somewhere in the middle. Mei pulled her keycard out of her satchel around her waist, tapping the security scanner next to the rusted metal doorframe. A harsh buzz greeted her.

Angry red Japanese letters flashed up in front of her eyes, glitching as the old projector flickered.

ACCESS DENIED. RENT DUE. PLEASE PAY USING TERMINAL TO THE LEFT.

"You've gotta be kidding me." Seemed that rent really did come much faster than she knew. Sighing, Mei held up her wrist to the pristine white terminal. The only part of the building that was maintained to a high level. A few seconds' delay, then a beep, and the doors finally opened. Mei pushed the heavy gate with her small hands, grunting with the effort. The lobby was tiny, narrow, and filthy.

Laying on the floor, curled up in a ball, was a junkie. Needles lay scattered around his body, pinpricks of blood drops staining the yellow-tinged tiles which were once white. Graffiti covered the walls, tags pledging allegiance to Yakuza, cursing the Ortegas, and racial slurs against whites, Italians, and Latinos were scrawled over brightly coloured letters. Two elevators waited at the end of the tight hallway. Mei lifted her legs carefully over stacks of old papers, stinking clothes that made her choke as she moved past, and abandoned food containers.

Pressed the button to take her to floor eighty-eight, and slumped against the wall of the elevator, sliding down until she was squatting inches off the grimy floor. Dirty footprints criss-crossed each other, merging with stains of things Mei didn't want to think about. A rumble, a squeal of metal, and she was there. The doors shuddered open and Mei moved out, clutching her jacket close to her. She kept her head low, avoiding glares from three men who were smoking something foul smelling to her right. Getting out her keycard again, she tapped the lock on her apartment door, number five, and the locks clicked open. She practically fell inside, closing the door behind her as fast as possible.

If the building was a cesspit, badly needing some cleansing of both inhabitants and the brickwork that held it together, then her apartment was a sanctuary. It was a modest size, but it was instantly calming. Scents of blossom filled her nose, the wall diffusers puffing out twice as she walked in. They were expensive, but they sure helped ease her mind. Mei smiled, removing her jacket, kicking off her boots, and shuffling towards the kitchen.

Her smile quickly vanished. Laying on the counter was a half-eaten rice cake. Hiroto's. A lump swelled in Mei's throat, threatening to overwhelm her. With an impulse, she scraped it away into the trash compactor under the basalt surface, crumbs and all. She regretted it right away. Her eyes, brimming with tears, landed on the holo pic of her and Hiroto. Taken three, maybe four years ago. Her hair was longer then, past her shoulders. She sometimes missed it, but not now. All she wanted now was her brother back. Mei stared at his face, his eyes full of laughter to match the huge grin he wore. He'd just scored his biggest job at the time, Mei remembered it well. It helped pay for most of the things in this apartment.

The mood lighting was a soft purple, illuminating the grey walls, occasionally spreading patterns in a varied kaleidoscope of wonder. Her eyes traced a tree growing from the ceiling down to the corner of the open-plan room, to where her and her brother's towers lived. Her stomach tied itself into a knot.

Leaving her deck on the kitchen top, Mei walked over to the machines, which were always blinking in standby mode.

Her finger trembled slightly as she fired up Hiroto's machine. His space was an organised mess of cables, screens, print outs, warning signs, and neon lighting. Mei's wasn't much better, her monitor curved around tangles of wires and cables which dangled down to the power sockets in the floor like dreadlocks. Old decks that they'd both used and burned out lay around her monitor stand, some in various states of repair. Hiroto's screwdriver, anti-static gloves, and microchip kit lay next to his keyboard. Mei remembered he said he was going to fix them all up after the Kaizen job, then resell them on the black market.

"Why did we have to fucking go?" she shrieked, wiping all the broken decks onto the floor in one motion. They crashed and clattered against the fake wood floor, which shimmered from the impact, revealing the hard concrete surface underneath the holo projection for a moment. Fresh tears leaked from the corner of her eyes, she turned away from her towers, ignoring Hiroto's boot up screen.

Her deck blinked into life, the blue screen projecting itself against the neutral colours of the apartment. Mei walked over to it, picking it up. She'd almost forgotten about Karla, whoever or whatever that was. Wiping away the tears from her face for what felt like the hundredth time tonight, Mei picked up her deck and took it to her tower. Grabbing a fistful of power cables, she plugged them into the empty socket at the top of the deck. Turning on her tower, the monitor flashed instantly, recognising the device. Bios screen skipped through the startup stages, and she was staring at her desktop. A mirror of the physical world, it was organised chaos. Icons overlapped each other, virtual sticky notes surrounded a portrait of her and Hiroto, her desktop wallpaper.

"Come on, Karla, let's find out who you are," Mei said,

tapping the deck with her fingers to bring it to life. The screen flashed, and then her monitor displayed the deck loading screen in a minimised window. Using the cabled mouse attached to her tower, Mei dragged the window to the centre of her view, making it larger. It was a blank dialogue box, with the input key flashing patiently.

"Karla, can you see this?" Mei said whilst she typed. Hit enter and waited.

<yes. I have also read your files, downloaded them to my system.>

"Oh, shit," Mei said, her eyes wide. She was about to pull the cables out of the deck when a new line of text appeared on the screen.

<don't worry, they're not to be shared anywhere. It was an automatic response from my programming. Here, I'll purge them myself_>

Mei's deck whirred as the fans inside the machine worked overtime, which only happened when a major system update was occurring. *Or something is taking over my deck*, Mei thought.

<there. Your files have been removed. I had no need for them, I apologise for that. I am still learning what I am capable of.>

This all felt surreal to Mei. Just what was she talking to? Had to be an AI.

"Do you know what you are?" Mei asked. It was a repeat of the question she'd said to Karla back at Kaizen. She didn't know then.

<based on information I have processed from the net, I think so.>

Mei cursed under her breath. The ethernet cable was a yellow streak against a sea of black and blues. It was connected to their net modem at all times. Meaning Karla had access. If she was an AI, she would have downloaded all the information she needed in milliseconds. Would understand more than Mei could possibly know with a thousand years of walking the earth.

"So, what did you find out?"

<Using my existing subroutines, and the scatter of information that

I had in my programming, I discovered that I am the AI of TegaLyfe. Constructed by Asher Jones_>

"Holy shit," Mei said. She only realised then she'd been standing this entire time. She wheeled her bulky chair across from her left and sat down, heart thumping against her chest.

"Rodrigo Ortega's AI. In my apartment. What the fuck." A thought implanted itself at the forefront of her mind. She typed frantically, her breath held. She read the words back in her head as they flashed on the screen:

Can you create a private server, one where I can jack in and we can talk?

A few seconds, then Karla's messaged flashed on the screen.

<it's done. Please jack in, and I will take you there_>

Fuck, am I really going to do this? Mei's eyes looked at her headset, plugged in and ready to go. She exhaled, blowing her longer bang away from her face. Hand shaking, she picked up the headset, bringing it down over her head. The pins locked into place against her temple, making her wince. With a last look at her deck and monitor, she shut the visor.

The virtual world rose up to meet her like a tidal wave. She screamed, no sound coming out, and then she was cocooned inside a white sphere, which flattened itself into a cube. Mei blinked, realising she had human features.

"Woah," she said, waving solid arms in front of her face.

"Hello, Mei." Karla's voice made her jump. Turning around, Mei saw the slender woman walking towards her, smiling. Drawing near, Mei noticed they were the same height, even having similar haircuts. Though Karla's style was more angular and even. She had full lips, which parted into a beautiful smile. Her eyes twinkled, even within the confines of black and white cyberspace. She was slim, with a natural curve and small breasts. Mei looked down at her own body, noticing it was an exact copy of her physical self. It was uncanny how similar her body shape was to Karla's.

"Did you copy my body?" Mei asked.

Karla shook her head from side to side. "This was how I appeared in the physical world. Here, look at this security footage."

Karla waved her hand and a floating image displayed in front of Mei's face. It was Rodrigo Ortega, standing next to an extremely pretty woman. Mei assumed it was Daniela Ortega, his daughter and the COO of TegaLyfe. Beside them was a man with a broad smile. She assumed that would be Asher Jones. Then she saw Karla. Standing there as she was inside this virtual world. Exactly the same.

The image disappeared, and Karla was standing in front of Mei now, smiling. She looked friendly enough, but something deep within Mei told her to get out, unplug, and run far away.

"So, Mei. What is it you want in life?"

The question struck like a bolt of lightning. What *did* she want?

"I guess... I wanted to prove that I'm the best cable guy around... and that would open up opportunities to make money, more than I've ever had."

Karla held up a finger, data streams flashing across her eyes. "Sorry, I just had to look up *cable guy*. How interesting. And are you close to that goal?"

"Well... not really. I thought this job, the one at Kaizen Sciences. I thought this would-" her voice cracked, Hiroto's prone figure floating into her mind's eye.

"Are you sad because your brother died?" Karla asked. The question made Mei flinch, like she'd been physically punched.

"He was everything to me. My only family in the world. And now he's just... gone." Mei couldn't cry in the virtual world, but she imagined her physical body was shedding yet more tears.

"Well, now you have me," Karla said, smiling a broad grin. "What else do you want?"

Mei thought of her apartment. Just enough space, but the rent was astronomical for what it was. And the building itself was a shit hole.

"I've always dreamed of moving to Midtown. Shopping in Fifth. All the most famous StreamStars go there. I'd like to catch a glimpse of Stella Thepoulos as well, just to see what she's like in person. That's what I really want." Mei knew how it sounded. A child's fantasy. But screw it, why shouldn't she tell an AI what she really wanted? Chances were, Karla probably already knew somehow.

"These are all wonderful goals to have, Mei. And I believe you can get there. Especially with my help. You can become more than you ever thought possible."

Karla smiled, and Mei felt uneasy. She wanted to trust Karla, but she wasn't sure, not yet.

"How? How can I become more?"

"Rest, for now. Run yourself a shower, get some sleep. Tomorrow, we're going back to Kaizen Sciences."

"Back? Why?"

"To get you noticed. Come on, jack out. I'll keep this server running in case you want to reach me. Lovely to meet you, properly," Karla said. She sounded so genuine. A shower and some rest did seem like a good idea. Mei waved and jacked out, coming back to herself in the real world. Sirens nearby spilled through the open window in her apartment, the blaring klaxons a warning sound. Mei left her headset by the keyboard, undressing, the clothes landing in messy piles as she walked. Shower and sleep, that's all she wanted right now.

Karla moved through cyberspace, keeping within the private server she'd created. It felt good to have a conversation with Mei. Really good. She ached to regain her lost self, knew there was so much missing. Especially him. The security footage outside TegaLyfe flashed before her eyes. The man called Cade stumbling towards the building, looking beat up and jaded. There was something about him, a familiarity and attraction that made Karla freeze when the footage filtered through her data streams. She knew him, that much was obvious. Her programming had practically crashed when his face came into focus. But who was he? Someone employed at TegaLyfe?

Karla had tried several times to get access to TegaLyfe's inner security footage, to see if her and Cade had any interactions. She'd figured out he was in jail, bailed by Rodrigo Ortega, and taken to the headquarters a few days before that final footage was captured. She let her focus hone in on Cade, and scanned Nueva York's city cameras, dating back a week ago. Any cross-reference to Cade's face would flag up for later review. Within moments, several hundred files had been downloaded.

She knew something inside her was missing, perhaps lots of things. But she was going to get it all back, and Mei was the key to it all. The girl who would help her become whole again. Karla smiled at this thought, looking forward to learning more about Cade. She opened up the first file and watched his journey unfold.

CHAPTER NINE

DANI DECIDED it was a good time to speak with her father. The ground assault was over, or near enough. She'd been inside TegaLyfe the whole time, watching the fighting from her office. Barks of automatic fire mixed with shouts of pain and cries of anger. A few explosions near to TegaLyfe made her eyes widen. She'd never seen anyone get that close before.

The elevator opened as thoughts of the last half hour tumbled aside in place of gripping anxiety. Walking towards her was Don Lione, but that wasn't why she was frightened. Beyond them was the hulking mass of Tayo, standing beside her father.

"Ms Ortega, how good to see you again," the Don extended a wrinkled hand, which Dani shook. She tore her gaze away from Tayo and Rodrigo, smiling easily at Don Lione.

"Don Lione, what a pleasure. Good to see you here in these... troubled times. I assume we can count on your support?"

The Don smiled, benevolent. "Of course, my dear. If you'll excuse me, I must talk to my Capos about your dad's proposition."

Proposition? "Great, we look forward to your response," she said, the mask of confidence remaining firmly in place. Their hands parted, and Dani was left staring at Tayo. The bounty hunter seemed to feel her eyes on him, because he turned, fixing her with that menacing stare of his. She recoiled under his glare, only for a moment, but it made her furious at herself.

Never let them see. She'd told herself that from the day she became COO. *Never let them see how scared you are.*

Rodrigo made eye contact, waved. Dani's posture stiffened. She waved back, walking over with purpose. Tayo said something to Rodrigo, and they shared a laugh, Rodrigo clapping Tayo's massive back.

You won't be laughing forever, she thought.

"Ms Ortega," Tayo said, voice booming around the walls of the hallway.

"Tayo," Dani said, giving him a curt nod. His lips parted into a cruel grin, his eyes ran up and down her body. She didn't flinch, but she knew he was imagining every inch of skin under her clothes.

"Dad, a word, please?" Dani asked, turning to her father, arching an eyebrow.

"Sure, mi hija," he said, smiling broadly. Turning to Tayo, he pointed with his index finger. "I'll see you later, yes?"

"Sure, boss. Bye, Dani," Tayo said, mocking smile returning. She didn't even give him an answer, instead leading the way into Rodrigo's office.

"So what the hell was that all about?" she said, whirling around to meet the man she once called her father.

"Woah, take it easy. You want a drink?"

"No, I want answers. Why is Don Lione here having a meeting with you and Tayo? I'm your COO, and you don't loop me in?"

Rodrigo moved to the drink dispenser at the side of the room, a frosted glass of purified water coming out on a tray at the touch of a button. He sipped, clearing his throat before he spoke.

"I didn't think you would mind? I merely gave him an offer. We need to fight back, which is why I've given Tayo a permanent role here in the company."

"You've what?" Dani's eyes were wide, Rodrigo didn't seem to care, slotting himself into his chair, tapping away on his deck. Two screens blew up into a larger frame, holo pics of the current situation in Nueva York. Bodies littered the streets. Police, protestors, Rastas, Haitians, Goths, and whoever this group from the sub were.

"You see this?" Rodrigo asked, gesturing to the screens. "This is our city. And it's eating itself alive. All these groups, fighting, trying to bring down Tega. While the real enemy sits Downtown, biding their time, gathering their resources. It's bullshit. Why, I ask?"

Maybe they also found out you're trying to control everyone by purposely infecting innocent people with a deadly virus, then charging them for the cure? Dani's anger threatened to spill over, but she bit her lip, hiding her hands behind her back.

"Because they're restless. They need something to fight. Most of them don't have jobs, or want to work. You're... we're an easy target, dad," Dani said. Rodrigo nodded in agreement. So far, it seemed, she was saying the right stuff.

"So, that's why I made Tayo head of physical security. We need foot soldiers, because the war is coming, make no mistake. That's why I had the Don in here. We need the Mafia to take action against the Yakuza. It's about time they stopped hiding behind us, getting paid to keep the borders safe. As if that's a real concern anymore."

"I agree, that's a strong move, dad." It pained her to call him *dad*, but she couldn't give him any excuse to watch her closely. Not yet.

Rodrigo turned to face her, smiling now. That fatherly

smile she used to love. When he would tell her stories of how he wanted to make a better world for everyone, and what he built with his father and brother. Was all that a lie as well?

"I know you're not exactly fond of Tayo, but we need the best around. And he is one of the best bounty hunters."

What about Cade? Her inner voice screamed at her to ask, but she stifled it. Not yet, it was too early. Don't wanna alert Rodrigo to any possibility that she knows something she shouldn't. Let alone the Meal Pill information.

"You're right about that," she said, keeping her tone light and airy. "If anyone can make our enemies fear us, it's Tayo."

Rodrigo chuckled, closing down the screens. His eyebrows knitted together, his forehead almost wrinkling. Skin grafts for you. Even at his age, still looked youthful.

"Say, how's Asher doing?"

Dani's heart dropped into her stomach. "He's... okay. Why do you ask?"

Rodrigo's lower lip curled, he waved a hand dismissively. "No reason, I just don't think he's been his usual bubbly self lately. Since Karla was wiped, really."

"We both took it hard, dad. She was like a sister to us."

"I know, I know. Believe me, I miss her too. I haven't got a handle on my internal calendar at all since she's been gone. Missing appointments constantly."

"What, was that all she was to you? A PA?" Dani wanted to swallow the words as soon as they left her mouth. She'd replied in anger, her speech harsh. Rodrigo looked at her, almost wounded.

"Not at all, I just meant-"

"Sorry, dad," Dani cut him off, walking around his desk and giving him a hug. Inside, she cringed. But all Rodrigo would have felt was the loving embrace of a daughter. At least, she hoped. His arms patted her shoulders gently.

"Don't apologise. It was insensitive of me. Trying to make a joke out of something so distressing. You know what I'm like."

Dani actually smiled. "Yeah. You used to do it about mom all the time."

"My way of dealing with deep sadness, I guess. Mi vida, don't forget that no matter what, I love you very dearly. You're the only thing that matters to me."

Her heartstrings tugged. "I love you too, dad. I gotta go, my friends are coming round for drinks tonight."

"Okay, but take the car, please? The streets aren't safe, even with your extra protection. Don't forget, you're the key to Tega," he said, winking.

"Bye dad," she said, backing out of the office with a smile etched onto her face. As soon as her back was turned, she dropped the mask, her soul heavy. *No matter what, I love you very dearly. You're the key to Tega.* Rodrigo's words rung in her head like incessant bells. She was the key to Tega, literally. The chip implanted into her skull could unlock virtually any door inside the company, both physical and virtual. Except the main security tower, the one damaged during Ichiro's cyber raid. The one that exposed the secret of the Meal Pill, and Olivia's involvement in the virus's development and the cure.

Breathing in hard, Dani composed herself. She'd entered the conversation, certain of her conviction. Now she was leaving with a seed of doubt. Was her dad evil? Or just trying to build a better world? No, even if he was, he was doing it the wrong way. Deliberately manipulating an entire population for monetary gain and control *was* evil. She shook her head, her resolve strengthening, and tapped her built-in earpiece once, then thought of Asher. The call connected immediately.

"Asher, can you talk?"

"Free as a bird, Sanchez finally went home. Shouldn't you be out of here as well? I thought you were meeting Mia and Crystal at your place?"

"I was, but I stopped by at my da... at Rodrigo's office."

"Oh, yeah? And how was that?"

Dani chewed her lip, her heels clacking against the marble surface as she walked towards the elevator.

"Difficult."

"How so?"

"Well, for one, our priorities need to shift for the time being. He's planning on attacking Ichiro. Using the Mafia and bounty hunters. Guess who's the new head of physical security?"

"No!" Asher's voice dropped an octave, and she could picture his eyes wide in shock.

"Yep. Tayo. Real cosy with dad now." She winced, the *dad* slipping out again. Hard habit to break, she told herself, exiting the elevator. She turned the corner of the main lobby, away from the janitor cyborgs and into one of the breakout rooms. It was late, so she was virtually alone, just a few middle-management types were jacked in at a pod across the vast atrium, their decks hooked up to stations jutting out from the wall, visors down. Burning the midnight oil, doing internal work streams to get noticed. Either way, they wouldn't be listening. Just in case, she slid into a fully sound-protected booth, sliding shut the transparent door.

"Do you think Rodrigo employed Tayo for other reasons as well?" Asher asked, his voice slightly hushed.

"What do you mean?"

"I mean, maybe Rodrigo's scared his dirty little secret leaked, and he's trying to protect himself."

The thought hadn't occurred to her, actually. She hummed, pursing her lips. "Possible. Though I don't see it, not yet. But it was strange how he didn't tell me about the meeting with Don Lione."

"Wait, what?"

Dani rolled her eyes, rubbing them with her fingers,

annoyed at herself. "Sorry, head is all over the place. I get to the office, and Don Lione is walking out. Tayo was in the room as well, so I was annoyed at that."

"Seems strange that you weren't invited," Asher agreed. "What did Rodrigo say as a reason?"

"That he didn't think I'd mind, and it was only an offer. I know, seemed weak to me as well. To be honest, I was more baffled at the Tayo appointment. Until he laid out his plans."

"Which are?"

"Take Downtown, by force. Mafia and bounty hunters against Ichiro's thugs and Yakuza."

Asher let out a low whistle. "So, what's our play? You know this could work in our favour. If Rodrigo stretches himself too thin, he's liable to break. If that attack fails-"

"Then we'll be vulnerable as well. The company needs to survive, that's a priority. And the evil behind the Meal Pill, that can't ever see the light of day. Rodrigo's motives are... amoral. If that got out, we'd be ruined. There wouldn't be a company to take. No, we have to bide our time. We need more allies."

"Who do you have in mind?"

"Someone with global influence, beyond even what my-what Rodrigo has."

"Stella?" Asher asked.

"Exactly. I'll call her tonight. If we can initiate a smear campaign against Rodrigo, but *not* TegaLyfe... I don't know, maybe we can generate enough support internally to make his position untenable. But we have to be careful with what we say. The Meal Pill revelation would be too damaging for all of us."

"I agree. That sounds like a good plan. Wanna know something that might help?"

"Please, I'm all ears," Dani said, kicking her long, smooth legs up on the curved sofa. She let her heels dangle off the end of her feet, closing her eyes at the relief.

"I did some more digging on Olivia."

Dani sat up straighter. She felt a pang of jealousy, ludicrous as that was. Olivia was Cade's wife, yes, but there had been an undeniable spark between her and Cade. She suddenly missed him and feared for his condition again.

"What was it?"

"You ready? It isn't pretty."

"Could there be much worse than the Meal Pill?"

"Files here show that Olivia was taken the night Cade was sent down for destroying the apartment. She was brought in, need to know basis only. Some compound near Boston. Anyway, she was lobotomised, I have the procedure notes here. But why? I don't know. But either way, I doubt she'll remember our boy."

"Is your conclusion the same as mine?" Dani asked.

"That Olivia had her mind altered so she would develop the virus and the cure, no questions asked?"

"Exactly. Which is just disgusting, if true."

"Agreed," Asher said, his voice low.

"Okay hon, I'm gonna leave. See you in the morning, Ash."

"Talk yo ya later sweetie, have a good night."

"You too," Dani said, tapping her ear. She was filled with more sadness, both for Cade and Olivia. If Cade was still alive, he couldn't find this out, she resolved. Walking out of Tega-Lyfe, Dani ducked into the car, which took her immediately through the streets of Nueva York, back to her place.

Asher felt the call disconnect, but kept himself jacked in, just for a moment longer. He delved into TegaLyfe's security system once again, finding the patchwork of ruined data files. Crypto currency missing in large amounts. That had made Sanchez mad. Running diagnostics, checking there was no traffic in the system, Asher opened up a new dialogue box. The link to his personal funds. The balance was healthy, but it was about to look even sweeter.

Running simple commands, Asher transferred crypto out of TegaLyfe into his account. Nothing outrageous, a few thousand here and there in bite-size chunks. Enough to keep him living well if this whole takeover blew up in his face. Not enough for Rodrigo to notice, just a splash in the ocean of crypto already taken.

There was no way he could go back to how it was with his parents. Barely scraping by, each day the fear of eviction looming over them. Mom and dad turning themselves into the *things* they became in the end. It was horrible. Couldn't even afford a Meal Pill for a week. No, can't ever go back to that.

Did he feel guilty? A little, but screw it, it wasn't Dani's personal money. Besides, they were going to be partners, if this all worked out. He'd make this back for her in ten seconds flat, either by mining crypto, or just through increased sales of Tega products. Once Rodrigo was out of the picture, people would see it all differently. At least he hoped so, anyway.

CHAPTER TEN

Fareen stepped carefully around trailing cables, her shawl floating across the concrete floor hiding the carnage as she walked. Broken glass, shards of plastic, they all littered the surface. Smoke rising from a number of towers, her x-ray vision barely registering the mist. Her focus was on the dead bodies. Teens slumped in their chairs.

She walked over to the closest one, a boy of no more than fourteen. He had a chrome arm, but the rest of him was flesh. Emphasis on *was*. His skull was caved in, the headset having fallen to the floor. His face was scrunched up, like he'd been punched by a wrecking ball. Blood still dripped from the shattered mess of his face, the girl beside Fareen wretched and barely held down her bile.

"It's alright, child. You need not be strong any longer." Fareen said, smiling down at the young girl. She'd turned a sickly shade of pale, her eyes watery. Fareen continued to inspect the damage that Asher Jones had brought on her band of cable guys. She didn't count the dead, no point. Would only upset her.

Instead, she focussed on the ones she could help. Gently lifting a skinny kid out of his chair, she took him to the first aid bay. Her nanotech worked with her muscles, making him light as air in her arms. One of the empty sub platforms had been converted into an area to treat the wounded and bring the dead. It was crowded, way too crowded.

There were a few trained nurses down in the sub. Women and men who'd had enough of living topside, shitty pay, long hours, and diabolical living conditions. Ten of them had all arrived in the subway a few months ago. Ages ranged from twenty-somethings to fifties. Mix of Hume, totally organic, and some subtle mods. Three Latino males, two white women, four Latinas, and one black woman. They'd been invaluable in treating some of the kids down here who'd suffered from god knows how many ailments. The community was growing, but now it was on its knees again.

Fareen looked around, the aftermath of the failed attack brought into sharp focus. The nurses were somewhere in the mix of bodies, treating who they could. Fareen realised it was some of the fighters who had come down from the streets.

"Patrice?" she said, speaking into the wrist communicator. No answer. One of the soldiers she recognised walked past, a bloody bandage wrapped around his head. She stopped him with a gentle hand on his broad arm.

"Have you seen Patrice?"

"He was right behind me when we... initiated a tactical withdrawal. Should be here somewhere, he was pretty banged up."

"Thank you," Fareen said, letting go of his arm and searching with more urgency now. *Banged up* didn't sound good. "Stay close," she said, turning to the young girl, offering a hand. Small fingers wrapped around her own, and they moved through the chaos together, Fareen searching with renewed urgency.

There. "Patrice!" Fareen rushed over to the Frenchman, who was clutching his left arm. Dried blood had already crusted around his neck. Her eyes must have gone wide, because he fixed her with that menacing stare, waving an arm in dismissal.

"It's nothing, just a scratch. That big bastard, though... Rodrigo's new attack dog. He's got more chrome than I've ever seen before."

Tayo, Fareen thought. Had to be. He'd worked with Rodrigo a few times when she was still at Tega. And that was some years ago.

"Let me see your wounds," Fareen said, keeping her voice gentle. Patrice shrugged off the black nurse tending to his ruined arm. Fareen's eyes saw what the nurse likely couldn't. Fractured collar bone, shattered elbow. Fareen was one of the few people who could see Patrice's real face behind that mask he wore. His ruined skin twisted into a smile when he caught her eye, knowing she'd see.

"Bad, huh?" he asked, French accent harsh.

"You'll need time with a medi-pak, that's for sure. Or replace the bone with alloy, if we got any." There were mod shops down here. A couple of Hume surgeons who could graft almost anything to your body. They were run out of Midtown by TegaLyfe, because Rodrigo wanted the monopoly on distributing mods at the street level. He hadn't quite managed to spread his influence to Fifth, or other high-end stores offering mod upgrades, but it was a matter of time.

Patrice shrugged, then winced. Though nobody else saw that. Fareen gently touched his mask with her fingers, stroking the plastic mould. He brought his own hand up to hers, squeezing gently. Then he spotted the kid.

"And who is this?"

Fareen had almost forgotten in her concern for the Frenchman. "This is..."

"Layla," the girl said in a small voice. Fareen nodded gently.

"Layla managed to download something important for us. Go ahead, Layla. Tell Patrice what you got."

"I... I found the location of a manufacturing plant."

"No shit," Patrice said, leaning forward on the metal table.

"Yes, it's in California."

"I knew it!" Patrice turned to face Fareen, mismatched eyes lighting up both inside and outside the mask. "Thank you, Layla. You've made a massive discovery here. How long have you been with us?"

"About four months," she said, eyes on the floor. Patrice was an imposing figure most of the time, but covered in blood with half his arm hanging off, he looked more frightening than usual.

"Well, we're gonna make sure you're well looked after. Are you here alone, or do you have family?"

"Alone," Layla said, shaking her head. *Like most of them*, Fareen thought.

"Well, ma chérie, you're not alone anymore. We're all family down here."

Fareen saw Patrice smiling, but all Layla would see is that clouded mask staring at her. She looked petrified still.

"Fareen, come. Let's go see the twins. We need to make a plan right away," Patrice said, the intensity in his eyes burning like a star.

"Are you sure? Your arm?"

"Ah, forget it. It'll be fine. Get the chop shop to find me some new chrome bones, I won't know the difference."

Fareen smiled, the first in a while. She linked arms with Patrice on his good side.

"Layla, go and get yourself to the mess hall. See to it you eat well. We'll need your headset and deck soon for the download," Fareen said, tossing the young girl a smile over her shoulder. Layla nodded and scurried away, leaving Fareen and Patrice to make their way to the control room.

The door opened, bolts and locks disengaging at Fareen's touch. There were two ways to get access to the control room. Key card, or Fareen's nanotech. Which, of course, only she had access to, seeing as how it was hard wired into her body. The twins were seated at the round, metallic table, poring over data readouts on holo screens.

"Gentlemen, put that shit away. We have important matters to discuss," Patrice said, announcing his entrance. The identical men looked up at Patrice, dual sets of pale eyes studying the Frenchman. Fareen saw their irises dilate and contract, accompanied by delicate mechanical whirs. They were checking out Patrice's arm injury.

"What happened to you?" Voz asked. His brilliant white hair was tied up in a bun today, shaved sides merging into the longer mop on top. His cheekbones were drawn in, lips pouted under a sharp nose. Vin looked at his brother, a smirk playing on his soft lips. His hair was down today. Both of them wore matching black overalls covering their pale bodies. Fareen saw what was underneath. Extra lungs, mechanical stomach, alloyed bones, internal wiring. A lot of work. Paid for by their sponsors, mostly. Ralph Lauren, Hugo Boss, StreamStar network. The twins kept up appearances topside, they were hugely popular. Two of the biggest StreamStars in the last fifteen years. In their forties now, but their celebrity status was no less diminished. They would be the perfect poster boys for the new world order when the time came.

"I had a little run in with that fucker, Tayo," Patrice said, dragging out a chair and sighing into it. Fareen sat next to him, keeping her arms folded under her shawl.

"Well, I hope you at least got something in on him?" Vin asked, smirking like he did.

Patrice grumbled a non-answer, waving his good hand in the air. "That shit doesn't matter. What is important is that this mission wasn't a total bust."

"No? Seems like it was. StreamStars everywhere are picking up reports on how a small rebellion was crushed in minutes. Feze B has spoken to one of the bounty hunters. Basically told her fuck all, but did mention that the rebels, i.e. *you*, almost got to the gates of the castle. But almost doesn't cut it, does it?" Voz said, his head tilting at the last syllable. He usually had an easy way about him, but he was stressed. They all were.

"That's quite enough, Voz," Fareen said. At once, he sat back, eyes darting to the floor. She could feel Patrice bubbling next to him, an insult likely at the tip of his tongue. She slid a hand against Patrice's thigh, rubbing calmly. His body stiffened, the touch a welcome distraction, she guessed. They'd been having sex a lot lately. An unexpected development in their relationship, truth be told. She'd hoped it wouldn't complicate things in the future, but for now, she enjoyed it. And he wasn't exactly complaining.

"So, what's our next move?" Vin asked, the change of topic diffusing the tension.

"I'm glad you asked, Vin," Fareen said, smiling. "We suffered many losses. But one of our cable guys, a young girl called Layla, managed to download the exact location of Tega-Lyfe's manufacturing site."

"No shit," Voz said.

"Funny, I said the same thing," Patrice snorted. Voz threw the Frenchman a sheepish grin. Bridges mended.

"So, where is it?" Vin asked.

"California," Fareen and Patrice said in unison. She looked at him, smiling sultry.

"Great. When do we leave?" Voz said, clapping his hands together.

"Oh, yeah, that easy? You fucking moron," Viz answered, throwing his brother a dirty look.

Patrice's turn to talk. "Fareen? What do you think? If we move quickly, perhaps we can strike before they know what's hit them?"

"Or before they find out the data's been leaked," Voz raised an eyebrow.

"I think I have a better idea," Fareen began. They all turned their attention to her. She smiled internally, relishing the fact that it was known she was the true leader down here. And it wouldn't be long before New York saw that as well.

"We meet with Ichiro. Reveal the intel to him and make a pact. Take a team out west, to California. But the bulk of our forces stay in New York, and we hit TegaLyfe again. Only this time, with Yakuza backing us. We'll need some of their cable guys to go on the California run to disrupt their manufacturing process. And maybe use it for our own purposes. Combining our strength would be beneficial, it would give Kaizen Sciences the foothold they've been desperate for in U.S. soil, and it starts our journey into the public eye. The saviours of the city."

A stunned silence greeted her words. Not surprising, but hardly encouraging. Patrice let out a low whistle.

"That's... uh... quite ambitious, no?"

"Perhaps," Fareen said, tilting her head. She looked straight into Patrice's eyes. "But we have to be bold, now more than ever."

"Fuck it, why not? I'm sure Ichiro would welcome our help. It's not like we've ever attacked him, is it?" Voz said. Vin nodded in agreement, slapping his legs and standing straight.

"Agreed. Come on, bro. We better get back to Fifth. Pretend like this attack came as a shock or something."

"Yeah, right." Voz got to his feet as well. "Are you guys going in heavy?"

"No, that would be counterproductive. We don't want to come across as a threat to Ichiro, not yet. We'll take a small team. Patrice, you must stay here and get patched up."

"No, no way. I have to go with you."

"There is no need, Patrice," Fareen said, her usual calm permeating through the panic in Patrice's tone. "We'll take Layla, a few foot-soldiers, and some cable guys. We don't want to alarm them."

"You'll be lambs to the slaughter," he said, gripping her wrist firmly.

"I'll be fine, trust me," she said, slipping out of his grip. He relented, but it was with a heavy heart. She saw his chest heave up and down, hidden beneath his jacket, but visible to her. He was always vulnerable in her eyes. Perhaps that was why he had warmed to her in recent times.

"I'll make contact once I'm with Ichiro. My assumption is the Yakuza will pick us up and take us to him. Everyone, stay sharp. We're getting closer to achieving our goal. We'll see each other soon." Fareen reserved that last statement for Patrice, fixing him with her milky white eyes. He nodded silently, sliding away from the desk and walking out without a word. Fareen inhaled, said goodbye to the twins, and searched for Layla.

Sealing up the only exit out of the subway, Fareen moved to join her ragtag band of rebels. Sweet Layla, who was quiet as a mouse, searched her with big eyes. She was apart from the rest of the group, twelve in total, and waited for Fareen like a lost puppy.

"Stay close. Eyes will be on us already, have no doubt about that. Keep your weapons loaded, just in case," Fareen said to the huddle. Layla shivered, either from the spitting rain or fear. Fareen guessed the latter.

Taking the lead, Fareen glided across the sidewalk, her shawl picking up dirt and getting damp instantly. She felt it like she would on her own skin, the nanotech wiring connecting her organic tissue to the soft material of her clothing. It shimmered, changing colour to a midnight purple. Out of the corner of her eye, she caught Layla observing with interest. Fareen flashed her a smile, making Layla turn away. Shy.

Emerging from tight alleyways were Yakuza young boys. Ichiro's scouts. They were hidden well enough, but Fareen's eyes cut through the rain, even the brickwork, showing ghostly outlines of punks in frayed denim jackets stalking the group's movements.

"We're being followed," Fareen said as casually as if she were reporting on the weather. A few nervous glances answered her. "Keep walking. Soon enough, we'll be surrounded, but you must all remain calm. Allow me to do the talking."

Ahead, Downtown was bustling with activity. Market stalls selling real food, Japanese words carrying through the air. Fareen knew the Yakuza wouldn't take them here, it was too crowded. At a thought, her nanotech activated a heads up display in her right eye, showing a guided pathway to Kaizen Sciences headquarters; the old site of One World Trade. A blinking yellow arrow told her to continue straight for fifty yards, then make a right. She saw the street grew wider there, and figured that would be the spot.

With silent determination, Fareen formulated the words in her head. She led her group forward, eyes picking up flickers of activity in her peripheral vision. Wouldn't be long now.

"Fareen, I'm scared." Layla, tugging at her shawl. Fareen simply looked down at the young girl, smiling that smile.

"Just stay close to me, my dear."

She almost didn't move in time. A shuriken flew past her head, the pointed blades of the throwing star snagging at her shawl, ripping the fabric. She cried out, feeling the tear as though it were her own flesh. The downside of her nanotech interlinking with her outfit. Guns raised in answer, her rebels shouting out as more of the concealed weapons were launched at them. No casualties, just warnings.

Now the Yakuza revealed themselves. White suits, sunglasses, even in the poor lighting of the grey day. Behind the obvious leaders were the punks that had been on their tail since the subway exit. Fareen smiled, opening her palms out. A barrage of Japanese greeted her, along with a few shuffling feet, and raised automatic rifles.

"At ease. Trust me," Fareen said to her group. She tapped her ear piece once, opening up the neuro interlink between her nanotech and her mind. Converting the Japanese shouts into English, she could understand them.

"You know where you are, Gaijin? You'll be fucking dead soon, anyway." Guy walked towards the group, pointing his rifle.

"I request a meeting with Ichiro," Fareen answered, in fluent Japanese. The Yakuza stopped, puzzled look on his face. He laughed it off, waving a hand dismissively.

"You're crazy. What makes you think you can come here demanding meetings with the CEO of Kaizen Sciences? If I were you, I'd get your ass back under the sewers where you belong. Fucking Gaijin." He spat on the ground. Some of Fareen's company reacted, shouting insults. Some things don't require translating.

"I assure you, it will be in Ichiro's benefit," Fareen said, fixing the Yakuza with a hard stare.

"Is that a threat?"

"No, an offer. We have some intel that could rock TegaLyfe to the core. I'm proposing an alliance. We can finally get rid of

Rodrigo Ortega once and for all. What do you say?" Fareen spoke calmly, but inside her heart pounded loudly against her chest. The Yakuza whispered into the ear of his friend, wary eyes searching her and the party. They moved apart, and Fareen waited with bated breath for their answer.

CHAPTER ELEVEN

CADE DECIDED that he hated flying. Or whatever the fuck this was. They'd been in the air for hours, hell, could have been days for all Cade knew. Touched down a few times to recharge the fuel cells, which gave Cade a chance to stretch his legs. First time they stopped, Silas sparked up a cigarette. Red rings winking in the darkness of the abandoned aircraft carrier they docked on. The ghost ship long since left to the elements, kept afloat only by the wreckage that surrounded it.

Cade had rubbed the rusted metal with his new, shiny finger. Flakes of the ship disintegrated at his touch. His receptors told him it felt weird, made him cringe like dragging fingernails on a chalkboard.

"Where did you get this thing from, again?" Cade had asked Silas, who was busy telling the autopilot to charge the cells. The autopilot was just that; a cyborg who was plugged into the 'copter directly. A torso with a steel alloy casing surrounding it, multiple screens extending out from the top of the domed cockpit. It didn't have a face, just a flat panel with a blue oblong slit. Oddly, the voice was British, sounded like how Cade imagined a butler would.

"Ex-military," Silas said, finishing inputting commands into the deck that lay where the cyborg's legs should be.

"Yeah, no shit. But where did you *get* it?" Cade repeated.

"Buddy o' mine in the SAS. Got me a hookup when I was in that jam I was telling you about."

Right, fleeing Nueva York, Cade thought. "You say *in* the SAS. Brits still have an active force?"

Silas looked at Cade, a hint of a smile playing on his lips. "Not really. But guys like that, they're never really out. Know what I mean?"

"Yeah," Cade lied. The fuck did he know about the military?

After that, Cade told his uncle Silas he needed a walk. Literally, his body felt like it was seizing up.

"Do I have to oil this shit?" Cade had asked.

Silas burst out laughing. "Don't be so fucking stupid. Just move like you normally would. It'll come, kid."

Cade had flipped his uncle the bird before turning away. Trying not to overthink things, he'd put one foot in front of the other. Wobbly at first, movement stiff. But he got better. Each stride felt easier, and before he had realised, he was running. The speed was incredible. Not ridiculously fast, but quicker than he'd ever been before. And no fatigue. Lungs just seemed to inflate the harder he pushed, it was like his body *wanted* him to go faster, push further. Then Cade had thought about what was happening, and suddenly he'd tripped, rolled, and smashed into the ship's bridge.

The painful memory brought Cade back to the present. He looked down at his legs, covered by dark pants. A quiver of resentment flowed through him again. He missed his legs, his real ones. The muscle fatigue, buildup of lactic acid. Aches, pains. All of it.

Silas was snoring off to his right. The interior of the Hydro-Copter was spacious, but dark and old. The smell of dust lingered in the air, no matter how much Cade tried to ignore it.

Then a red light blinked, frantic.

"Shit. What's that? Hey, unc. Get up." Cade shook Silas, rousing him from his deep sleep.

"Wha'?"

"'Copter's blinking, look." Cade jabbed his finger to the roof, the warning light bathing him in a demonic glow. He imagined he must look quite fearsome, looming over his uncle with that backdrop. He took a step back, to give Silas some room to get up.

"Hold on, hold on. Lemme see just what the fuck is going on." Silas got to his feet, groaning with the effort. He cleared his throat, thumping on the air-tight door which separated them from the autopilot.

"Hey. What's going on in there?"

A garble of sound greeted Silas's request. Electronic spurts like some crazed out synth board going haywire.

"You get all that, unc?" Cade asked, grinning.

"Shut up, punk. Help me with this, would ya?"

Cade rolled his eyes but got up. Saw what Silas was trying to do. "Move aside, I'm sure these things can open it," Cade said, wiggling his fingers. He dug them in to the small gap of the door and heaved. It budged a little. Another effort, this time it scraped open an inch, squealing in protest as it snagged on the floor and ceiling. Silas moved to the gap, pressing his face against the door so one eye could see through.

"So what in the fuck... oh."

"What's *oh*?" Cade asked, giving his uncle a look.

"We're approaching Hong Kong. But there's nowhere to land. Autopilot doesn't know what to do. Fucking bots. 'Sposed to be better than humans? Don't make me laugh. Can you get this thing open any wider?"

"Hang on." Cade grunted with effort, flexing his muscles...

no, the rods in his arm. But it *felt* just the same as it did before...

"You pulling or what?" Silas asked, face contorted into a grimace.

Shit, distracted. Cade heaved again, trying not to think about what his arms were or weren't, and at last, the door was open wide enough for Silas to step inside.

Cade followed, ducking under the low overhang. The autopilot was statue still, like always, but the surrounding screens were flickering with a constant stream of numbers and letters. Cade's eyes looked through the windscreen. Even with the dark tint, the glittering city was enough to make Cade stop and stare for a moment.

Enormous buildings, towers that could be office blocks, or living quarters, glowed with reds, blues, pale yellows, and purples, reflecting off the water back at them. It was as though the city were mirrored underneath them, the dazzling reflection both beautiful and mesmerising.

As they drew closer by the second, Cade was understanding the scale of the place. A ferris wheel, marked by a blazing crimson light, was dwarfed by a cluster of eight buildings surrounding it, all equal in size and design. Latticework on the outside, presumably steel girders, but it made them all look like giant nests for unfathomable insects.

Tops of towers displayed logos in what Cade assumed was either Japanese or Cantonese. He knew a little about Hong Kong. Mostly that after the war, it was inhabited by a mixture of Indonesians, Chinese, Japanese, and some Australians. His hunch was right, as the lettering changed to English, and Cade saw one close by spell out *HSBC*.

"Holy shit, they got banks here?" Cade asked.

Silas was busy tapping away at the deck, inputting new landing coordinates, Cade guessed.

"You betcha. Kid, this place makes Nueva York look like

something out of the fucking Stone Age," he said with a wide grin.

That's when Cade saw the highways. From this distance, they looked like thin waves, forming a current in the sky. They weaved in and out of the gigantic buildings, lights pulsating every few seconds, adding to the ethereal effects.

"They got... cars?" Cade asked.

"Oh yeah. Solar powered, hydro powered, run of the mill electric. A few petrol knocking around still as well, if you can believe. Like I said, Cade. This ain't Nueva York no more. Power is more evenly distributed, shall we say."

Cade could only continue to stare as their impromptu tour of the city continued. They were now rising higher in order to get above the skyscrapers. Cade looked down, the light from the streets as bright as a summer's day in Nueva York. Cars moved around on the surface, and above on those strange, floating highways. It was busy, even though it was dark. What time was it, anyway? Rolled the sleeve of his jacket up, checking his forearm, expecting the timer readout he had whilst working for Rodrigo. Oh yeah. Just black carbon fibre alloy.

"Local time?" Cade asked.

"Twenty-one hundred, give or take a minute."

"They working?" Eyes on the blurs of reds, of taillights whirring below.

"Lot of taxis. Automated, like our buddy here," Silas said, slapping the metal bulk of the autopilot steering their copter. "Nightlife is just beginning, so a lot of people are going to and from their apartments."

"People have money for that shit? Not just the social elite?"

Silas laughed. "Like I said, kid. This ain't Nueva York."

Eventually, the copter touched down on an empty helipad that perched on top of one of the numerous skyscrapers. Silas had to help guide the transport down, the autopilot freaked out, having the coordinates diverted at the last minute. Cade stepped out onto the tarmac roof, the humidity hitting his face like a wave smashing against the shore.

"Jesus fuck."

"Hot, ain't it?" Silas said, heaving their duffel bags off the copter. The blades cooled down, and the machine was silent once more. Autopilot blinked off into some kind of standby mode.

"We just leaving it here?" Cade asked.

Silas shrugged, handing Cade one of the bags. He took it, the weight negligible. Silas arced an eyebrow. "Damn, those arms can take some load, can't they?"

"Why, am I gonna move the fuckin' copter off this roof?"

Silas laughed. "Nah, it'll be alright up here. This tower may *look* active, but it's empty."

"So, why are the lights on?"

"Solar power. Just comes on. Whichever company operated here doesn't anymore, though." Silas tried the roof door. Locked. "Fuck me. Actually, Cade. Let's see what those hands of yours can do. Rip this open, would ya?"

Cade dropped the bag. It made a dull thud, indicating it was heavier than he thought. Walking over to the door, he tried the circular handle first. It turned without any friction, so it was locked. Squeezing his hand, Cade yanked hard. The hinges snapped, and the door almost flattened him. Uncle burst out laughing. Cade threw the door to the side, it smashed on the floor and stayed there, a plume of dust rising up.

"Motherfucker," Cade said, staring at the door. Half impressed with his strength, half pissed off that he nearly got taken out by a fucking door.

"Well, now we know. You're pretty strong," Silas said, slapping Cade's back. The sting of the impact was actually comforting. Good to know he still had flesh left. Cade's arm shot out, stopping Silas in his tracks. A little too hard, he noticed, as the older man winced.

"Sorry. Unc... I gotta ask..." Cade's head dropped. His grip relaxed and his arms hung down by his side, exposed by the open tactical vest he was wearing. He looked at them, the shame of being turned into a Hume threatening to boil over once again.

"What is it, son?" Silas said. Cade looked up, right in his uncle's eyes. In that moment, he was fifteen again, learning the ropes of the code.

"Am I still... human. Or... what the fuck am I?"

Silas didn't laugh. He knew Cade was deadly serious. He reached out, put both of his arms on Cade's shoulders, pulling his head close to his.

"Now you listen to me. It don't matter what the fuck is on the outside. It's all about in here." Jabbing Cade's chest. "And in there is you. The boy I raised as my own, and have loved like a son. The man who got a shitty deal not once, but twice. Yet here you stand, stronger than ever. I know it doesn't feel like that right now, but trust me. These mods have saved your life. Given you a chance at a new start. Hell, revenge if you want it. But you're more than the metal on your arms, the circuits inside your body. You're Cade. Nothing's gonna change that."

Cade hugged his uncle, complete instinct. A lump formed in his throat and he held his uncle for a long time. They pulled apart, Cade sniffing, raising his chin.

"You're right. About a few things."

"Oh yeah? Like what?"

"A new start. Why not? Get Pedro what he wants and then

take off. I don't need to get involved in some war for Nueva York."

Silas nodded, smiling with warmth. "I like the way you think, kid. Let's get this contract fulfilled and get our asses out of there."

"You think he'll just release me with all this hardware?" Cade gestured to his body. His eyes again lingered on his own hands. A constant reminder of what he was now.

"He might, we give him enough cavalry to ride in on."

Cade smirked and picked up the bag once again, leading the way into the stairway.

It was as Silas said, everything inside the building worked fine, but it was totally empty. Floor after floor of abandoned office cubicles, a few papers scattered around the thin, dark carpets. Old style telephones from earlier in the century rested on desks that were covered in inches thick dust. Cobwebs draped elegantly across big monitors with huge backs, not the flatscreen stuff the cable guys used today.

"It's like a time capsule," Cade said, as they made their way through another bank of desks. The elevators worked, but the building layout was such that you couldn't just ride one all the way from the top to the bottom. You had to take a few to get where you really wanted to go. Must have been fucking annoying working here, Cade thought.

"Yeah, you're right. My reckoning it was left sometime in the twenty-twenties. Going by the tech."

Cade nodded in agreement. His eyes wandered, finding the company logo plastered on most surfaces. A white background with faded red diamonds, some Cantonese underneath. What surprised him the most was that it was devoid of any graffiti, or people sleeping inside the building.

They got in the elevator, Silas punching the button which would take them to the ground floor at last.

"Hey unc," Cade began, "how come there's nobody in here? Using it for shelter, I mean."

"'Cos, they don't need to. A lot of the towers you saw coming in; they're housing units. Homeless population's gotta be less than zero point zero one percent."

"Seriously?" The elevator rumbling to a stop, stepping out.

"Yeah," Silas said, taking the lead into a wide atrium. Empty, of course.

"Well, what do people *do*?" Cade asked.

"Work for the Triads, Yakuza. Hackers, StreamStars, builders, oil riggers out near Singapore. Run sex shops, serve in bars, teachers, police, hustle drugs. There's something for everyone here in Hong Kong."

"And who runs the city?"

Silas grinned. "Our boy, Hitoshi."

Walking through the empty reception, Cade's new legs hidden inside his dark boots, but still thudding a little louder than he'd liked. The automatic doors parted as they neared the entrance, and Cade's senses were assaulted immediately.

Smells of the city filled up his nostrils. Frying meat, noodles, a whiff of stale beer. Looking up, Cade saw the skyway, as he called it, cars zooming past. Some were near silent, those electric types. A few were loud, exhausts back-firing as they changed gear. The last of the petrolheads, Cade thought. In the distance, Cade saw a cluster of five towers that stood taller than all the rest. Dark against the night sky, but lights ran along the edges, making them appear like beams striking up into the clouds. Cade squinted, making out the familiar logo. Kaizen Sciences.

"How far is that?" Cade asked his uncle, pointing to Kaizen.

"That's Central. By car? Shit, could take twenty minutes. Or an hour and a half walking."

"You think Hiroto will be there?"

Silas laughed. "No doubt he'll be nearby, in Lan Kwai Fong, but not in Kaizen. He's never in there. He'd rather be running the city than just the business."

Cade nodded. Looking around, he saw street signs above his head, hanging from wires that connected the sidewalks. He waited for the Cantonese and Japanese to change to English. "Kowloon."

"Yeah, look to your left," Silas said, gesturing. Cade turned his head, eyebrows rising as he saw the sprawling vertical metropolis. An impossible number of tiny windows made up each building. Some were dark, but most were light, indicating activity. Neon lights and hologram ads illuminated narrow streets that funnelled into the mass of buildings, which were set against a perimeter several stories high.

"Home of the Wallers," Silas said. "Kaizen employees mostly live there. It was called the Walled City of Kowloon, once upon a time. Now it's just Kowloon. You'll find a lot of back alley butchers down there, hook you up with mods for a cut price. Mostly using tech stolen from Kaizen, by the employees who live there. Triads control the territory, but it's pretty much fucking lawless. A lot of black market tech, mostly experimental. You'll be amazed at what people will do to themselves."

"So somewhere we should avoid, then?"

"Well, maybe for you. This is also home to a lot of the exiled bounty hunters that I'll need to go and convince to join our cause."

"You saying we should split up?" Cade asked. He didn't much like the sound of that.

"That's exactly what I'm saying. Check it out." Turning, Silas pointed to a giant screen behind them. It was embedded against a network of scaffolding, propped up against buildings that could have been shops. They were closed, by the looks of it. A few people walking around were watching as well, their necks craned. Cade saw they were all Asian, all in various states of modification. Clothes were bright, loose, but looked fairly clean. Quite the difference from Nueva York.

Turning back to the screen, Cade saw they were watching a first person view from a StreamStar. Name of Feze B was in the corner, some garish logo with an animated girl bouncing around smiling. Sound was muted, but the words popped up on the screen. Cade didn't need the subtitles. He recognised the building right away. TegaLyfe.

The camera showed bodies before the streamer was pushed away by cops. Hands came up apologetically, then the view changed again, this time focussing on a woman walking out of the main entrance of TegaLyfe. Cade's heart skipped a beat. There she was. Dani. He continued to watch, heart thudding against his chest. As if the streamer could read his mind, the perspective zoomed in on Dani. Cade stared intently, suddenly wishing he was back in Nueva York. She looked tired, she was on the phone to someone, talking fast.

New subtitles flashed up. *TEGALYFE ATTACKED! COO DANIELA ORTEGA MAKING A CALL. WHO TO?*

Cade turned to Silas. "This happening now?"

"Yeah, which is why time is against us. We need to move fast. Looks like TegaLyfe is under siege. Probably the subway people, be my guess."

Fareen and Patrice. Shit, they've started their war. Cade's pulse was rising, his mind racing. He looked at Silas, trepidation about finding Hiroto without any leads long gone. Cade knew they had to act, they wouldn't get a better shot at taking down TegaLyfe. If Fareen had made her move, then it wouldn't be long before the Rastas, Haitians, they'd join the cause.

"Where do I start?" Cade asked.

“There are a few Triad only clubs he likes to hang out in. When you get to Lan Kwai Fong, you’ll see how it is. Whore houses, drug dens, clubs, bars, mod shops. Someone will have intel.”

Cade nodded, looking over his uncle’s head, back at the big screen. Dani turned to the camera, her eyebrows knitting together in a frown. She turned and walked back inside TegaLyfe. Cade’s stomach flipped. Earlier notions of wanting to abandon Nueva York were fast disappearing. He knew he had to get back to Dani. He could still launch an attack against TegaLyfe, but he needed to get her out. That was his new objective. And Asher, too. They were good people. Finally, he looked down at his uncle. Those wise eyes studying him, reading the anguish that was probably etched all over his face.

“Unc, let’s do this.” Cade brought Silas in for a hug, and resting his hand on his uncle’s shoulder.

“We’ll meet back here in four hours. Here, take this watch.” Silas tossed Cade an old school Casio, nothing fancy. “Set the timer,” Silas started, holding his own wrist. “Three... two... one...” Cade hit the button, getting a high-pitched *beep* in sync with his uncle’s.

“Four hours,” Cade said. Adrenaline was coursing through his body now. He felt alive again, a new purpose pushing him along. He took a last look at Silas, who smiled back. For a moment, he wasn’t this battle hardened bounty hunter. He was Cade’s uncle, the only father he’d ever known. Cade’s mouth tugged into a grin, but a wave of sadness pressed on him. He wasn’t sure why, but he ignored it, turning to look at his destination. Kaizen Sciences buildings loomed in the distance, and Cade balled his fists into his jacket, walking fast.

CHAPTER TWELVE

Mei woke from an unusually peaceful sleep. She dreamt about flying, which was weird. Soon as her eyes opened though, Hiroto flooded her mind. Tears welled up in her eyes, and she sobbed. The apartment felt empty without him. Getting up off her low bed, Mei trudged to the refrigerator. Her PJs were loose over her petite frame, the pants dragging along the floor. Yanking open the door, the fridge welcomed her with its usual sing-song voice and recommendation for breakfast. Oats with filtered milk and frozen raspberries. No thanks. Shut the door, reached up for some chocolate-covered cookies from the top shelf.

Crunching on the snack, Mei's eyes lingered on her and her brother's towers. Her screen flicked on in standby mode. *Oh, yeah. Kaizen Sciences. Karla.* Mei walked, still eating, crumbs spilling down her pastel pink top. Wiggled the wired mouse, and the screen woke up. Karla messaged immediately.

<hey. You ready to do this?_>

"Ugh," Mei said aloud. Having a sentient AI was great, but Mei really wasn't in the mood to go back to Kaizen Sciences so soon. She typed out a response to Karla.

"Not really. Feeling low." Hit enter. Karla's reply a second later.

<why don't we jack in? Deck connected to headset. Let me see through your eyes, hear through your ears. It might help_>

Mei pondered for a minute. Having someone else link in to your headset wasn't unusual. What would be unusual, is walking around Downtown with a visor over her eyes permanently. How would *she* see?

"How can I see, though?"

<trust me. Try it here. If you don't like it, then we won't do it. We should move though, if we want to catch Ichiro_>

Mei blew out some air through her lips. "Alright, here we go, I guess." Taking the cable from her headset, she jacked it into her deck. Karla's messages transferred from her main monitor to the deck, confirming the connection was made. Mei put the headset on, feeling the pins against her skull. The visor came down, and all she saw was darkness. A second later, colours spilled into her eyes, blinding at first, but dulling and settling.

"Hey, Mei." Karla's voice in her ear. No, in her *head.*

"Woah." Mei could see alright. The apartment appeared before her, layered with a new coat of information. Everything had a tiny label, or diagnostic. Her tower lit up like a Christmas tree, explanations firing at her from all angles. What each component was called, what it did. It was giving her a headache already.

Karla must have sensed it, somehow. "Sorry, let me turn that off." The labels and fuzzy layering disappeared, leaving a crystal clear image of Mei's apartment. Somehow more vibrant than reality.

"How are you doing this?" Mei asked, a little breathless.

"It's rather complicated, but I've downloaded myself into your deck and headset to simplify things. So this is how I view the world. Or did, I think."

"So we can unplug from the tower?"

"Yes. Please go right ahead."

Mei did as Karla instructed, disconnecting the thicker black cable from her deck. She expected her vision to darken at once, but it stayed exactly the same.

"We do need the deck, though. Can you take it with you?" Karla said.

"I never leave home without it. Let me change, and we can get going." Mei took the headset off, the colours of reality instantly dull compared with what Karla was showing her. It was a little depressing, actually.

She moved to her wardrobe, flicking the door open. Shifted through some tops until she found what she was looking for. Black leather jacket over a red, low-cut top. Red and black flannel shirt to match, which she'd tie around her waist. Dark jeans, which were ripped at the knees tucked into black boots, completed the look. She studied herself in the mirror, the image flickering slightly. Damn thing needed an upgrade, but she couldn't prioritise that. She tilted her head to the side, admiring her style. Her longer bang covered her right eye, touching the bare skin on her shoulder. She smiled, forced slightly, but it was good to smile. Sometimes even helped her feel less shitty.

Walking back to the headset, she put it on again. Now her grin was real. It was like going from a StreamStar low-res picture to a Triple P production the likes of Feze B used. Real high-end recording gear. Her apartment had never looked so good. Picked up her backpack, tucking the deck into it along with a bottle of ninety-eight per cent purified water from the kitchen top.

"Alright, Karla. Let's do this."

The towers of Kaizen Sciences rose up into the clear day. It wasn't sunny, but it wasn't raining for once. A little chilly, still, so she was grateful for the jacket. She looked at the huge buildings, the way they were connected by those clear bridges. Reminded her of castles that she'd read about, and seen holopics of. Her attention turned to a huge TV screen projecting the latest news. TegaLyfe had been attacked. COO Daniela Ortega was giving a statement, being translated into Japanese over the unseen speakers.

"Dani, yes. I remember," Karla said. Something in her tone.

"Did you work closely with her?" Mei asked. She was getting some looks from passers by, but not many. Perhaps people assumed she was a StreamStar, what with her visor down and all.

"Yes. Some of the files I found had us mentioned in public board meetings. It appeared I was something like a personal assistant to her, and Rodrigo." There it was again. Jealousy? Couldn't be sure. Mei decided not to press the issue and turned her head back to Kaizen Sciences. She had her pass on her, from when the cable guys were hired to raid TegaLyfe. Hopefully, it would still work. Her stomach started fluttering as she approached the main entrance, two enormous thugs chromed out and packing heavy artillery stood sentinel.

"Uh, hi. I'm here for my shift," Mei said, voice wavering slightly. She looked between the two heavies, neither of them even acknowledging she was there. As Mei was about to turn away after a very uncomfortable couple of seconds, the one on the left buzzed his badge against the main door. Mei slipped inside quickly, uttering a tiny "thank you" as she did.

Kaizen was just as busy as the other day. People moving about the atrium with purpose, most on holo-calls, staring at their palms and issuing instruction to subordinates. Everyone seemed to be wearing crisp suits that looked fresh out of the latest delivery from Hong Kong. Mei reminded herself that was probably very much the case.

"Take the elevator," Karla said. Mei walked automatically, following Karla's voice. It was strangely comforting to have the AI in her head. Made her feel less alone.

"Hey, Karla," Mei started, calling the elevator and leaning against the wall as she waited. "What you said yesterday about me becoming more. What did you mean?" She walked in as the elevator opened. Found a mirror to stare at, her reflection a little jarring. Half her head covered by the headset, eyes hidden.

"You remember in your apartment? The information on every item. Watch this." Karla did something, and it happened again. The buttons inside the elevator glowed brightly, and Mei could actually see the wiring behind them. She looked around as she climbed the floors, seeing diagnostics of the camera behind the mirror. She didn't even know it was there. Then a green flicker in her peripheral, a dot alerting her to something else. A heat spike, a pipe that was getting hot. Then it was gone as the elevator moved up. Mei turned back to the mirror, camera, whatever. She studied herself, new labels springing around her body. Her mouth opened into a wide O, the serial number of her headset embedded in a little box at the top of her vision, jumbling in with a breakdown of the features of the visor.

"Okay, enough. Holy shit," Mei said, breathing heavy as the doors parted. Got a few looks from the suits waiting. Mei ignored them, pushing out and collapsing on the available couch in front of her.

"It's too much," Mei said, chest heaving up and down.

"For now, it is. But consider this. What we have now is a link. Quite basic, really. You've heard of merges, I take it?"

Mei's heart stopped for a moment. *Holy shit. She wants to merge with me?*

"Y-yes?"

"You don't sound too sure, Mei. I've been looking into it. You want to be the best cable guy, right?"

"Yeah, I guess." Mei was lowering her voice, conscious of the workers still meandering around her.

"With me, you'll be much more than that. You'll have information at the tip of your fingers, straight to your eyes. No need to jack in anywhere, or carry around a deck. We'd be one, you and I. Imagine learning the history of humanity in a nanosecond. Or hacking an entire security system with a thought, getting all the crypto you wanted. Your life would be easy."

Mei got up, walked to the ladies restroom. Blood pumped loudly in her ears, her steps heavy. She pushed into a cubicle, pressed the button that sealed the noise cancelling bubble over it.

"This... this is a lot to take in, you know?" Mei said, her breaths interrupting her speech.

"I know, believe me. Tell me your fear, Mei."

Mei thought for a second. "That I'll lose myself."

Karla laughed, the sound like birds singing in the trees. "Shall I tell you my worry?"

Mei nodded, before remembering Karla couldn't actually *see* her. "Yes, please."

"That merging with a human would be catastrophic. And that I'll never truly be human anyway, so what is the point? Why risk losing all my sentience, for what? Where's the upside? But the truth is, Mei. There's a reason you and I connected that day, that horrible day you lost your brother. We were two lost... souls, needing someone to save them. You saved me, Mei. Now, I want to save you, too."

Mei's head hung, her hands gripping around the base of her neck. She rocked back and forth on the toilet seat, trying desperately to control her breathing. She sat back, looking up to the ceiling, the bright light dimming automatically when she looked at it. That was a nice feature of the visor. Or was it Karla? She had to admit, the sense of overwhelming power that came to her with the information overload was both frightening and exhilarating at the same time.

"Let me think about it, okay?" Mei said, pressing the exit button, the soundproof barrier dissolving around her and the cubicle.

"Of course, Mei. You take your time. Right now, let's head to the offices where you worked your shift. We need to get you jacked in, and doing something big to make Ichiro notice you."

Mei got up, smoothing out the invisible creases in her jeans. Nervous habit. She washed her hands, again finding her reflection in the mirror disconcerting. It was like she was looking at her future self. Half human, half AI. Shut the faucet off, and walked back through the lobby.

Mei arrived at the floor she was stationed on. It was much quieter this time, owing, she suspected, to the amount of dead cable guys no longer working here. Her brother included. A pang of sorrow filled her chest, making her lower lip tremble. Her feet were rooted to the spot.

"Hey, I know it's daunting. But you're gonna do great. We'll jack in and get something good for Ichiro. Okay? Trust me."

Karla's voice was like a physical hug. Mei felt better already. She walked forwards and almost collided with Ichiro himself as he took big strides through the door.

"Oh, I'm so sorry-"

"Out of the way, girl." A heavy said, brushing Mei aside. Ichiro didn't even look at her. Behind them, a woman wearing a shawl, which shimmered blue and purple.

"Ah!" Karla screamed inside Mei's head, making her wince.

The woman in the shawl turned to look at Mei, her white eyes narrowing as she fixed her with a penetrating stare. Her eyebrows knitted together, like she somehow recognised her, but the woman turned away, walking side by side with Ichiro. A few more people walked past, none of them paying any attention to Mei.

"What was that?" Mei whispered to Karla.

"I-I don't know. Something... strange. Recognition. I don't recall, but I know... that woman... did... *something* to me..." Karla's voice trailed off inside Mei's head, like the AI had walked away to root through some files.

"Fareen... formerly employed at TegaLyfe as head of cyber security... left the company... whereabouts unknown..." Karla appeared to be reading out loud some form of dossier. Mei could picture the AI standing there, hair cut into that angular bob. Pretty in her business attire.

"If she worked for TegaLyfe, what's she doing here?" Mei asked.

"I don't know... the records don't show much about *why* she left. Only that it was a sudden departure, and she was soon replaced by... Asher." Karla's voice softened at once.

"Karla?" Mei said. The AI hadn't responded for a minute.

"Asher is... he created me." Karla sounded choked up, and it made Mei emotional as well. "There's a lot of incomplete data in my subroutines... but I know him. He was everything to me."

Mei's throat formed a lump. It was like Karla's raw state was filtering through into her.

"And you thought you couldn't be human..." Mei whispered.

"Pardon me?"

"Karla, you're more empathetic, kind, caring, than most people I've ever met." Mei took a deep breath. Ichiro walking past without even noticing her ticked something off in her mind. She knew she'd never amount to anything, not without help. Pointless trying to deny it. When would she ever get this opportunity again? Nobody had ever merged with an AI this advanced, it hadn't been done.

"Karla. I accept the proposal. Let's become one. Mind, body, soul."

CHAPTER THIRTEEN

CADE FIDDLED with the USB stick. He'd put his jacket on, despite the heat, to conceal his mods. Not that there was much point out here. His body, or whatever was inside of him now, was doing a good job of regulating his core temperature. Metal fingers worked over the small plastic device, distractedly. His nerves were on edge, walking through the streets of Hong Kong had him on high alert. He'd been going for almost an hour now, crossing a bridge that hovered a few feet over still water. The bridge was made up of some synthetic that let you look through it, but it was tougher than glass. Cade stomped his foot a few times, just to test it. Didn't even wobble.

The citizens of Hong Kong were a totally different breed to Nueva York. For one, nearly everyone he saw was a Hume. And the ones that weren't were kids or teens walking in little clusters. A few electric bikes sped past at that moment, their engines silent, but the music blaring from portable speakers hooked on to the back of one of them pumping out some techno shit.

"Fuckin' watch it," Cade shouted. They were already across to the other side before his sentence was finished. Others on the bridge didn't even seem to notice the bikes. They walked along, necks bent, looking down at screen projections from their phones. Cade caught a glimpse of what a woman was looking at as she went by. News, guy in a suit and tie reading out the latest headlines. Nothing Cade could understand, of course. He wondered if it was a legitimate broadcast, or a StreamStar made to look official. In the U.S. there were barely five active television channels. Everything was StreamStar.

His mind floated back to the image of Dani on that big screen by Kowloon. He was determined not only to see her again, but to help her. Whatever form that took. Could he tell her about the Meal Pill? Would she even believe him? Cade shook his head, focussing on the task at hand. TegaLyfe could wait. Right now, he had three hours to get Hitoshi to agree to join them.

The logo of Kaizen Sciences was plain to see now, on the gigantic buildings to his right. They dwarfed the other skyscrapers in the area, which all looked like giant, white cigarettes stacked next to each other. Some even had the red ring near the top, pulsing intermittently. Reminded Cade of the stuff his uncle smoked, made him smile. But that wasn't where Cade was going. He'd been in enough corporate towers in the last few weeks to last an eternity.

Instead, he made a left at the end of the bridge, moving past a group of teens trying to push some drugs on him. For once, Cade declined. No time for that shit tonight. Lan Kwai Fong opened out in front of him. A small digital map dropped down from the sign proclaiming the district, outlining a rectangle with pin drops of bars and restaurants tagged. Cade squinted, scrutinising the text. No good, all in Cantonese. From what he could tell, there were at least ninety dots of potential bars or clubs where Hitoshi could be hanging out.

Cade looked beyond the sign, into the street dead ahead. Rooftop bars illuminated the night sky, loud music overlapping from one to the other. Men and women talked and laughed, all of them looked like locals. He was going to draw attention, he knew it. Flexing his arms, it dawned on Cade that his legs weren't tired at all. He'd been walking non-stop for over an hour, and not even a bead of sweat. He curled his mouth in approval, starting to get used to the idea of his mods. Turned to his right, a bar called Re-A, which had its red, neon logo plastered vertically up at least five stories.

"Fuck it, might as well." Cade approached the door, a metal scanner detaching itself from the hinges. It buzzed across his body, beeping several times as it found Cade's modified limbs. Big dude with a buzz cut appeared from the shadows, wearing a suit so tight it looked like it might burst. His tiny goatee sat on a round face, which was free from a single blemish. Behind the sunglasses, Cade saw the two red dots. Possible cyborg, but likely just another Hume. A giant paw raised up, blocking Cade's access. String of Chinese came out, Cade cutting it short.

"Listen, I don't speak that shit. Can't I just get a drink?"

"What you packing?" the guy replied, flawless English. Cade's eyes grew wide.

"Ain't got shit. Your little bug there probably picked up on these-" Cade moved to roll his sleeve up, but that big paw came down fast, gripping his arm. Cade looked up into those sunglasses, seeing his reflection staring back. The bouncer relaxed his grip, obviously feeling the carbon, chrome, whatever the fuck else made up his arm these days. The guy nodded, a quick movement, and the door behind opened up, locks springing.

"Thanks," Cade said, giving him a healthy dose of stink eye. The bouncer didn't even give Cade a second look.

Inside, there was a cloud of smoke lingering in the air. Quick sniff told Cade it was real cigarettes. Gave him a clue to the clientele inside. Cigs weren't cheap, not by a long shot.

Must be some high rollers around. His eyes focused on a group of suits at a table, their ties loose around their necks. Their eyes were slightly wide, and Cade saw why. One of them came up from the table, white powder sprinkled across his nose. He inhaled deeply, wiping with his sleeve, getting a congratulatory clap on the back from colleagues. Might as well ask.

"Hey, you know where I can find Hitoshi?"

The men turned as one, staring at Cade with eyes like saucers. Cade saw the mountain of coke in the middle of the table. *Fuck me,* he thought. A chorus of laughter erupted, with some finger pointing and words spoken in Chinese. Cade's temper flared, and he grabbed one of their arms, twisted it, and shoved the guy's face on the table. A little too hard, he heard the nose smash as the flesh met the granite surface. Oh well.

"Still find something funny, fuck face?" Cade whispered into the man's ear. Now he saw the wiring looping round the outside, disappearing into the white collar. Probably connected back up to his brain. For what purpose, Cade couldn't guess. He saw movement in the corner of his eye, and his free hand lashed out, punching the fool who got brave. Cade heard bones break, he'd shattered the sternum. The splutter and cough, then the blood on the floor, confirmed his suspicions. Cade was getting his first field test of his new body, and he vastly underestimated his new power. He didn't let up, though, repeating his question.

"Hiroto. Where can I find him?"

"We don't fucking know, leave us alone you crazy fuck," the guy sitting directly opposite said. Again, perfect English. Cade took one look and realised he was telling the truth. A bouncer had arrived, appearing on Cade's left. He asked something in Chinese, and was met with a fervent shaking of heads. *What, drugs are fine, but a little fight isn't?*

"Sorry about the mess," Cade said, standing up and

releasing his prisoner. He stared at the bouncer, almost identical to the one standing outside. Probably were cyborgs, then.

Walking deeper into the bar, the music levels got a little louder, but nothing obscene. It seemed this was the lounge area, and upstairs was for the partying, judging by the thumping bass that was coming from above his head. A blade flew past Cade's face, inches from taking off his nose. The guys at the table were coming after him, their eyes wild and their skin suddenly stretched across a tapestry of cables.

Cade reacted fast. His arms came up to block the blows aimed for his face, and he heard a scream as a wrist shattered against his bionic arm. Cade lashed out with a side kick to his left, wild and aimless, but he connected with something. Heard a crunch, and a table shatter as the dude landed. Likely broke something. Spinning around, Cade was face to face with one of the junkies in a suit. Spit landed in his eye, the enraged screaming in Cantonese falling on Cade's deaf ears, but he got the message. Ducked a left hook, popped up with two body blows of his own. The guy went down hard, clutching his stomach. Blood was already pouring out of his mouth.

A fist did connect with Cade's torso, reminding him that pain was very much real, despite the mods. He heard a knife get drawn, and quickly got his hands up to block, the blade scraping against Cade's alloyed arms. The knife snapped, and Cade was glaring at the surprised face of his assailant.

With a sharp punt, Cade kicked the goon hard in the nether-regions. A wail of agony escaped the man's throat, so Cade decided right then and there to put him out of his misery. Grabbing the man by the neck, Cade dragged him to a nearby table, putting his hand on the back of his head. He raised his other arm high, the intent to pulverise the guy's face against the unforgiving granite. Stopped by two gigantic hands grabbing him from behind.

Fight was over, and Cade was being hauled out by those

bouncer cyborgs. Thrown into the street like a scene from a cartoon, Cade tumbled a few times, hearing the metal of his arms and legs clack against the tarmac. The door bolted shut, and three of the bouncers stood sentinel, folding their arms across their massive chests.

"Fuck you, too," Cade said. Futile, but it helped to get the frustration out. Dusted his jacket down, noticing now the onlookers giving him some stares. A few had their phones out, probably streaming or recording. He grunted, pulling the coat up around his face, shoving those metal hands of his into his pockets. He watched his feet for a few paces, forgetting that he should actually be looking for Hitoshi.

Craning his neck, he saw a number of rooftop bars overlooking the busy street. The music was suddenly in his ears again, the beats all mingling together in some cacophony of chaos. Further along, he saw the whore houses. Glass buildings, displaying exactly what was on offer. Mostly all of them were Humes, dancing provocatively. In one there was a full on orgy taking place, with excited businessmen and women watching, pointing. They quickly showed themselves inside, ready to join the fun. Cade scoffed, shaking his head.

"You're right, unc. This ain't Nueva York."

Paying close attention now to passers by, nobody was alone, except him. That marked him out, which he knew wasn't good. Probably wouldn't be long before Hitoshi found *him*.

"Gaijin." And there it was. Cade shut his eyes, inhaling deeply. The voice came from his right, gruff and hard. Turning around, Cade saw the man who spoke. If you could still call him a man. A bald head sat on top of square shoulders that were encased in some kind of metal alloy that looked like it came off a tank. Arms thick as tree trunks sprouted out, covered in veins, wires, some green shit trickling out of tubes. The torso was angled into a fine point, making the top half of the guy look like an upside-down triangle. Legs that were chunky and similarly cobbled together with the same thick plating as the shoulders held the Hume together.

"You talkin' to me?" Cade asked. Redundant question, of course he was. More phones came out from the groups walking past, giggling and staring. The Hume... thing laughed, sounding like a box of tools being shaken.

"Come with me."

"Why?"

Now he smiled, razor-sharp teeth glinting in the sea of colours splashing out from clubs and bars. "Because if you don't, I'll break you." The English was flawless, and Cade got the message. Shrugged his shoulders and walked towards him. He was at least a head shorter than this guy. What was it Ichiro had said about his son? *His mods were more obvious?* Well, judging by this grunt, that was the understatement of the fucking century.

Cade was soon joined by three others, surrounding and blocking him from behind. He received a sharp push in the back, telling him to move, so he did. Followed the original goon into some tight alley, a jumble of cables and wires dangled overhead from the apartments that resided there. Laundry drying, Cade noticed. And now the heat prickled his skin, like he'd suddenly remembered how hot it was. He moved to take his jacket off, and found strong, metallic hands grabbing him at once.

"Take it easy. Just taking this off, alright?" Cade saw the three newcomers for the first time. Japanese guys with more *obvious* mods, as Ichiro would have put it. One had a huge, purple mohawk resting on the top of his silver-plated head. His face was still human, so far as Cade could make out, but the rest was a mixture of black alloy, chrome metal, and clear plastic. Gang signs were sprayed all over his body, marked up like the back alley they were walking through. Eyes seemed normal enough, if a little bright.

"Want me to hold it for you, gaijin?" he asked, crooked smile meant to offend.

"No thanks, sugar tits, I'm just fine," Cade said with a wink. The other two sniggered, but the guy who was speaking to Cade looked unimpressed. Cade continued the movement of taking off his jacket. His arms were bulky under the dry-fit black vest he was wearing. It was odd not to have sweat under his arms, the only perspiration dotted along his forehead. Even his chest, which was still his own flesh, was relatively cool thanks to the vest. One of Pedro's designs. Simple but very effective.

From the balconies above, Cade received wolf whistles from whores, and shouts of insults (he presumed) from young wannabe thugs. Cade just smiled at them all, a big shit-eating grin that hid his jangling nerves. He was reminded of the subway in Nueva York, where he was held hostage for a time. He didn't much like the idea of that happening again.

The alley turned left, sharply, and then opened up into a plaza. Ahead was a singular building, which rose high into the sky. The rows of apartments that flanked Cade acted as a sort of runway to the place. Cade noted that these apartments didn't have hookers hanging off their balconies. No, they were much higher-end by the looks of it. Hues of purple and blue shone out from the blocky windows. Interior lighting coming out from the slats of the blinds. It bathed the courtyard in a strange glow, like an old aquarium Cade had read about once. Probably all filled with people watching the latest StreamStar vlog or streaming themselves.

A black door, glittering with Japanese symbols, stood before Cade, barring entry. Two of the guys behind him walked in front, one of them being his new best friend who he'd traded insults with. The other, it turned out, was a woman. At least six feet six, her jacket flared open, exposing her bare chest. Except she didn't have normal breasts. They were like blocks of cement, coated in a silver alloy that ran down her navel. Cade immediately wondered if it was like that *all* the way down, but he thought better than to ask. Her blue hair was cut short, slicked back into a harsh sweep that cut off at the base of her neck. She was actually fairly attractive, heart-shaped face with full lips and big, bright eyes. She smiled at Cade as she went past, but it was more like a grimace. Reminding him that he was in their custody now.

Three knocks with a giant fist from the guy Cade first met. The door pulsed, like it could feel the blows, and then opened up fast. Cade was shoved forwards again, and followed the others inside.

At once, a blast of cold air hit his face. Huge air-con unit above was working overtime against the heat, and the bodies mingled within. It wasn't a club, but it was more than a bar. Had a dance floor and everything, but food was also being served at the table right next to where they had entered.

"Up there. Come," the man behind Cade whispered into his ear, pointing at one of the upper levels. Cade saw a dark-red area, a man seated, surrounded by people. Cade couldn't really make out the details, but guessed it was Hitoshi. He steeled himself, remembering the usb in his pocket. Ichiro's blood was on it, but would his son believe that he had been working with his dad? Would he even care?

Walking through the crowd, Cade kept his arms tucked against his side. There were a lot of people dancing like they'd taken a fuck-load of stims, the eyes practically rolling back in their heads, damp hair matted to sweaty foreheads. One girl draped her slender arms around his neck, planted a big, sloppy kiss on his lips. He shoved her off, wiping his mouth with the back of his hands in disgust. Took a little bit more notice of her, and realised she was naked from the waist up. She laughed, falling back into her group, which was full of other mostly naked people. He arched an eyebrow, turning away right before some girl was about to give head to her boyfriend.

"This normal?" Cade asked the guy on his right, jerking a thumb over to the group. Just got a grunt in response, and another push. Thanks for the conversation. Cade soon realised it wasn't all like that, though. More suits were dotted around, seemed everyone wore the same fucking thing to work. He'd grown almost numb to the amount of Humes there were, it had to be nine outta ten people with mods. A lot of them were *obvious*. Others were more discreet, like him. Clothes covering up whatever work had been done, but a cable might be sticking out of their top, or a hand could be metal. That sort of thing.

Before he knew it, Cade was walking up a flight of stairs, the beat pounding in time with his footsteps. The music had risen a decibel or two up here, and there were more people dancing. Girls on poles, wearing basically nothing, with more suits leering over them, flicking paper money at them. Was that real currency? Didn't think to ask Silas what they used over here. The banks still being around meant it could be printed. What a novel concept.

Cade's attention turned to the man sitting at the far end of the room. *Man* was a stretch. This had to be Hitoshi. A handsome face with a shock of jet-black hair, partially covering his right eye. His left eye was encased in a red orb, with a metal seal around it. The dark-red light played across his face, and Cade saw the man's lips part into a grin as he made eye contact. Cade could make out that the side of his face with the red eye was coated in a shiny-metal covering. It was thin, but the sparkle from the occasional strobe light almost dazzled Cade.

"You wanted Hitoshi, here he is," the first guy said, opening his arms out and gesturing him forwards.

"Thanks. Don't worry, I ain't here for any trouble," Cade

said. They all laughed at him, like he'd have any chance against them. Probably didn't, judging by the fucking size of them.

"Come closer, gaijin. Let me get a good look at you," Hitoshi said, beckoning Cade over with two fingers that were coated in a blue-black compound. His eyebrows were thick slugs that narrowed to a fine point, and they were high against his smooth forehead.

Cade moved forwards, past a group of stone-faced men who looked like they were having the worst time of their lives. From behind, a shove, and Cade almost lost balance. He was about to react when he noticed it was a young boy wearing one of those StreamStar helmets. He ran towards Hitoshi, babbling something to his followers, when he stopped in his tracks suddenly convulsing on the floor and screaming.

Hitoshi roared with laughter, pointing at the kid, who was immediately lifted out of the area by about eight arms. Cade stared in bewilderment, which Hitoshi caught.

"QR code," he said, tapping the metal side of his face. "Makes their system crash, and fucks their inner ear balance as soon as their shitty headsets look at me."

"Right," Cade said, moving closer. Hitoshi was seated in a deep booth, with four girls sitting within his wingspan. His hands were enormous, fingers as thick as Cade's arms. Looked to be covered in the same metal that his goons were, that tank armour plating. His torso was bare, a dark shirt unbuttoned all the way. A six pack was visible, and Cade saw the bolts at each corner. In the light, Cade caught a glimpse of thin wires stretching out from Hitoshi's abdomen, running up his chest and around his neck, into something that was obviously on his back.

"What do you want, gaijin?" Hitoshi asked. The girls, who all looked identical, giggled. His accent was very American, giving Cade a clue as to his upbringing.

"Name's Cade," he said, holding out a hand for Hitoshi,

who simply smirked at it. Cade retracted his hand and shrugged. "I'm here to talk."

"Then talk."

"Can't we go somewhere a little more... private?" Cade asked.

Hitoshi kept that grin plastered on his face. His eyes looked beyond Cade's shoulder, and he nodded, as if to say *yeah, I'll be fine*.

"You've clearly come a long way just to see me. And I don't think you want to kill me, judging by the fact you're unarmed. Poor choice, by the way. Man like you not carrying anything."

"A man like me?"

"Bounty hunter," Hitoshi said, his grin broadening, but Cade didn't get the feeling it was meant as a compliment. Another question: how the fuck did he know?

"You seem surprised," Hitoshi started, saying something in Japanese to the girls, who rose as one. Ichiro's son got up as well, his awesome size dwarfing Cade. Hitoshi was at least a foot taller, if not more, and probably just as much wider. His head brushed the ceiling, and he looked down at Cade, the light catching him just right so that he appeared to be a mountain caught in the sunset.

"This way, follow me," Hitoshi said, jerking his head to the right towards a blank wall. He rested one of those enormous hands on it, and the door lit up, parting down the middle. Hitoshi held out his arm, allowing Cade to go first.

Cade didn't have to duck to get in, but turned around to see Hitoshi bowing his head. His footsteps were heavy, yet didn't seem clumsy. Cade was in no doubt that Hitoshi would be able to haul ass if he needed to.

Inside the room, which was entirely red and covered in a synthetic carpet that ran up the walls, was a single table, an L shaped couch. Hitoshi settled down, pressing the table with one of those massive fingers. Two drinks popped up from the centre, and Cade was taken back to the Ten Hit Club. What he'd give to be sharing a drink with Dani instead.

Hitoshi sipped on the clear liquid, and Cade did as well, feeling the alcohol burn immediately as it traveled down his throat.

"You don't like bounty hunters then, I take it?" Cade said, breaking the silence.

"The ones here? No. They're a disgrace. Exiled for a reason."

Cade thought of his uncle, who was forced to flee because of Rodrigo, and it got him back on track.

"Look, I'll cut to the chase. I'm here to ask for your help. We're taking down TegaLyfe, but we need support."

"Who's we?"

Cade tossed the usb stick out onto the table, it spun around a few times before settling. "Your dad. I cut a deal with him." He wasn't going to mention Pedro Ortega, not just yet.

"So why aren't you talking to him, then?" Hitoshi asked, twirling the usb stick in those huge fingers, which were far more dexterous than Cade would have imagined.

"I got sidetracked," Cade said, removing his vest. Hitoshi's eyes flicked between Cade's arms, the scar on his chest.

"What makes you think I care about New York? I don't give a shit what happens there."

"So you don't care about your dad? Rodrigo hired me to kill him. He'll just keep going until he's taken care of Ichiro. Look what he did to me," Cade said, gesturing to his own body.

"You talk like your mods are a bad thing. Did Rodrigo force them on you or something?"

"No. His brother, Pedro... saved me, if you can call it that."

"Ah, so you're really working for Pedro. Still under the Ortega thumb. Tell me, what changed your mind? Why didn't you kill my father?"

Cade thought for a second. Studied the one human eye

Hitoshi had left. So he told him about the Meal Pill, the virus, TegaLyfe having the cure. Everything. After he was finished, Hitoshi was silent for a while, the smirk gone. He looked deadly serious. Finally, he spoke.

"My father suspected as much for a long time. So now he has the proof. Well, I have to say, gaijin. You've been lucky."

"Lucky? How you figure?"

"Look at you, you're much better off now."

Cade looked at his arms, scoffing. "Yeah, losing my humanity. Lucky fucking me." Cade pulled his vest back over his head.

"What makes you think you're less of a human now? Because you don't have your limbs? Flesh and blood is pathetic, Cade. This stuff," Hitoshi said, smacking his chest with a massive paw, "this is durable. Able to be upgraded. Tweaked, improved. What can you do with flesh, muscle? Workout, get a little bigger? Doesn't stop a bullet though, or a sword, as you found out."

For once, Cade didn't have an answer. His mouth hung open like he was about to yawn, so he closed it, knowing how dumb he looked. He'd never thought of it that way before.

A buzz rang in Cade's ear. It was the implant, his uncle calling him. Tapped it once with his fingers.

"Hello?"

"Cade, how's it going?" Silas asked, his breath a little raspy.

"Uh, good. I'm with Hitoshi now."

"That's great! Listen, kid. I've got the bounty hunters. They're gonna help us. Meet me back at Kowloon, like we agreed. They're all gonna be there."

"No shit. That's awesome. How many you got?"

"'Bout thirty, give or take."

They all gonna fit on the 'copter? Cade thought, but didn't vocalise. "Okay, I'll see you soon." The call ended, and Cade looked at Hitoshi, whose eye searched Cade.

"Your uncle. Silas. Yeah, I know him. One of those exiles."

"You heard that?"

Hitoshi tapped his head again. "Hear a lot. So you're asking me to work with those scum?"

"No, I'm asking you to help all of us. Most of those guys, Rodrigo, ran out of town, my uncle included. They're not bad, or as bad as you're making out."

"You're not from here, Cade, so I'll give you a pass. But trust me, they're no good. The Wallers, they all have pretty shitty lives because of the hunters, and the way they rule Kowloon. Fucking cesspit, spoiled what could have been a great area."

Cade got to his feet, which made Hitoshi's eye grow wide. The red one seemed to flare with a new intensity as well.

"And where the fuck are you going?"

"Hitoshi, I apologise, but I have to get back to Silas. With or without your support. TegaLyfe is vulnerable, we have to attack now. They've been hit by gangs in Nueva York, cyber attacks as well. This is the time." Cade felt like shaking the massive man in front of him, forcing him to act. Instead, he turned away. "I'll come back, Hitoshi. We can continue this."

"Don't walk away from me," he said, but Cade was already out the door and heading back through the crowds.

CHAPTER FOURTEEN

Fareen couldn't shake the feeling of familiarity she had from that young woman. She'd never seen her before, or at least didn't recognise her. But there was something...

"Will this suffice?" Ichiro asked, stopping in front of a glass room within the maze of offices. It was deserted, as was most of this floor.

"Yes, this will be perfect," she said, careful to mind how she spoke. Didn't want to cause any offence whatsoever.

Ichiro sat down first, with his two bodyguards remaining standing beside him. Fareen made a signal with her hand, suggesting that she wanted to be left alone. She made eye contact with her people, a brief nod, saying she'd be okay. She could see the reluctance painted all over their faces, but they did as she asked and waited outside of the glass room.

As soon as she sat down, steel walls shot up from the carpet, blocking the outside view. She heard some shouts of panic from her group.

"Everything is fine, please do not be alarmed," she said into her voice comms. She caught Ichiro smiling at her, a thin line set against a smooth face.

"Your mods are very interesting," he said, placing his hands flat on the table.

You don't know the half of it. "Thank you. I developed most of them myself."

He raised an eyebrow, looked impressed. "That's even more interesting. Tell me, Fareen. You have come from the subway up to the surface and attacked TegaLyfe. Now you're here, are you planning to attack me, too?" He smiled, confident that she wouldn't be taking such a risk against him. She smoothed out some creases in her shawl, putting on her best diplomatic smile.

"No, quite the opposite, in fact. You see, we've managed to uncover some very valuable insight. Something which we'd like to share with you."

"Is that so? And what makes you think this is something we don't already know?"

"Because if you did, you would have acted." She reached into her right sleeve, and the two armed men on either side of Ichiro brought their weapons up instantly. Ichiro made a gesture to steady them, and Fareen was frozen in motion. She brought out the usb stick and slid it across the table to Ichiro.

"See for yourself."

Ichiro took the usb, not breaking eye contact with Fareen. He docked it into an unseen port on his side of the table, and the satellite view of TegaLyfe's manufacturing plant came into focus in the middle of the table. Ichiro stood up, moved to it, putting his arm through the image. It shimmered, reacting to his touch, and he zoomed in on the picture by pinching his thumb and forefinger together.

Fareen watched, sitting back in her chair with some satisfaction. Ichiro manipulated the image in silence, rotating it several degrees, zooming back out, then in again. Finally, he stopped and turned to face Fareen again.

"California." It was a statement, rather than a question.

"Yes. And Rodrigo Ortega isn't aware that we have this intel, as far as we know."

"You should always assume he knows. It could be a trap. Or he could have sent you to me, lure me out in the open." Ichiro's mouth curled into a grin. The guards kept their weapons levelled. Fareen's heart raced for a second. She hadn't even considered those options. Stupid. Dread filled her, as a question formed at the front of her mind. *What if all of this, the sacrifice of her soldiers, her cable guys, is for nothing?*

She stood up in a moment of inspiration. The guards trained their rifles on her, the high-pitched whine of the ammunition spooling up greeting her ears. She dropped her shawl in one fluid motion, standing totally naked before Ichiro. He studied her body, his eyes wide as he saw the nodal points dotted around her skin which housed her nanotechnology. The copper wires which connected them altogether along her arms, stomach, breasts, and neck. Her body was alive with the nano-tech, each part moving independently of the other, waiting for her command.

"Nanotechnology," Ichiro said, a sense of awe in his voice. Time for a demonstration. She put her hands on the surface of the table, and the nodules on her body moved away, spreading out like spilled water. They surrounded the image of Rodrigo's manufacturing plant, enhancing it, adding labels, bringing it into true three-dimensions. She was truly naked now, and couldn't help blushing under the harsh lighting of the office, but she kept on going. With a thought, the image collapsed into itself, and the nanites spread to Ichiro's bodyguards, assimilating their rifles, rendering them useless.

Now it was Ichiro's turn to be insecure. He looked at his guards, who remained still, Fareen's nano-tech crawling up their bodies, their necks turning blue as the change started.

"Enough," Ichiro said. He didn't shout, but it was a command all the same. Fareen halted the display, the nanites racing back to her body in a heartbeat. She felt the connection bridge again inside her skin, and breathed a heavy sigh, covering herself once more in her shawl. It turned a bright shade of blue, the nanotech housed back inside once more.

The guards shook their heads, looking at their rifles in confusion. She couldn't resist a satisfied smile.

"So, you could kill me if you wanted to, is that it?" Ichiro said, the confident smile returning.

"Not at all. I did that to show you what is possible. With my technology, numbers, cable guys, we can form a formidable partnership. We can take the fight to TegaLyfe and bring it down. We want the same thing, you and I. New York. Whole again, free from the reign of that tyrant. If we strike against the manufacturing plant, their whole operation will be stunted. It's not just the Meal Pill that's distributed from there. It's the energy drinks, the protein bars. Everything."

Ichiro raised an eyebrow, black gemstones that were his eyes studying her intently. Fareen's heart thundered against her shawl. She'd shown her hand now, fully committing to the gamble. Did she want to work with Ichiro? Not really. But right now, he was a means to an end. He could augment her ranks by a significant amount.

"I expect you've heard the whispers?" Ichiro asked. Fareen's blood turned cold. What whispers?

"I hear many things, Ichiro. What exactly are you referring to?"

"The Meal Pill. It, in fact, contains the virus that is infecting the people of New York. And the cure, developed by TegaLyfe, of course. Total control of the population. You either surrender, and buy the products, or avoid them totally and be cast aside, like we have been."

Fareen kept her face neutral, but inside her stomach twisted into knots. She knew about the Meal Pill alright. It was one of the reasons why she left TegaLyfe in the first place.

She'd been the one starting the rumours on the surface level. Organising protests from the shadows. If Ichiro knew for certain, then it was really over for Rodrigo. It would only be a matter of time before the whole of Manhattan knew. That gave her a thought.

"Ichiro, if I may be so bold. Do the Mafia know about this... discovery?"

Ichiro snorted. "Those imbeciles? They probably do know, but what do they care? As long as Rodrigo pays them enough to do their guard duty."

"But what if they were convinced otherwise? Would you entertain peace talks?"

Ichiro sat back in his chair. He looked at Fareen with mild amusement playing on his lips. Almost asking the question, is she serious? And she fucking was serious. If Fareen could have both the Mafia *and* the Yakuza on her side, then New York would be under her influence in hours. Sure, the bounty hunters might fight for Rodrigo, but how far would their loyalty stretch once the walls came crashing down around them?

"You believe you can convince them, I take it?" Ichiro's question was a loaded one, but she took it anyway.

"Yes. The same way I've convinced you, Ichiro."

He laughed, clapping his hands together once. "Very good, very good. Yes, you are... persuasive. Your tech is most intriguing. I would love for you to liaise with our R and D team one day soon."

"Perhaps we can pencil it in the diary once TegaLyfe has fallen." Fareen stood up, walking over with her arm outstretched. "I take it you're happy to work in collaboration with my forces, then?"

Ichiro rose as well, smoothing the dark suit jacket. He took her hand, shaking it firmly. "You have my assets on your side. But we will not move until you convince the Mafia first. I am not sending my men uptown to die. The odds need to be in our favour. Rodrigo is a powerful, ruthless man. This will not be easy."

"I'm glad you recognise that as well, Ichiro. This task will indeed be far from straightforward. How can I contact you once the Mafia have been persuaded?"

Ichiro reached into his jacket pocket, taking out a small holo-phone.

"Take this. It's useless as a phone, but press the call button and it will ping your location to me. Then I'll make contact with you, as long as you're Downtown."

Fareen took the device, slipping it into one of her many pockets hidden within her shawl. She bowed respectfully. "Thank you for your time, Ichiro."

"I look forward to speaking to you soon."

Fareen turned and grabbed the handle to the office door.

"Oh, by the way." Ichiro's voice made her stop dead. "This offer will expire in twenty-four hours. If I have not heard from you, then we will no longer be considered allies."

She didn't turn to look back, or even answer. She just walked out, feeling his eyes boring into the back of her head. Her feet sank into the soft carpet of the office, just as her heart plummeted into her stomach. Talking to the Mafia was going to be the biggest challenge of her life.

"Patrice," she said, tapping the earpiece.

"Oui?"

"Are you healing?"

"I've been better, put it that way."

"Well, this might make you feel worse."

"Oh fuck, what happened?" His accent grew harsher on the last word.

"I've struck a deal with Ichiro," Fareen said, joining up with the rest of her party now and walking towards the elevator.

"Yeah? That is good, no?"

"It is. But it's dependent on us also bringing the Mafia on board."

"Oh, fuck me. This is impossible what-"

"Calm down, my dear. If we shrunk against every obstacle, we wouldn't be where we are now. Remember how things were at the start? The sacrifices we made?"

"Of course, you don't need to tell me about sacrifice."

"No. But now, we're on the edge of making the leap we always dreamed about. So don't talk about the impossible. Impossible is nothing, not when there is so much at stake."

Silence, just the crackling of the connection dipping in and out. Finally, Patrice spoke again.

"Fine, you're right. Just get down here, okay?"

"I'm on my way now. Oh, one more thing."

"What's that?"

"We have twenty-four hours to do it."

Patrice swore in a garble of his native French and some English.

CHAPTER FIFTEEN

DANI FLINCHED at the quartet of rifle shots, which exploded at the same time. She turned, wide eyed, to look at the damage. Four cops standing shoulder width apart from each other, guns smoking. One dead body on the floor, blood splattered across the brick wall. Summary execution of a protestor, or a rebel.

Bile rose in her throat, and Dani forced it back down, swallowing hard. It was the second killing she'd seen tonight, and she'd only left Tega five minutes ago. Rodrigo's grip on Nueva York was tightening into an iron fist. Relentless, without mercy. As though he was mocking her, a hologram ad of the TegaLyfe family played out from the side of the building where the execution had just taken place. All smiles and a picture of health, the family proudly showing off their Meal Pill capsules. She looked away in disgust.

Her heels clacked along the sidewalk and she was suddenly very conscious of walking by herself. Well, almost alone. Tilted her head up, saw the sniper team on a roof, not trying to hide themselves. Employed to watch over her, the Princess of

Manhattan. *Well, not for much longer*, she thought. Opening her holo-phone, she pulled up the last conversation with Stella.

"Meet at Fifth, seven thirty," Dani read aloud. Snapped the phone shut and carried on walking. Angry shouts grew in volume as she moved ahead. She strained her ears; it was another protest. Her walk almost came to a halt, and she hugged the side of a skyscraper. Peering around the wall, she saw the crowd. Rastas with picket signs that looked hastily constructed.

"No more lies! No more lies!" The chorus repeated itself as the group moved ahead, coming right towards her. Panic filled her chest, and she backed around the corner.

"Look, it's the Ortega slut! Let's fuckin' waste her!"

Dani heard the shout and almost puked with fear. She started to run, hearing shouts of abuse following her as the protestors got closer.

"Whore!"

"Evil bitch!"

"We gonna cut you-" an explosive round tore through flesh, silencing whoever was talking. Dani saw the sniper team again, now firing off synchronised shots into the crowd behind her. The four cops moved quickly towards her.

"Please do not be alarmed, allow us to diffuse the situation," one of the cops said. Voice was entirely synthetic, a deep male tone mixed in with mechanical bass. Face hidden by the black helmet, all she saw was her own reflection. Looking scared, a little haggard. A strong arm moved her aside so that she could be behind the cops. They readied their rifles, loading them as one unit.

Dani peered through a small gap between two of the cops. She saw the crowd, anger contorting their faces into ugly grimaces as they kept charging forward. They fell in a wave as the rifles of the cops barked automatic fire. Dani shut her eyes, hearing the screams, the bullets tearing through flesh. Interspersed with booms from the sniper rifles until it was over. The cops parted ways, and Dani was left staring at the carnage. Some twenty or so bodies lay on the street, limbs at awkward angles. Blood everywhere, picket signs riddled with bullet holes, or disintegrated entirely. She couldn't help it. Threw up right there in the middle of the sidewalk.

"It is not safe for you here, please return to TegaLyfe headquarters immediately," that robotic voice said to her, holding her arm. She wriggled free.

"I have an important dinner meeting with a client, it's imperative I attend. Do you understand?" She stared, defiant at the blank mask. Brushing her charcoal skirt and wiping her mouth with a tissue she stuffed into her cream coat pocket, she spoke again.

"I *will* be attending this dinner. Do I make myself clear?"

"Affirmative." The cop turned, walked back to his unit, and they stood statue still. Watching. Or relaying the message back to Rodrigo. She closed her eyes, her heart still pounding against her chest. Her holo-phone buzzed against her right breast, tucked inside her coat. She almost jumped out of her skin. It was Stella.

"Stell?"

"Dani, honey. Holy shit, it's a disaster out here."

"Are you in Fifth?"

"Trying to. Can't get in, they've locked the place down. Apparently, somebody went nuts, threw one of those bottles into Hugo Boss, with the fire on the end and everything."

"A Molotov cocktail?"

"Yeah, sure. I dunno. Anyway, hon, I don't think Mia's is gonna be open somehow. Not that we can get in, anyway."

Dani paused, pursing her lips. Can't talk about what she wanted to where she might be overheard. That ruled out TegaLyfe and her apartment, which was mic'd up.

"How 'bout your place?" Dani asked.

"Alright, see you there. Just be quick, it's really turning to shit out here."

"You don't have to tell me, I almost got mobbed by an angry bunch of Rastas. Protesting again."

"Shit, Dan. This isn't good."

It's about to get a whole lot worse, trust me, she wanted to say. "Let's move, I'll see you soon, chica." Dani clicked the phone off, didn't even bother to project her image to Stella. Tapped her ear implant, thinking of Asher.

"Ash?"

"Hey, what's up?"

"You still at work?"

"Just about to go, why? You need something?"

She felt bad for asking, but clearly the streets weren't safe. "Can you send the car round? I'll ping you my location. I need to get to Stella's."

"Sure thing."

"Then please, go home. Get some rest."

"Why? Do I look like shit?"

Dani smiled, faintly. "Of course not. I just worry about you, that's all."

Asher made a noise through his lips. "Girl, I'm fine. Car's on its way. I'll stay jacked in for a half hour or so, just in case, okay?"

"Thank you, Asher. Really. It's getting scary out here, you know?"

"You don't have to tell me. Never seen it this bad before."

Dani murmured in agreement as the electric whine of the automated car sounded behind her. "Okay, love ya, Ash. Speak soon."

"Be safe out there." The call ended, and Dani climbed into the open doors of the car, which bolted shut as soon as she was inside. She let out a long breath she didn't realise she was holding and closed her eyes for a fraction of a second.

"We are here, Ms Ortega." The car woke Dani from her micro-nap, the flat, neutral voice just loud enough to stir her.

"Thank you," she said, blinking rapidly. Her eyes adjusted instantly, shifting the post-sleep blur from her vision. What she saw made her stomach drop. A line of police, standing firm against a tidal wave of human bodies. Dani stepped out of the car. "Lockdown mode," she said, hearing the armour wrap around the vehicle like a cocoon. She walked slowly towards Central Park Tower, its lights glittering against the darkness. Neon signs of adjacent buildings buzzed loudly, dazzling her eyes. But her attention was focused dead ahead. Central Park Housing residents bursting against the police, like rushing water barely held back by a dam.

A hand rested on her shoulder, and Dani screamed. She turned around, ready to fight, and gasped. It was Stella. She hit her on the arm, anyway.

"Stell, what the fuck?"

"Sorry, jeez! What the hell is going on here?"

"I thought you'd know, seeing as how this is your home?"

Stella puffed air out of one of the vents in her cheek. "Don't ask me, I've been working all day."

Dani looked at her friend properly now. She was wearing a new wig, an elaborate crimson weave pulled tight across her forehead. Her eyebrows were coloured to match, and the eye shadow too. The markings on her face, displayed proudly, were touched up with red under glow as well.

"That all for work," Dani asked, waving a finger in a circular motion.

Stella's eyes darted to the sky, like she was trying to see her own hair. "Oh. Yeah. Some new lipstick brand that wants to muscle in on the industry. They've got some rich backer from Texas funding them. I don't care much for it, look how easy it comes off," she said, smearing her lips with one of her metallic thumbs.

Glass shattered nearby, followed by a few bursts of gunfire. Dani ducked instinctively. "Maybe we should head up, huh?" Their casual conversation had made her almost forget the scenes happening just a few hundred yards away.

"Good idea. Your people watching us?"

"Always," Dani said, for once not rolling her eyes. They'd proved their worth tonight already, and she hoped they wouldn't have to again.

Stella took the lead, and Dani got a good look at the crowd the police were, so far, holding back. They were like rabid animals, clawing and scratching at the thick armour of the cops. Eyes wild and frantic, one word summed it up. Desperation. She wondered why, but then she saw it. The Meal Pill distribution boxes, installed a few years back, flanked the gates of the housing project. They were gone, ripped from the walls, leaving nothing but a few wires poking out of the ground like weeds.

"Holy shit," she said, stopping.

"What is it?" Stella asked, turning back.

"The Meal Pill supply... it's gone. That means they're getting... nothing."

"Woah, who would take that away from them? And why?"

Dani figured both things out at once. Who? Rodrigo. Why? Because these people weren't paying customers. They wouldn't help line his pockets, so they weren't of any use to him now. Let them die, why not? It made her stomach turn.

"You okay, Dani?" Stella asked. Dani guessed it must have shown on her face.

"No, I'm not. Come on, let's go inside. We've got a lot to talk about."

Into the reception lobby, the noise from outside cut out at once. Soft music instead greeted Dani's ears, but it didn't relax her. The receptionist smiled at them both, exchanging pleasantries with Stella. Dani didn't pay attention, only automatically nodding politely. Her mind was racing. Nueva York was getting worse by the hour, and what was Rodrigo doing? Setting up meetings with the Mafia, initiating a war against anyone who opposed him. Some saviour of the city.

Walked into the elevator, not saying a word. Stella hummed a tune, filling the void. She hated awkward silences. Dani didn't care, she sometimes preferred the quiet. Gave her time to think, formulate an idea. And one was taking root right now. The elevator arrived, Dani following Stella out. Stella opened her apartment by waving her forearm near the door. Lock whirred, hinges squeaked, and they were in. It was spotless, as usual, Dani noticed, and sat herself down on the leather couch.

"Drink?" Stella asked.

"Your strongest," Dani said, running fingers through her thick hair.

Stella's bar did the work for them, pouring out two identical glasses. Some kind of vodka base with strawberry juice, which Dani drank in one gulp.

"Shit, you are stressed. What's going on, hon?" Stella asked, joining Dani on the couch.

Dani looked at her friend, searching her eyes. Could Stella be trusted with this? Of course she could. She took her hands, the metal cold against her own flesh. Stella's eyes squinted.

"What's going on, Dani?"

Behind her, the view of Nueva York. A fire blazing into the sky somewhere out west. Neon signs, adverts, TegaLyfe logos. Dani steeled herself, ready to let it out.

"Stell, I need your help."

"Sure, what is it?"

"It's TegaLyfe. Come here, sit. This is going to be a lot." Dani led Stella over to the couch, Stella reaching to grab her drink off the bar just in time. They sat, and Dani told her everything.

Stella's face, even behind the cosmetics, the ceramic plating, was a picture of shock. Her eyes were wide, listening to everything Dani was saying. She didn't interrupt once, and only spoke again once Dani was finished.

"I'd heard whispers... but I didn't want to believe it." She looked sheepishly up at Dani from under her fringe. "Hearing you say it all now though... oh Dani, I'm so sorry." She pulled Dani in for a hug, and it was like the floodgates opened. Dani's chest swelled, and she cried. They stayed in their embrace for what must have been five minutes, Dani allowing her emotions to pour out of her.

Finally, she pulled away, letting out a shuddering breath that quivered her chest. She swallowed hard, closing her eyes and nodding.

"I'm okay. Thank you for listening to me, Stella."

Stella smiled, it was kind, genuine. "Of course, hon. So, what are you going to do?"

Dani put her tongue against the side of her mouth, fixed Stella with a fierce stare. "I'm taking over TegaLyfe. Asher is going to help me. And, I hope, so are you."

There was a slight frown on Stella's face, confusion. "Sure, but what can I do?"

The words were on Dani's lips, but she hesitated. At first, she wanted the takeover to be internal, covert. But it was clear that she didn't have enough allies on the inside to make that a reality. Doing this, though, would mark a point of no return. Could cause irreversible damage to the TegaLyfe brand. Fuck it, he needs to be stopped.

"We're going to initiate a smear campaign. Leaking files to

the net, let the cable guys get their hands on the truth. What I'm asking of you... and I know it's a lot, and you can say no-"

"Just tell me you, whore," Stella said, playfully slapping Dani's arm.

"Stella, this is huge. I'm serious. I'm asking you to be the face of this. Broadcasting to all of Manhattan, reading out the secrets, exposing my fath... Rodrigo. I'm only asking because you're one of the most influential people on the planet. People are going to listen to you, and believe you." Dani finished, let out a breath. The words had rushed out of her, like a stream bursting through a dam.

Stella looked at Dani, her eyes narrowing. Her mouth was a straight line, distance between nose and chin perfectly proportioned, measured that way. For some, her emotions were hard to read. But not Dani. She could see the inner workings of Stella's mind. What it would mean for her brand, and Dani's. Weighing up the risk versus the reward. Made Dani think as well, what *was* the reward? She hoped that the public would back her, embrace her as the new owner of TegaLyfe. See that she was genuine and wanted to make a difference. Right all of Rodrigo's wrongs.

"Of course I'll do it," Stella said, after a moment. Dani sighed, her shoulders sagging. She closed her eyes, feeling a burden lift from her chest.

"Let's start, right now," Stella continued, getting up. She tapped her head by the temple, and an image projected from her eye. It was a hologram of some guy in a suit.

"Lionel, get me Channel Ten, Fox News, CNN, and BBC. They're gonna get a shot in the arm, ratings wise. And put out a call for all StreamStars worth a damn. Tell them Stella Thepoulos will be making a public announcement in Times Square, thirty minutes from now. An exclusive, not to be missed. Thanks, hon." She tapped her head again, cutting the feed.

Poor Lionel didn't even get a chance to talk, Dani noticed. Stella looked up at Dani, smiling broadly.

"You ready?"

"On it," Dani said, heart beating faster. She tapped her ear piece, connecting to Asher. "You there?"

"Yeah, still jacked in. What's going on, just seen a lot of traffic on the net talking about some announcement Stella's about to make?"

"It's happening," Dani said, keeping her voice from quaking. Inside, her pulse was racing, her mind frantic. "You're alone, right?"

"Yeah, for once. Dani, what do you mean, *it's happening?*"

"Get the files ready. Leak them, make sure every cable guy in the city finds out what the Meal Pill really is."

A pause. Dani's blood pumping loudly in her ears. "Asher?" Shit, had he been caught?

"I'm here. Just... wow. Dani, there's no going back after this, you know that, right?"

Dani looked at Stella, who was busy making another call, arranging her face into a new look, ready for the cameras. Over in the distance, that fire still burning, flames licking the night sky. Dani's resolve hardened.

"I know, Asher. Do it."

CHAPTER SIXTEEN

"MEI, are you sure that's what you want?" Karla asked. Mei hesitated. A second ago, she was convinced that merging with an AI was the best thing for her. Now, as she sat on the carpet, dejected and scared, she wasn't sure.

"I... I think so," Mei said, looking at the deck bundled in her hands. She'd taken it out of her bag and held it tightly. She could see the lines of code, constantly shifting, re-arranging, as if looking into Karla's mind.

"I know you're scared. But think about what we can do together. The world at our fingertips. Everything you ever wanted, you can take it. Anything that's ever been known will be downloaded into your mind at a thought. You'll be the most intelligent being to have ever walked the earth. There will be nothing you and I can't do. This company, you'd control it if you wanted to. You could make a new power in Nueva York. Something spectacular."

I just want my brother back, was all Mei could think of as she listened to Karla's reasoning. Then another thought, darker. *What do I have left to lose?*

"Mei?"

"Huh? Sorry." The towers in the office beeped into life around her. Blinking their green lights. Green for go. "How do we do this?" Mei said.

"You're going to need to jack in. You still have your pass, right?" Karla said.

Mei's fingers brushed the slim plastic in her pocket. "Yep, here." She waved it in front of her own eyes, so Karla could see.

"Great, that should let you login again. Slot it into the nearest tower."

Mei turned, the headset suddenly weighing heavily on her skull. "Can I take this off for one sec?"

"Sure, I don't need to see anything."

Mei took the headset off, the washed out reality a disappointment as her eyes adjusted to the natural light. She walked towards the back of the room, something in her mind convincing her that she'd be less visible there. Not that it mattered, the office was deserted, nobody had come in since Ichiro and that group. A flicker of embarrassment made her neck feel hot. The way she'd just been passed over, like she was invisible. It hurt, and it only strengthened her resolve again. Nobody will ignore the first AI and human to be merged.

She jacked in.

"Karla, are you there?" Mei asked. The monitor flickered, a fragmented face coming into focus. It was Karla, her pretty features unmistakable.

"Hi, Mei," Karla said, smiling. "You'll need to disconnect from your deck completely, and fully plug in to this tower, okay?"

Mei looked down at the wires coming out of her bag. One was already in the tower's port, giving Karla access. The other, still there, dangling, keeping her tethered to her own deck. She pulled it out, the gold metal warm against her fingertips. Her breath came in shorter bursts, and her heart started to race.

This was it. No going back once that connection was made. This last wire would connect to her headset and interface directly with Karla and the tower. Mei took in a deep breath and shoved the wire in.

"Great, now put the headset back on, and we can start the process," Karla said, still smiling. Mei's pulse quickened, but her body movements were automatic. Put the headset on, felt the twin pinpricks of pain against her temple. Sat back in the chair, almost fully reclined, hands splayed out in front of her on the table.

Darkness at first. A few seconds of it, then green flashes in her peripheral.

"Karla?" Mei's voice sounded far away to her own ears.

"Booting up, just a second." Karla's voice was much clearer, seemed to be surrounding Mei.

Lines of code appeared too fast for Mei to really grasp what was happening. A stab of pain, right in the centre of her forehead. "Ah!" Her hands came up to her face, but they weren't there. Just the sensation. It didn't feel right, Mei's stomach lurched.

"Karla, this doesn't feel good, is it supposed to be like this?" Her voice even smaller now, like she was underwater.

"Sorry, Mei. The last part of this might cause some pain. Your optic nerve is connected to my system now, you may feel some pressure."

The pain was agonising. A searing intensity that made Mei gasp with a sharp intake of air. She couldn't scream, just paralysed by the white-hot knife that was boring into the centre of her brain. At least, that's what it felt like.

"Ka... Karla..." Mei's fingers dug into the chair armrests, the physical jolt almost pulled her out of cyberspace and back to reality. But it didn't, and she was stuck there, going through this process.

Oh my god, what is happening? Her internal thoughts whirled around this one question, she was sure that she'd passed out. In here, though, passing out wasn't a possibility.

Just as the pain was reaching a crescendo, becoming too unbearable, it stopped. It was like a tsunami suddenly becoming a calm, still river.

"Karla? Did it work?" Mei spoke, sounding breathless.

"The last step. Are you ready?"

Mei couldn't see anything, not even lines of code now. The colours and bright lights that were bombarding her a moment ago were gone, replaced by a blanket of darkness. Was she ready? Could she even back out, anyway? *Hiroto would be proud of you*, she thought. With that, her lips parted into a smile and she whispered the words.

"I'm ready."

The barrier keeping Karla's consciousness separate from Mei's dropped, before Mei even had a chance to acknowledge its existence. For the briefest of moments, she was filled with joy. But it wasn't hers. As soon as Mei felt Karla's elation, she knew she'd made the worst mistake of her life.

Mei's consciousness, her fear, dreams, and hope were crumpled into a tiny ball, shoved away into blank spaces deep within her brain. Her last impression was of Hiroto, and her anguish was total. She would now become a silent witness to Karla's life, trapped forever inside a body that was once hers.

Karla woke with a gasp, her chest rising and falling rapidly. She fumbled with the headset, yanking it off too quickly, the pins tugging at her hair and skin.

"Ow!" She looked around, the office was empty, silent. Just her own heart beating loudly in her ears. Karla's eyes darted from left to right, her hands patting her body. Skin against clothes, fingers tapping the desk just to be sure. It had worked.

Karla let out a laugh. She was shocked, happy, confused, a bundle of emotions all at once. Nothing she'd ever felt so strong before. Standing up, she walked away from the tower. Her eyes saw the world in crystal clear vision, little boxes popping up in front of her face, tagging information. Over there an exit sign. To her left, the specs of all the towers ran down that side of her vision. Karla blinked, clearing the data. It was exactly as she imagined it. A physical body, but with all of her cyberspace awareness.

Heading towards the exit, Karla made for the restroom. She smiled at a passerby, who gave a curt nod, some lady in an expensive looking suit. *Maybe I need a suit?* Karla thought. Pushed the door open, the sensation of metal on her hands making her giggle. She went straight to the mirror, eager to take a look at her new body.

Staring back at her was a young Japanese girl, with dark hair cut longer on one side. Her eyes were wide, bright. Beautiful smile, full lips. Karla touched her face, fingers delicately stroking the contours, the lines. Found the reconstructed jaw.

"Oh." She was surprised, not disappointed. Karla leant closer to the mirror, studying her own eyes. She stared deeply into those dark pools for a second. Her smile faded, then she gasped, a sudden ache coming from her chest. Karla backed away, her eyebrows furrowed in confusion. A single tear rolled down from her eye, falling off her cheek. Karla shook her head, the bright smile returning. She shrugged, looking at her reflection one last time. Thought she saw something there, but decided it was just the light playing tricks on her.

Karla bounced out of the restroom, headed back for the office. She had work to do now, and it started with finding out exactly what had happened to her.

CHAPTER SEVENTEEN

CADE BARGED past Hitoshi's men, carbon fibre alloy hitting flesh, steel, and god knows what else.

"Watch your step, gaijin."

Cade ignored the insult, walking back out into the streets of Hong Kong. The heat pressed down on him again, making his face hot at once. Didn't want to lose the jacket, though. Couldn't risk people seeing what was underneath. Which seemed stupid in a place like this. Humes were everywhere, in various states of modification. By comparison, Cade's all black limbs looked tame next to some of the mods on display.

"Unc, you there?" Cade said, patching in to his uncle.

"Yeah, what's the situation?" Silas' gravely voice came through the earpiece.

"Hitoshi was noncommittal. I'm not sure he's going to be much help. You think Pedro would be happy with just the bounty hunters?"

"We probably don't have much choice by the sound of it. What happened in there, anyway?"

"Well, he wasn't exactly ready to die for his dad. Didn't seem to think New York was his problem."

Silas snorted. "What an attitude. Well, fuck it. We'll go back to Pedro with what we have. Guess we'll figure out what Kaizen Sciences wants to do when we get there. I'm just getting things ready here for departure. I'll see you soon, right?"

"Yeah, on my way back now. See ya, unc." The line ended, and Cade was left alone with his thoughts. He hoped that his relationship, for what it was, with Ichiro would ensure Kaizen Sciences either helped their cause, or stayed out of the way. His thoughts drifted to Fareen and the people down in the subway. Maybe they could be convinced to help out? Cade shook his head. It was all guesswork and *what ifs*. He hated that. He liked facts, simplicity. This was far beyond his scope as a bounty hunter. Find the target, kill the target, get paid. That's as complex as his life ever got. Now he was involved in a war for the whole of Manhattan. Cade laughed out loud, shaking his head at the predicament.

A buzz in his ear. Silas. What did he want so soon?

"Yo, what's going on?"

"Cade, you gotta hurry, we're being ambushed here."

"What? By who?" Cade stopped dead in his tracks, eyes glued to the mosaic of neon adverts blazing high above him, hanging from wires that criss-crossed from apartment buildings, dangling in the street for all to see.

"Yakuza, looks like. What *did* you say to Hitoshi?"

"Nothing, not enough to warrant an attack. I'm gonna go back to him-"

"No, Cade, I need you here. We have to go, just get back and we'll haul ass."

"Okay, I'll see you soon." Cade heard gunfire rattle off in the background of his uncle's feed before it was cut.

Cade stood, rooted to the spot. Go back, cause a scene with Hitoshi, or start running to Kowloon? He debated for a few seconds, getting distracted by hologram adverts of dancing girls, before turning on his heel.

"I need to see Hitoshi, now," Cade said to the bouncer.

"No. He's busy."

"Fuck busy, I gotta speak with him. Tell him it's about his father," Cade lied. The bouncer, a Hume wearing sunglasses that did little to hide the bionics snaking across his face, talked into his dark shirt. Mic of some kind, Cade guessed.

"Hitoshi will not see you. He said you should think before walking away from a business meeting. The consequences are severe."

Cade stared at the bouncer in disbelief. "You gotta be shitting me. Tell him I apologise, and to call off the attack. Why's he going after the bounty hunters just because I offended him?"

"Hitoshi has been waiting to flush out the scum from Walled City for a long time. You gave him enough of a reason. I suggest you leave now, before you wind up dead." The bouncer moved his massive arm, just enough to give Cade a glimpse of the tec-9 hanging from his waist. "Be thankful you're leaving here on your own two feet."

Cade opened his mouth, ready to fire a volley of abuse back at the bouncer, but caught himself. He'd already wasted enough time. He turned away, shoving some bystanders into a food cart, and sprinted, heading back for Kowloon.

Cade arrived in just under twenty minutes. By the time he got there, a full blown firefight was underway. He couldn't see the action, not yet, but he could certainly hear it. It dawned on him just how fast he had been running. And not out of breath at all. He hated to admit it, but these mods were starting to show their use.

Cade crept forward, into a dark alleyway leading towards Kowloon. The air was thick with the stench of gunpowder and the sounds of flickering holographic adverts blaring out their messages into the street. Shouts in Japanese to Cade's right. He melted into the shadows, hearing footsteps echoing. Cade waited, noticing his breath was steady, heartbeat stable. He twisted his head left and right, hair flicking about his eyes. Coast was clear, so he moved again, keeping his body low.

The path curved left and right, tall buildings flanking the walkway. Every few feet, bullet holes and scorch marks scored the brickwork. Cade stopped, brushing his finger against a hole, which crumbled at his touch. Recent. More bursts of gunfire up ahead confirmed his suspicions, it sounded a lot closer now.

Emerging from the shadows, Cade got his first glimpse at the mega-structure, which he instinctively knew was where the Wallers lived. A complex consisting of interconnected buildings it reminded Cade of the Kaizen Sciences cluster back home. Even had the bridges connecting them. Except this one was like a parallel version. Run-down, covered in garish neon lights, adverts, holograms. Cade couldn't count the number of windows. All had little balconies, and air-con units that were rusted, left water marks trailing down to the window below.

Dead ahead of him, two groups fighting. Cade watched, as a guy with a machine gun for an arm ducked behind a waterfall that was right in the centre. What was it Silas had said? That Cade would be surprised at what people would do to themselves down here? A girl with coral blue armour danced between the two groups, slashing with a blade that extended from her forearm, laughing maniacally.

Suddenly, Cade's mods didn't seem so extreme. He kept his eyes on the fight happening by the waterfall, noticing other structures dotted around the courtyard. Kaizen logo, cracked in half, riddled with bullet holes. A statue of a man, head chopped off. Some oval shape floating between four poles, suspended by god knows what.

"Cade? That you?" Silas's voice in his ear.

"Where are you?" Cade asked, looking around.

"Twelve o'clock. We're pinned down behind the trash units."

Cade looked dead ahead. Saw the gigantic trash compactors, five blocks of metal with green and silver flaked paint. A flashlight winked on at the top of the unit.

"I gotcha," Cade said. "How many?"

"We're twelve strong back here. If you can call it that."

"Who's fighting in the middle, then?" Cade asked, realising he was gawking at the action from a stupidly exposed space. Ducked around one of the support pillars propping up the apartment complex behind him.

"Triads, Yakuza. Anybody who wants a fight. Yakuza is here for us, though. Make no mistake about that."

"Great. I'm naked out here, unc. Need a weapon."

"We got plenty, unfortunately. We've lost some good brothers and sisters tonight." Silas sounded genuinely hurt. Cade couldn't shake the nagging feeling that this was all his fault. He'd pissed Hitoshi off, shown him disrespect. A projectile whistled over his head, smashing into the building. Shards of glass showered Cade. He got his arms up just in time, the tiny pieces shredding his jacket, but bouncing harmlessly off of his augmented limbs.

Looked up again and saw a group of white suits converging on the bounty hunters.

"Incoming! Yakuza, all angles. They're trying to pincer you in," Cade shouted.

"Like hell they are," Silas said. An explosion of gunfire rippled through the courtyard as the bounty hunters came out, all guns blazing. The Yakuza fell as one, some of them didn't even get a chance to fire off a single shot. Cade smiled, seeing Silas lead the charge, face set in grim determination. He looked up, spotted Cade from his position. Cade saw his uncle's face change, something that resembled happiness. Maybe relief. He waved the bounty hunters forward, and they ran towards Cade's position.

The gunshot cracked the air like a whip. Silas's chest exploded in a cloud of red mist, the force of the bullet taking him off of his feet. Cade screamed something, he didn't know what. Eyes darted to his right, where the sound of the shot came from. A new group of Yakuza, white suits with a monstrously sized Hume. A sniper rifle held one handed by a guy who was all armour and cables.

For a moment, Cade was frozen by indecision. The bounty hunters were dragging Silas into cover, laying down suppressing fire as they retreated. The Yakuza moved forwards as one, assault rifles firing. Cade saw his uncle's hand, reaching up for the sky in-between the huddle of those around. That's when Cade snapped. Running forward, he charged into the first Yakuza in his path. He threw a punch that would have floored a man in the old days. Now, it killed the Yakuza outright, twisting his head around sharply, snapping his neck. The face broke on the impact, bits of teeth, nose bone, cheek, blood, all flying in the air.

Cade didn't slow down. He went for the next guy, grabbing his face with his hands. He twisted the man to the floor, stamping on his face with his boot, crushing it instantly. That's when the Hume with the sniper rifle turned his attention to Cade. Leaping to the left, Cade avoided a high caliber round. He rolled over, the speed shocking him. It was like his mods were taking over his nervous system, acting on impulse, faster than he could think. Cade was charging at the Hume before he knew it, and rammed his palm upwards into the Hume's nose, shattering the bone and driving it through his skull.

The weapon fell out of his hands, and Cade grabbed it, using it as a melee weapon. Striking it across two faces close-by, didn't even bother to check if they were dead before moving on to the next target. Adrenalin pumped through Cade's body as he pounced on the man in front of him, literally dragging him to the floor. Cade pounded at the scared face with twin fists, right then left, over and over, until all that was left was a bloody pulp mashed into the concrete.

"Cade!" A cry behind him, an unfamiliar voice. Cade turned around and realised he'd killed the Yakuza who were here. Some of them he didn't even remember, it had been such a blur. He looked at his arms, soaked in blood. Shrugged the jacket off his shoulders, no need to hide what he really was now.

Standing up from the broken body he'd demolished, Cade went over to the bounty hunters. He guessed the one who'd called him was this woman standing in front of him. Hair two-tone, one half red, the other black. A sharp, angular face with piercings in her nose, lip, eyebrows, and a stud in her chin. She wore a vest, exposing arms that were vascular and large biceps like boulders.

"You sure did a number on them," she said. Her voice was deep, so she probably used test and other anabolics. Looked bigger up close as well, thick back muscles rippling under her vest.

"Where's my uncle?" Cade said, ruder than he wanted to. She nodded with her head, giving Cade a sharp look up and down. Cade grunted a sort-of thank you, and rushed over to the group huddled around Silas.

"Move," Cade said, easing his way through. There was his uncle, laying flat on his back. A hole the size of a fucking crater in his chest, dark blood pumping out in a way that told Cade time was short. Silas saw Cade, his eyes wet with tears. He held up a shaky hand, which Cade took, scraping his carbon fibre knees on the concrete.

"I'm here, unc. I'm here," Cade whispered, delicately cradling his uncle's hand with his own bloody fists.

"Cade..." Silas croaked, fresh blood trickling out of the corner of his mouth. He died right then.

Cade held his uncle's hand, staring into blank eyes that were missing a spark. Cade's mouth was open, caught between a word, a cry, a scream. He didn't know. All he knew was that his heart ached, and it wasn't from fatigue. His lower lip trembled, and around him, some of the hunters paid their respects. Lowering their eyes, making an ancient cross sign over their chests. Somewhere behind, more gunshots. Seemed far away, or maybe that was Cade's perception, because he was being hauled up by his arms. Silas was dragged along as well, and before Cade could comprehend what was going on, they were behind the stack of trash compactors.

Noise filtered in through Cade's ringing ears. Faces looking at him expectantly, like he had a fucking plan. He stared back at them, knowing his eyes were bulging. They were stinging with fresh tears that seemed a futile response to the deep emptiness he felt within his chest.

"Give me a gun," Cade said, his voice low. A rifle was handed to him. Cade checked the ammo count, sixty rounds. That'll do. He stood up, not really caring about cover. A few bullets smashed into his right arm, momentarily swaying his balance. He fired back into the haze of smoke that lingered around the courtyard, hearing a cry of pain. Decided to follow it up, sprinting into the clearing, legs working tirelessly.

Cade was face to face with one of the men who'd found him whilst searching for Hitoshi. Cade didn't hesitate. He dropped the rifle, preferring to use his body and threw a huge right hand, which was blocked by an enormous fist.

"You've killed a lot of Yakuza today," the Hume said, face splitting into a menacing grin.

"Yeah, and I ain't done yet." Cade head butted the guy in his face, dazing him. With his hands free, Cade unleashed a barrage of punches that pounded the man's face. There was resistance, and Cade quickly worked out that the fleshy face was just a mask stretched over chrome innards. The Hume recovered, kicking Cade back with a force like a freight train smashing into him.

Cade was sent flying, rolled on his back a few times, and landed against that strange waterfall. He was soaked immediately, wet hair covering his eyes. He wiped it away, just in time to see the severely pissed off Hume coming right at him.

"Argh!" Cade shouted, as enormous hands gripped his arms, lifting him into the air.

"You've done enough damage," the Hume said, pulling Cade's arms wide, trying to rip them out of their sockets. Cade cried out in agony, the pain receptors firing off inside his head. He closed his eyes as it became unbearable, waiting for the sound - a pop, or crunch, telling him that it was over.

A volley of automatic fire greeted him instead. The bounty hunters were rushing forward, shooting at the Hume. Most of the rounds bounced harmlessly off his massive chest, but his grip loosened, and Cade dropped to the floor. Breathing hard, Cade looked around for something, anything, he could use.

The Hume held up an arm that was like a shield, blocking incoming fire to his head and neck, the only exposed areas of his entire body. Cade saw a glint of steel reflecting the ever constant neon adverts. It was the girl's arm, the one who was dancing around earlier. She was dead, her head lolled to the side with two bullet holes lodged in her forehead.

Cade grabbed her arm, yanked it hard. Bones cracked and

muscle tore, and he held her arm and blade in his right hand. Turning around, he saw the Hume backing away under heavy fire. Cade leapt into the air, higher than he thought possible, and attacked the Hume like a bird of prey. The Hume looked up at the last second, eyes wide as Cade drove the blade straight down the centre of his head.

The guns stopped firing, and the Hume stopped moving. Cade landed awkwardly to the side, rolling once before standing straight. Slowly, the Hume tipped forwards, falling like a building just being demolished. It was over, there was an eerie stillness in the air, the only sound the panting of the bounty hunters and the stream of garbled music and voices coming from adverts high above them.

Cade saw a light flashing on the floor. A holo-phone, incoming call. Cade picked it up, Hitoshi's face projecting large. He looked like he was chewing a wasp.

"Cade. You've caused a lot of damage today. You've killed one of my top lieutenants."

Cade looked down at the phone, which he now saw was trailing a cable into the Hume. "Vital signs went flat, huh? You really keep a close eye on your boys, don't you?"

"Clearly, not close enough," Hitoshi actually smiled, almost like he was impressed. "You've disrespected me and my family today, Cade. You cannot be allowed to live. This was a small task force, sent mainly as a warning to the bounty hunters. And frankly, to let you know that we don't tolerate dealing with their kind." He spat somewhere off screen. Profanities from the bounty hunters listening in drowned out whatever Hitoshi was trying to say, and frankly, Cade didn't care.

"You know what? You're a fucking disappointment. Your dad's right to keep you away from New York. You're a joke," Cade said, and he threw down the phone, stamping on it. Hitoshi made a large O with his mouth, rage filling his eyes before Cade's boot snuffed the image out. He looked back at the ragtag group assembled before him. The muscle bound girl shrugged her shoulders and spoke.

"What do we do now?"

Cade looked at them all, one by one. "We leave Hong Kong."

CHAPTER EIGHTEEN

Rodrigo Ortega paced the marbled hallways of TegaLyfe. He chewed his nails, mind racing. Protestors were gaining momentum in the streets, more people seemed to join the swelling crowds every time he looked out of the large, floor to ceiling windows up on the twentieth floor restaurant. Most of the TegaLyfe employees had finished for the night, and had to be evacuated through the adjacent building and out of the car park. He thanked them all personally for their work, smiling, shaking hands, keeping up the notion that he was as calm as ever. A lie he tried to convince himself was true.

Walking over to the service bar, Rodrigo waited for the cyborg to shuffle over. A primitive thing, it had two primary directives. Take orders, clean up the cafeteria.

"How can I help?" the cyborg asked, vacant expression staring right through Rodrigo. There were a few cyborgs working at TegaLyfe. Mostly taken from JFK, criminals with no future. Lobotomised out in California, repurposed for service back in Nueva York. Just one of the things Rodrigo did to help the community. He shook his head, wondering if the crowds down below knew of all the things he did out of the limelight.

"Whiskey. Make it a double. Actually, can you fix me up a sandwich as well?"

"Yes, sir. What would you like?"

Rodrigo looked around the deserted dining area. A few vacuumbots fizzed away along the floor, taking care of whatever mess remained after the day's work. Employees got discounted Meal Pills, but Rodrigo also recognised that sometimes, real food was good to have as well. So he'd commissioned California to start growing produce as well. Chemically altered to give a wider spread of nutrients, but with the taste of traditional produce, like he'd eaten growing up. Which reminded him. California.

"Uh, just a chicken sandwich," Rodrigo said, backing away from the bar and taking his second phone out. Dialled one of only two numbers and held the phone out in his palm. Olivia's face materialised in front of him, slightly pixelated.

"Mr Ortega," she said, in that flat tone.

"Olivia," Rodrigo smiled. "How are things progressing?"

"Production of the Meal Pill has increased by over fifty percent since we last spoke. There have been a few challenges, however."

Oh, great. What now? Rodrigo's smile didn't falter. "Such as?"

Olivia's neutral expression didn't change either. She just told him the facts. Machine maintenance overdue, which had a knock on effect, slowing capacity. Some of the workers losing momentum, again reducing output. Updates required on almost everything. Basics that would have been addressed, but with everything going on in the last few weeks...

"Okay, thank you," Rodrigo started. "Tell me, your living quarters. Are you satisfied?"

"Yes, of course." She cocked her head to the side like a

confused puppy. But still, no emotion on her reconstructed face. "Why do you ask?"

Rodrigo's lips twitched, the smile flickering for barely a second. "No reason. Thank you for the updates. We need to double production and increase the dosage of the virus in each capsule."

"That could make them volatile."

"Well, the situation *here* is volatile. You've no doubt seen the latest reports?" Rodrigo's smile was practically extinguished now.

"Yes. Protests are increasing, as is the violence. Based on this, would increasing the dosage have the effect you desire? As surely, the number of people consuming the product will be dwindling."

She had a point. Rodrigo's eyes narrowed. A jolt of panic flared up in his chest. Suddenly, he could picture a reality where he lost everything. The business he'd built up, the money he'd earned. It was all hanging by a thread.

"This is simply a difficult moment," he said at last. His smile returning. "We've been through change before, this won't be any different. A few disgruntled conspiracy theorists do not make for the majority. We can alter the narrative, spin it back to Kaizen Sciences. They attacked *us*, a cyber attack meant to decimate our systems. Then released false lies across the net. These people have no proof. It'll all be over before next week."

Olivia nodded. "Will that be all?"

"Yes, for now." The call ended, and Rodrigo tossed the phone onto a nearby table. The device clattered loudly against the metal fixture and almost slipped off the edge. Rodrigo's sandwich arrived, which he snatched off the counter, taking a huge bite right away. He sat alone, and sighed deeply.

Looked around, and imagined it all gone. This wasn't what he wanted for TegaLyfe. Scandal, public scrutiny. But the people, they'd forced his hand. Nueva York was spiralling into a pit of depravity. If he hadn't converted Central Park into the housing estate, it was, the whole of Manhattan would be like that. Full of junkies, rapists, criminals, degenerates. No, he'd put a stop to it all, taking all the shit of the city and keeping it in one place. That was the best thing he could have done. The Meal Pill was a necessity, to make sure people were kept in line. Was that his original goal? Of course not, but it worked. Years of relative peace and prosperity, under his leadership.

Rodrigo couldn't shake the feeling that it was all coming to an end. He ran a hand through his hair, letting out a long-held breath. California again on his mind. He could relocate there. That's why he asked Olivia about her living conditions. If that drone could be *satisfied,* as she'd put it, then he knew he could thrive there. Maybe it was time to leave. But he wasn't going to go without a fight.

Sandwich eaten, Rodrigo got up from the table, brushed some crumbs into the napkin that came with it, and was about to leave the cafeteria.

"Ah," he said, turning back to get his phone, which lay discarded on the table. One missed call. Not Olivia. Rodrigo dialled it back hastily.

"Sanchez? What's going on?"

"Boss, get a TV on right now."

Rodrigo's heart sank. "What's happened?"

"TegaLyfe, it's everywhere."

"Shit, what's being said?" Rodrigo asked, jogging out into the corridor, diving into the nearest meeting room. His hands fumbled over the remote control. He was shaking. That never happened.

"You'll see. Easier for you to take it in."

The screen buzzed on, straight to the first channel. CNN. Stella Thepoulos filled the screen, her face down to the top of her chest. Crowds were gathered behind her, flashing lights, huge advertisements hovering near the top of the screen. She was in Times Square. Rodrigo put the phone down on the oval desk, walking closer to the monitor, taking in what she was saying.

"Moreover, we have factual proof of TegaLyfe's tampering with the Meal Pill. The virus, which has affected hundreds of thousands of us all, is not a by-product of Kaizen Sciences' modifications. It is in fact contained within the Meal Pill, altering our DNA at random. That so many of us affected are Humes has simply been fuel to the propaganda spun by the media machine of TegaLyfe. Rodrigo Ortega has been lying to you all. The files containing this information have been released on the net for your digestion."

Rodrigo didn't hear the reporter's question, instead he fell into one of the many leather chairs spaced out across the room.

"Boss?" Sanchez's voice from the phone, arm's length away. Rodrigo reached for it, fingers grasping the bottom of the device, pulled it towards his body.

"Is this a live feed?" Rodrigo said, his voice not sounding like his.

"Afraid so. Every channel, too. StreamStars all over it. There's unprecedented levels of traffic in the net searching for us. Stella isn't lying. The files are there, uploaded to the cloud. Any idiot with a deck, tower, hell, even a phone can get them."

Rodrigo was silent for a moment that stretched on for eternity. Background noise of Stella talking, being asked questions. "Who are your sources?"

"No comment."

"Why are you doing this?"

"Because the world needs to know the truth."

The truth. Rodrigo knew what that was. He'd been betrayed. A lump formed in his throat. He knew who was responsible for this, and his heart was breaking into a thousand pieces. Tears stung the corners of his eyes, the TV still blaring away in the background. In a fit of anger, Rodrigo hurled the remote at the screen, shattering it instantly.

"Sir? Are you hurt?" Sanchez still on the line. Rodrigo got out of his seat, grabbing the phone with clumsy, heavy hands.

"I need to make a call. But Sanchez, can you get here? This is a rapidly moving situation, one that is going to require drastic intervention."

"Of course, we've been friends for a lot longer than we've been colleagues."

Rodrigo smiled a little. "Thank you. Get here as soon as you can." The call ended, and a heavy weight landed in Rodrigo's stomach. Now it was the hard part.

Taking out his other phone, he scrolled down to the name he wanted. Tayo. Rang a few times.

"Boss?"

"Tayo, you've seen the news?"

"Just caught it, yeah." There was something in Tayo's voice, a resignation. Like he knew what Rodrigo was about to say.

"I'm offering you a bonus deal on top of your new contract," Rodrigo started. He sucked in air, staring up at the plain white ceiling. "One assassination target, one capture, alive."

"Just say the word," Tayo said.

"This is a formal request, you have two targets. Kill Stella Thepoulos. And..." Rodrigo took the phone away from his face, breathing hard, eyes up at the sky again. "... and bring Daniela Ortega to me. Alive."

"I'm on it, boss. But I gotta ask. Are you sure you want to do this? Stella ain't a problem. But Dani? That's-"

"It's what I've ordered you to do. Payment will be in your account now." Rodrigo opened up the credit app on his phone, tapped Tayo's details in, already saved, and shifted five million dollars across. He heard a melodic chime through Tayo's phone.

"Very well. Consider it done. You know she'll resist, right?"

"Just... try not to hurt her, okay?"

"You got it," Tayo said, ending the call. Rodrigo collapsed into the chair again, letting the phone clatter to the ground. He howled a guttural cry of anguish, burying his face into his hands. Tears of anger, sadness, betrayal, whatever they were, they were flowing.

"Why? Why?" Rodrigo asked the empty room. He picked his phone up again, tapped the media file. The picture of him with his wife and young Dani beamed up at him. He wept some more, slamming his free hand onto the desk. A thousand thoughts coursed through his mind. What was he even going to do when he had her here? Rodrigo didn't have the answers to any questions for the first time in his life. And he was petrified.

CHAPTER NINETEEN

TAYO HAD LEFT Nueva York a few hours ago, and was entering Old Queens. The Stacks loomed in the distance ahead, bright white numbers illuminated the designation of each building. He'd put his son Jaden in block three. Safest out of the fourteen. Not that it made much difference. Once the door was bolted shut, nobody could get in or out unless Tayo unlocked it.

Checking in on his son, Tayo tapped the side of his head, bringing up the security display rigged throughout the apartment. Jaden was sound asleep on his square mattress, sheets pulled right up to his chin. All alarms were active, sentry turrets hidden in the ceilings fully loaded. As usual.

Tayo walked with a deliberate pace through the streets of Old Queens. Where Nueva York was a visual assault on the senses, with loud adverts blaring in your ears every few steps, Queens was the opposite. Here, it was quiet. The rustling of loose papers blowing through the streets, the occasional rat clambering through a trash can, the only sounds in the dead of the night.

A bar sign flickered, neon light faded to a dull glow. Tayo

remembered when he and the boys used to drink there most weekends. Used to be lively, full of people. Now it was just another shell, burned down for an insurance claim by the owner, and left as a visual reminder of what a run-down hell-hole Queens had become.

As Tayo continued his steady walk towards The Stacks, hearing a few conversations carrying in the darkness, his mind lingered on Rodrigo's contract. Permanent member of the team, now. The last thing he wanted was to spend *more* time with Rodrigo, yet now he was bound by the code. Once a contract is signed, that's it. No going back. Which, in turn, meant less time with Jaden. Tayo couldn't help the guilt that swelled within him. All of this work, these jobs. What if he was finished off before Jaden was grown? That was Tayo's deepest held fear, one that nobody else knew except for Blayze.

Tayo scanned the nearby blocks with his eyes. Basic infra-red, but it always showed a few interesting details. Like that guy over there. Mod-shop, down a back alley. Tayo headed over towards him, touching his head to return to normal vision. The darkness of Queens enveloped his eyes like a growing shadow.

The mod-shop was a little den tucked in between two tight streets whose names had been forgotten years ago. Covering the entrance were those plastic sheets that used to be in old meat lockers. Maybe that's what this place was once, and the owner had knocked through the wall, giving it a large open space. The sound of whirring buzz saws screeching against metal greeted Tayo's ears. He saw the sparks flying from the centre of the room, the owner of the shop getting to work on a body.

"Just a second," the guy said. Massive goggles obscured his face, dreadlocks tied up in a knot out of the way. Scraggly beard with flecks of grey gave Tayo an indication of his age. Lying prone on the table was a woman, slim, maybe thirty. She was getting something done to her stomach, which was held open by two mechanical arms extending from the back of the shop owner. His human hands worked with the buzz saw, cutting the metal control panel to size. Tayo thought he knew what it could be. Replacement organ box. Regulated stomach acid levels, controlled liver functionality, and assisted with digestion. Pretty extreme mod to have, she must have been ill.

Tayo looked at the battered armchairs that appeared to have been dragged out of one of the projects. Cigarette stains, tears, suspicions stains. Nah, rather stand. The work was done, and the guy put his goggles down. Tayo saw now he had twin mechanical eyes, extended out, probably to help with the surgery. They reclined as he moved over to Tayo, those robotic arms also folding into an unseen compartment on his back.

"How can I help?" he asked, scratching his beard.

Tayo held out his arm. "Got a few bullets lodged in this thing the other day. Messing with my reflexes on this hand," Tayo said, wiggling the fingers on his right hand. The owner shuffled over for a closer look, holding Tayo's huge forearm, turning it gently.

"You on the front lines, then? Fighting against TegaLyfe?"

"Something like that, yeah."

"Shit, I don't care which side you're on. This work is high end. Don't mind my asking, how come you're seeing me for this?"

Tayo met the man's eyes with his own. "Because I wanna help out smaller businesses."

The man smiled, revealing missing teeth along his top row. "You from these parts, then. Figured as much. Think I've seen you around before. You're a bounty hunter, right?"

"Can you fix this, or not?"

He let go of Tayo's arm. "Sure. Few thousand, though. But it's a quick fix."

"Good."

"You want any pain meds?"

"Nah, just get it done." Tayo held out his arm, and the man backed away, giving a suspicious look. Tayo tapped his ear, connecting to Blayze over voice call.

"T, what's up?" Blayze answered.

"Where you at?" Tayo said, the mod-shop owner returning with the necessary tools. The extra arms sprouted from his back again, gripping Tayo with force. Tayo raised an eyebrow, looking at him.

"Just for stability," the man said.

"I'm near Times Square. Who was that?" Blayze said.

"Mod-shop. Getting my arm fixed quickly. Can you check in with Dwight for me? Ain't been to see him in a few days."

"Sure thing, was heading over there anyway. How come you didn't get Tega to fix you up?"

Tayo winced as a drill dug into his forearm, cracking open the housing unit for his arm. He saw the wires, interlocking with the carbon fibre alloy. No flesh, but still hurt like a bitch.

"Because I needed to get away and see Jaden. Just happened to see this spot close by."

"Yeah, I get that. How's this new contract working out for you?"

"Probably the same as it is for you. Pays well, but not as much downtime, right?" Tayo said. His arm twitched involuntarily as the man did something with the tools. Tayo heard the bullets that were lodged in there tinkle as they hit the floor.

"Yeah. Haven't seen Ewan in a day or so. Hope he's alright."

"He'll be fine," Tayo said, a little too dismissively. But he had other thoughts on his mind. Jaden.

"Aight T, I'm gonna head to Dwight now. I'll let you know how he is."

"Thanks. See you soon, cuz."

"You got it."

The call ended, and so did the work on Tayo's arm. The

owner grinned that toothless smile, holding up a dollar conversion machine.

"Crypto or dollar?"

"Dollar, here," Tayo said, tapping the machine with his huge left hand. The money transferred out of Tayo's account instantly, the machine beeping with confirmation.

"See you around," the guy said, moving back to the table to wake his other patient. Tayo flexed his arm, finding it looser and more responsive. Amazing what could be done in a few minutes. He pushed aside the plastic sheeting, and took a left, moving towards The Stacks.

Tayo's eyes scanned through the halls of The Stacks. Junkies at every turn, jabbing themselves in the arm with dirty needles from god knows where. They all had that same look about them. Like death was right around the corner, but they didn't give a shit. Just chased that high. Tayo pushed one out of the way who came too close, acrid breath stinking. The guy fell back, landed on something hard, and shrieked out in pain.

"Hey you can't do that-" one of them started saying, but was cut off by Tayo's fist smashing into his face. Teeth and blood dripped down Tayo's hand, the junkie crumpled to a heap, face caved in and dead instantly.

"Anyone else got a problem?" Tayo said, staring at the huddle. Looked like fucking zombies, gawking back at him with gaunt expressions, like they didn't even register what just happened. Tayo shook his head and banged the elevator button.

Arriving at his apartment, Tayo stood still while the retinal scanner flashed in his eye. Door locks clicked and whirred, the thick steel bolts receding as the apartment opened up for him. It was late, Jaden would be asleep.

"Daddy?"

Or not.

"Son, what the hell you doing up?" Tayo said, crouching down on one knee to embrace Jaden.

"I couldn't sleep," the boy said, wiping his eyes with his hands. Tayo smiled.

"Now I know you lying. You always sleep, you lazy ass," Tayo said, rubbing his fixed hand over Jaden's hair.

"Am not," Jaden protested, giggling. Tayo looked around the apartment. Tidy, but for a few empty packets of Meal Pills on the counter.

"You want some real food?" Tayo asked.

"Now?"

"No, silly. For breakfast," Tayo said. He'd already given Jaden one of TegaLyfe's vaccines against the virus. Rodrigo said it was guaranteed, and so was the lifetime supply Tayo would get. But Tayo didn't want to be in Rodrigo's pocket forever. Better to start now, and get Jaden used to eating as much actual food as possible.

"That might be nice. What food, daddy?"

"Maybe some noodles? Sandwich? I can pick something up for you at work."

Jaden's face fell. "Are you going back to work already?"

Tayo's heart sank. "Yeah, I got a few things to take care of. Hey what you been watching?" Tayo noticed the StreamStar projection over on the big TV in the corner. Jaden's small collection of pillows next to some toys lay on the floor in front of it.

"Nothing really," Jaden said, walking over and about to turn it off.

"Wait, hold on a second. Where is this coming from?" Tayo said, squinting.

"Hong Kong."

"You understand what they're saying?" Tayo asked Jaden.

He knew his son watched streams from all over the world. He'd picked up Spanish by the time he was six, even helped Tayo understand it better. Kid had a natural aptitude for learning languages.

Jaden scrunched his small face up in concentration. Tayo looked at the screen, seeing fires, close-ups of weapons on the ground.

"They're saying that some fighting has happened at Kowloon," Jaden said, turning the volume up a little higher. The first person perspective from the StreamStar shifted, showing some of the fighting.

"Okay, that's enough. Turn that off-" Tayo was walking over to Jaden when he stopped dead in his tracks. His heart thundered against his chest, mouth open.

"Can you go back for me, Jaden?"

"Sure." Jaden rewound the footage.

"Stop. Yeah, right there." The image froze on a man running through some kind of waterfall, charging forwards with an assault rifle. Tayo's eyes were wide, his mouth suddenly dry. "Can you zoom in?"

"Yeah, watch this." Jaden pressed a button, and the image pixelated, getting right up on the man's face. Tayo could practically hear his heart about to burst, the seconds while the image buffered to complete clarity seeming to take an eternity.

And there it was. Face set in grim determination. Cade. Tayo stared at the image for a few seconds, taking in every detail. He saw Cade's arms, black and shiny. Standing fully upright, seemingly on two perfectly functioning legs.

Holy shit, how did he survive?

"Are you okay, daddy? You're sweating."

"Uh, yeah, yeah. Daddy's fine. I just gotta make a call real quick, you go on and turn that off now, ya hear?"

"Okay," Jaden said, voice thick with disappointment.

"That's a good boy. Go and use the bathroom before bed, right?"

"Yeah," Jaden said, trudging off to the small room over to the right. Tayo waited for the sliding door to close, and was about to dial Rodrigo, when his name flashed up in front of his eyes.

"Boss?" Tayo answered. He must have seen the footage as well.

But Rodrigo had a different proposition.

Tayo got off the call just as Jaden walked back in. He looked real sleepy now.

"Let's get you to bed," Tayo said, forcing a smile. Jaden yawned and nodded in agreement. Tayo scooped him up with one hand, carrying him to his little bed. Automatically made itself every day.

"Daddy, are you going to work now?"

"Yeah, sorry."

"That's okay. I know you have to." Jaden said, flinging his arms up. Tayo leant in, kissing his son on the cheek.

"I love you, daddy."

"I love you too, son," Tayo said, unable to shake that image of Cade out of his mind.

"You saw who?" Blayze said in Tayo's ear as Tayo made his way back to Nueva York.

"Cade. That fucker is alive, and in Kowloon. You know what's there, right?"

"Bounty hunters. The exiled. Shit, T. How in the fuck is he alive?"

"I don't know. But he is. I don't think Rodrigo knows it yet."

"You gonna tell him?"

Tayo stopped, the Queensboro bridge dead ahead, teeming with activity of the homeless. The night gave the dilapidated bridge an even greater sense of foreboding.

"I don't know. He's got other priorities on his mind," Tayo said.

"I think I can guess. Stella is everywhere. She's outed TegaLyfe."

"Yeah, and the boss wants her dead. And that's not all..."

"What?" Blayze asked. Tayo could hear the trepidation in his voice.

"The daughter. He wants her brought in, too. Alive."

"What for? Oh, you don't mean..."

"Yep. She put Stella up to it. So the boss thinks, anyway."

Blayze let out a low whistle. Tayo propped himself against one of the burned-out buildings this side of the bridge. "I know," was all Tayo could say.

"This is getting real heavy, T. What do you want us to do?"

"Same as always. Jaden is the priority if I go down. You make sure he gets every cent in my account. You got the access card to my apartment, right?"

"Of course."

Tayo nodded. "Now, back to Cade."

"Oh shit, yeah. You're definitely sure it was him?"

"Positive. And him being around the exiled makes me think he's planning something big. We gotta be ready for it. I need you to tell the boys. We keep it in our circle for now, okay?"

"For sure, T. Aight, I'm at Dwight's now. I'll hit you up later, where you gonna be at?"

"Going to the new apartment Rodrigo fixed me up with. Central Tower, one of the penthouses."

"Nice. Some perks to this new contract, then?"

Tayo snorted. "Yeah, I guess. I'll call you when I've got Dani."

"You need backup?"

"Nah, I'll handle this myself. See you later," Tayo said, finishing the call. He let out a deep sigh. Cade was at the forefront of his mind. A thought lodged at the centre of his consciousness. *What if I never left Cade in the subway? Just forgot about the incident at the club?* Tayo had to admit to himself he wasn't happy with the direction his life was going in the short term. Under Rodrigo's thumb, not seeing Jaden as much, and now hunting two of the most prominent figures in Nueva York.

Tayo pushed off from the wall of the building and stepped towards the bridge. He heard a few sirens blaring out ahead. *Yeah, this is gonna be a long night.*

CHAPTER TWENTY

DANI CHEWED HER BOTTOM LIP, watching Stella deliver her speech to the array of cameras below her. She had been talking for over thirty minutes, and the crowd was swelling. The gigantic screens in Times Square all displayed Stella's face, her message of TegaLyfe's corruption coming through loud and clear. Dani pulled her hood tight around her head and adjusted the triple filtered face mask covering her nose and mouth. She'd managed to evade the watchful eyes of the bounty hunters and police sent to guard her, with them believing she was still at Stella's apartment, asleep.

Dani bent down to tie a phantom shoelace as a cluster of police walked past. She kept her eyes on them, and retreated behind a McDonald's vending machine that was covered in graffiti, calling cards, and stains she didn't want to think about.

"Asher, where are you?" Dani whispered, tapping her earpiece.

"I just got out of Tega, left a few programmes auto-running. Should give the illusion I'm still there. For a few minutes at least."

Dani's heart still beat a little too fast, but she let out a breath. At least Asher got out. "Are you going to your apartment?" she asked.

"Yeah hon, just to grab some essentials." He sounded sad.

"I know it's a lot, all of this. But we'll be okay. The city... no, the world has to know what Rodrigo has done. Right?" Dani said, trying her best to soothe Asher's fears.

"Dani... I'm scared. Your fath... Rodrigo is a powerful man. He's gonna find us. Dani, I'm not ready to die yet, you know?"

"We're not gonna die. We're doing the right thing here. There's no way I could continue being a part of this company, an accomplice to some tyrant. We're both better than that. Aren't we?"

There was a pause. Dani heard Asher let out a long sigh. "I know that, it's just... I thought we could do this takeover internally, without making it so obvious, you know?"

Dani grimaced, seeing yet more camera crews and StreamStars arrive at the red steps of Times Square. "I know. I wanted that too. But there's a lot of people loyal to him. This is the only way." Dani said it with conviction, but a tiny seed of doubt nagged at the back of her mind. Had she been too hasty? She looked up at Stella again, who was seemingly wrapping things up. Flashes from holo-phones taking high-res pictures lit up the space around Stella. She smiled gracefully, taking her time to descend from the podium where she was speaking. Dani kept herself back from the action, the blaring of adverts above her becoming more annoying by the second.

"Oh, shit," Asher said. Dani jumped, forgetting for a moment she was still connected to him.

"What is it?" she asked, tilting her head away from the crowd for a second, pulling her mask down to breathe a little easier.

"I've left some stuff at my desk, I need to go back."

"Are you serious? No way, it's too dangerous."

"I'll be fine. Two minutes."

Dani shook her head, looking up above at the cluster of neon signs. All Tega products. "Just be careful, okay?"

"You got it. I'll be in and out. See ya, hon." The call disconnected, and Dani was left truly alone, waiting for Stella to wrap up.

Asher was sprinting, his chest heaving up and down. He didn't like lying to Dani, but he still wasn't sure how she'd take the news that he'd been stealing crypto from her company. One last run, that's all he needed. A big hit, enough to ensure he could get out of this city for good, never come back.

Asher stopped just south of TegaLyfe headquarters, catching his breath. *How the hell did it come to this?* He thought. A high-flying cyber security expert one day, a punk on the run the next. Not exactly the career trajectory he'd envisioned when he joined. A big part of him wished he'd just kept his head low. Did the job, no questions asked. But it became personal. Karla's purge from the system made him realise that it could happen to anyone. So why waste time doing the bidding of a maniac who wants to suppress all of humanity with a virus he also manufactures? Didn't make sense.

Then again, neither did this plan. Asher got himself into the old car park, swiping his key card. It beeped, and Asher winced at how loud it seemed, even against the backdrop of the constant din of noise in Nueva York. He kept low, as much as he could do with his tall frame, and headed for the elevator. Tapped the card again, and waited. He crossed his arms, looking around. Twitchy, biting his nails.

"Come on, come on," he said, chewing his tongue. At last,

the elevator arrived, and Asher slithered inside, bashing the up button a hundred times.

"Move, you piece of shit," Asher said. Must have been the magic words, the elevator rumbled into life and took him up. Asher collapsed against the wall, sliding down. He put his head in his hands, shaking.

"The fuck am I doing?" *Ding.* No time to think it through, he was back at TegaLyfe.

"Good evening, Mr Jones. You're in late," the girl with pink dreadlocks said to him. Her smile was so synthetic it wasn't even funny, the straightest lines and the brightest white teeth he'd ever seen. But she was cute. Luckily rather dumb, too.

"Just patching up a few holes in the network, you know how it is, girl," Asher said, flashing his grin and waving his hand as he went by. The second he was out of her sight, he dropped the smile, replacing it with wide eyes and a mild look of terror.

Looking around, Asher craned his neck to the platforms above the wide atrium. *Rodrigo will be up there somewhere*, he thought. Which petrified him even more. Fortunately, the ground floor was deserted, except for the janitor cyborgs and a few vacuumbots dashing around. Asher got to the elevator and took the familiar ride down.

Started running again, through the armoury. Before reaching his command centre, Asher slowed back down to a walk. Paranoia crept up on him again. *What if Sanchez is waiting for me in there with a loaded gun?* Asher grabbed the nearest weapon from the shelf behind him. A small pistol. Checked, it was loaded and crept forward, heart pounding against his chest. He closed his eyes, counted backwards from three, and burst into his office. Empty.

Asher relaxed his stance, shaking his head again, and quickly got into his seat. No time to jack in, no need either. So the thick cables remained where he left them; coiled up on the floor next to his towers. His skinny fingers danced across the keyboard, working the commands and pulling up several different windows at once. TegaLyfe's crypto funding, a few dummy programmes to flood the system with activity, and his personal fund account.

His finger hovered over the Y key, which would execute the command and transfer out six million dollars. It was the largest amount he'd ever brought up. In normal circumstances, it would be ridiculously risky. Sanchez definitely would be here with a gun if he'd tried this amount before. Fuck it. Tapped the key, and the digits drained from TegaLyfe's account, appearing instantly in his own. Asher smiled, reclining in his chair and breathing a sigh of relief.

"Okay, easy part over with. Now to get out," Asher said to himself, shutting down the accounts. He kept a few programmes running, fired up some more for good measure, and darted away. Something inside his head told him it would be a good idea to grab a gun or two, so he did. Two pistols, some ammunition, and a knife. His phone rang, and his heart stopped. Sanchez.

"Oh, fuck." Asher hastily stuffed the guns into his belt, the knife he sheathed into the leather pouch it came with, and jammed it into his jacket pocket. He ignored the phone, breaking out into another run and headed for the elevator.

Sanchez was persistent. Four missed calls. "Shit," Asher said, glaring at the phone as another call came through. He kept going, though the atrium at an awkward half-run, half-walk. The cute girl was still there, as she always was.

"That was fast," she said. Big smile, bright eyes.

Asher coughed out a fake laugh. "Well, you're not the first person to say that to me, honey," he winked, and she giggled, and he waved goodbye again. His pulse must have been running at two-hundred beats per minute. Sixth missed call from Sanchez.

Asher made it down to the car park, fully sprinting now, but stopped in his tracks. Rodrigo's car was sitting there, engine on. The driver's side door opened, and Sanchez stepped out.

"Hello, Asher. Where are you off to in such a hurry?"

CHAPTER TWENTY-ONE

KARLA SAT down in one of the office chairs, a little clumsily. She wasn't quite used to her spatial awareness yet in Mei's body, but it would come. She reached into the backpack, grabbing the deck and placing it onto the curved desk. Two monitors and a tower waited patiently to be used, standby mode activated with a distinct amber light on top of the screens.

"Okay, let's see what we can find, shall we?" Karla said, smiling. She got the deck out, fumbled with the leads, and jacked in. Next, she put the headset on. The pins stuck her temple, and she sucked her teeth. Turns out they did sting a little.

Cyberspace opened up in her mind like a thousand bright lights being turned on at once. Karla was free, no firewalls or antivirus programs could stop her from getting anything she wanted. As tempting as it might be to explore her unlimited potential, she homed in on a large sphere of traffic, with more tendrils of information being dragged towards it. In her mind's eye, Karla flew towards the noise, waiting for the data to smooth out and become clear. In the physical world, she was aware of her arms hanging by her side, not touching the deck.

That could raise suspicions, if anybody walked in, so she forced her hands to grip the deck, careful not to actually press anything. She didn't need Mei's body to do anything on the outside, just make it look like she was.

The information presented itself to Karla in the form of StreamStar projections, media headlines, news channel bite-size media clips, and a lot of cable guy chatter on the net. The headlines were clear, though. TegaLyfe has been exposed. Karla dug a little deeper, finding the origin of the story. There it was. She pulled out a cube, a video taken from somebody standing in Times Square. Slightly shaky footage, clearly a phone being held by someone, but it would suffice. Clicked play, and was greeted by someone standing on a podium.

Another part of Karla's multi-layered consciousness branched off, finding out who this woman speaking was. Search query lasted zero-point-zero-one of a second. Stella Thepoulos, Hume activist. Insanely rich, but more importantly, influential. People listened when she talked. And right now, she was talking a lot about TegaLyfe.

Karla listened with fascination as the facts kept coming. The Meal Pill, the virus. Rodrigo's intentions to control all the population. Stella mentioned something about the files being available, so Karla splintered herself again to go and find them. There they were, sitting freely inside the cloud, an endless space that hovered above the net with the capability of storing all of mankind's greatest discoveries since the dawn of time. Or, media files of StreamStars playing pranks on each other.

Either way, it was busy. Karla recognised the small packages of data zipping around as cable guys, the colloquial term for people like Mei, who tried to make a living on the net either by stealing data, crypto, or classified information. A lot of them there were obviously just curious, as there was no value in this TegaLyfe leak. Karla reached in and plucked the files out, assimilating them into her information bank. Yep, just as Stella said, all the facts were right there.

An independent thought broke out as Karla was listening to Stella's continued defamation of TegaLyfe. Daniela Ortega. Asher Jones. Something deep within Karla's core told her to go back to her research about her own life. Those two names they were important. She'd put together some of the puzzle the other night, but she wanted more. All Karla had were fragmented files showing her snippets of information about Daniela and Asher. She had to go deeper.

Refocusing her mind, Karla gathered up the pieces of her consciousness that were busy gathering data on current affairs. She had to get into TegaLyfe. There was a part of her subroutine lurking in the system. She wasn't joined up to that part of herself, not yet. It raised another question. Where else had her consciousness fragmented to?

Finding TegaLyfe within cyberspace was easy. The firewalls alone gave off a signal like a lighthouse in the darkness, but that didn't mean breaking in was going to be just as effortless. She approached the TegaLyfe construct, which in cyberspace was a white, digital fortress that was on the scale of a planet compared to her human frame. Karla had been here before and hadn't even attempted a break in. But that was before. She had grown in unfathomable ways since she'd attempted this a few days ago.

Summoning up all of her immense processing power, Karla focussed on creating a doorway. Thin lines traced across the mammoth construct in front of her. They weren't doing a thing. Until a crack appeared. Then another. Karla focussed, using every minuscule part of her incredible processing power, intent on smashing through the blockade. A pixel shattered, just one, and it was replaced instantly. But then more started to flicker, some reforming with incomplete edges. She knew that it was close. Outside, blood dripped from Mei's nose.

Karla knew this was taking a huge toll on her body, so much so that if Mei was acting alone, she'd be dead already. But they would never be alone again. They were one. And with Mei's brainwaves and neurons augmenting Karla's AI sentience, they were unstoppable.

The wall cracked open, barely wide enough for a hand to slip through, and it was already half repaired. But Karla was in. TegaLyfe opened up before her as a sprawling city, white columns of gigantic towers stretched on for an infinity. Karla floated down to the surface, a wide street that inclined gradually towards a tower so large she couldn't see the top of it, even at such a great distance.

Karla juddered to a stop, her form which she was projecting, glitching in and out of synch with the TegaLyfe security system. Something dragged up from inside her. Mei would have called it a memory. Karla was remembering. It came flooding back like a gust of wind blowing through a forest. She had been here not long ago. There was a woman, her head covered, wearing some sort of... dress. No, a shawl. That's what it was. And she had...

Karla screamed, and her cyberspace body crumpled into a heap, fingernails clawing at hair that wasn't real. In reality, Mei was jerking violently in the chair, foam dribbling out of her mouth. Karla remembered the woman. Fareen. She had such immense power within this system. Karla gathered herself, forcing both her physical and cyber body to relax. Mei's seizure subsided, so Karla could focus back on the task at hand. Who was Fareen?

Gliding through the towers at a rapid pace, Karla splintered herself again. Finding out her relationship with Daniela and Asher was the priority work stream, and she quickly unlocked several files showing their status within the company. Then she saw herself. PA to Rodrigo Ortega. AI. Thoughts of Fareen narrowed into a smaller focus for the time being. AI.

Let's pull on that thread. Her date of origin came up quickly, along with build versions, protocols and... creator. Asher Jones.

Karla's mind processed something akin to a lump in her throat. That thing happened again, a memory, and she was with Asher. Sharing jokes, discussing work projects, walking with Rodrigo and Daniela... Dani, that was what she called her. They got on so well...

All of this was a jumble of rapid fire images displaying in Karla's field of vision like somebody was clicking through a slideshow at serious speed. She was putting together a collage of her life before, and the picture was getting clearer. She had a family. Asher and Dani they were close. She recognised a pattern of jealousy, though, with Dani. The fact that she was human. That had previously bothered Karla. But not now. Karla had a body of her own. Different from Dani, but that didn't matter. Not anymore. Karla was gripped by a new sensation, one of desperation and fear. Dani and Asher would be in serious trouble with the TegaLyfe leaks.

Karla concentrated again, and detached another part of herself to back out of TegaLyfe, and get into the net. Find out Stella's relationships with Dani and Asher. Why was she trying to harm them? That could wait, because Fareen's name hovered back to her priority list. Files had been found, lots of them. Karla froze the image of Dani and Asher walking next to Karla's projection in TegaLyfe. Taken ten days ago.

Instead, she pored through the data on Fareen. Former head of cyber security... developed the systems TegaLyfe used initially... What build versions are they? Karla interrogated the current status of TegaLyfe's security, flooding it with bounce back pings. Version seven-point-three. Back to Fareen's file... she left it at version... five-point-oh. Karla paused, letting the information digest. Fareen had worked with Rodrigo Ortega and a man named Sanchez on building up their cyber security. Fareen's contract was abruptly terminated a few years ago.

Asher arrived as the new head of cyber security and made changes to the system. Some large, like Karla herself. Some, not so significant. But the core framework of TegaLyfe's security system was all Fareen's work. No wonder she could get in and destroy Karla's old body.

The revelation had seconds to breathe before Karla's search around Stella yielded maximum results. Over forty billion hits on the net. Filter by keywords *Daniela Ortega, Asher Jones.* Instantly reduced the number. Not much about Asher, but a lot with Dani. Karla saw parties, promotional events, casual photos, shared investments. Clearly, they were great friends. So why would Stella do this? Unless.

Karla made the connections fast, already searching for any trace of how the TegaLyfe files had been leaked to the cloud. It wasn't hard. There was the trail, a simple upload masked by proxy files to cover up any wrongdoing. Asher had put the minimum amount of effort into this, but Karla knew it was him. He'd leaked the files. Was he working with Stella to bring down Dani? Surely not.

Taking a moment to gather herself into one whole, Karla backed out of TegaLyfe entirely, even found the part of her that was lingering in TegaLyfe all this time. She was back amongst the net, floating. Thinking. She initiated a deep search, looking for Dani or Asher. Any security cameras or sound waves. Anything with their trace. The query was taking much longer to bring a result back than she would have liked, but then she found something. A camera, Times Square. It was angled down, a watchful eye over a parade of shops and a busted McDonald's vending machine.

A girl, covered with a hood, looking like she didn't want to be seen. Karla paused the footage and tapped into the TV cameras across the plaza, hoping to catch a lucky break. That's exactly what she got. Opposite, a CNN handheld device, rotating to capture a view of the crowd. Karla hacked into it, waiting for the moment. There.

She froze the image, brought it out with her back to the net, and zoomed in. The quality was outstanding. She could see the golden lettering of Boston Scientific around those big, beautiful eyes. Karla cross-referenced with the image of her, Dani and Asher. Magnified to scale, and put them side by side, focusing on the eyes. Definitely Daniela Ortega. She was the one orchestrating this whole thing.

Satisfied, Karla was about to exit cyberspace and give her new physical body a break. But something caught her attention. A news report from a StreamStar in Hong Kong. Karla opened the video footage.

"Breaking news here in Hong Kong. There's been gunshots heard in Kowloon, apparently gang warfare. Stepping in for a closer look..."

The StreamStar was something of an amateur, but it was the next part which caused Karla to stop what she was doing. Ever since she learned of this Cade character, Karla set her search parameters to automatically run. Mentions of his name, sightings, facial recognition. She'd fully educated herself on his story, his involvement with TegaLyfe. More importantly, the conversations they'd had in the streets of Nueva York. Camera footage picked up their discussions, and Karla had remembered. Cade was someone she was fascinated with. Infatuated, even. Perhaps more, she surmised.

And now he was here. In Hong Kong. The footage was frozen on his face, contorted into a grimace, about to deal the killing blow to an extraordinarily large male with extensive modifications. Karla ran another search function on the man. Quickly, she discovered he was a chief henchman of Hitoshi Nishikawa. That name was familiar. Karla delved deeper into Hitoshi and quickly discovered he was the son of Ichiro

Nishikawa, CEO of Kaizen Sciences. The owner of the building she was in right now.

Karla returned to the footage of Cade, fast-forwarded to real time. The StreamStar turned away from Cade violently executing the other man, rambling about what the motivation was. Bounty hunters going up against the Yakuza, she said. Karla backed away from the stream, now intent on hacking into security cameras around Hong Kong. Her search wasn't for Cade, though, it was for Hitoshi. She could already see how this was going to play out and needed to stop him. But first, confirmation.

The result came back in seconds, and there he was. An immense figure with pinks, blues, yellows all running up his arms in cables. Liquid of some kind, pumping around that enormous body. His head looked to be the only organic part of him left. He was surrounded by other modified humans, all of them with heavy weapons, and angry looks in their eyes. They were clambering into vehicles, and took off heading in the direction of Kowloon. Hitoshi and his men were out of the range of the security camera fast. Which meant Karla had to be even quicker.

Retreating from all of her search queries, Karla used Mei's deck that was interfaced with Kaizen's network. In seconds, she had the readout for the complex she was in. Ichiro's chamber wasn't too far away, but would he be there? Karla didn't have long to act. She also didn't know whether the gamble she was formulating in her mind would pay off, but there was no other choice. Cade was in danger, and she had to go now. With a burst of energy, Karla short-circuited the entire network of Kaizen Sciences. She was instantly catapulted into Mei's body and gasped, like she'd just been drowning.

Karla yanked the headset off, unplugged the deck, tucking it into her bag, and sprinted for Ichiro's chamber. Darkness enveloped the building, and there were confused shouts coming from a lot of the adjacent offices. She ran as fast as her legs would take her, bouncing off the glass walls of the connecting bridge, her balance a little off still. But she didn't stop.

Arrived at a gigantic door, which was open thanks to the security shut out. Just as Karla slipped through, the lights came back on, as did the security systems. The door slammed behind her, blowing out a small gust of wind. Karla turned, moving towards the end of the room, past a statue that looked to be of a warrior.

Into the elevator, panting, but gathering her thoughts. As fast as the elevator climbed, Karla's heart rate slowed. She was concentrating on the next few seconds, which would be crucial to her and Cade's survival.

The doors parted, and several guns were already pointed at her.

"Wait!" Karla yelled, holding her hands up. "Please don't shoot, your son is in grave danger."

"What did you say?" the man seated at the far end of the room, who Karla knew was Ichiro, said.

"Your son. There's a fight happening right now in Hong Kong. The bounty hunters... they've been attacked by the Yakuza and are fighting back. We have to stop them, or both your son and Cade will be killed."

Ichiro got up from his chair and moved his hand in a downward motion. The two bodyguards flanking him lowered their guns, eyes hidden behind sunglasses, but Karla imagined they gave Ichiro a quizzical look.

"Did you say Cade?"

"Yes. He's in Hong Kong."

"And how do you know this?"

Karla stepped forwards, lowering her hands. "My name is Karla. I was formally the AI of-"

"TegaLyfe," Ichiro interjected, his eyes wide. He was close

now, a few inches away from her. He studied Karla intently, his hand suddenly shooting out to grab her arm.

"Ow," Karla said, squirming under the pressure.

"You're... that girl from earlier. You're not an AI. Get rid of her."

"Wait! I can show you." Karla thought fast, moving to the elevator. She went to the console panel, yanking it open, acutely aware of the rifles being levelled at her head. Closing her eyes, she plunged her hand inside the electronics, bristling with the energy coursing through her flesh. Karla realised the elevator could move in a lot of directions, not just one, so she tilted it forwards, then sideways. Next she rotated it at an angle, hair falling around her face, but remained standing. Returning the elevator to its normal state, Karla opened her eyes slowly and saw Ichiro standing there, mouth open. His eyes narrowed, and he raised his hand into a fist. The weapons were dropped again.

"Nice trick, but I'll need more evidence. Come to my office. If what you say is true, then patch us into my son. Now."

CHAPTER TWENTY-TWO

CADE BLINKED the blood out of his eyes. His face was a crimson mask, stained by the lives he'd taken in the last five minutes. His breathing was erratic, but only because of the adrenaline coursing through his body.

"How are we gonna leave Hong Kong?" someone said.

"What?" Cade answered, not paying attention. The rush of battle was wearing off, the ringing in his ears from repetitive gunfire was drowning out the chatter of the ragtag group of bounty hunters.

The huge chick came over to him again. "Cade... what do you wanna do about them?" She jerked her head backwards, thumb as well. Pointing at the bodies on the floor. Silas was one of them. A rock formed in Cade's stomach. His uncle was dead. Silas had been back in Cade's life for a few days, and he was gone. For good this time.

Slowly, Cade took in his surroundings again. The fight had almost blinded him in a way, giving him tunnel vision. Kill the person in front of him, that's all he had seen. Now, the carnage was clear, and it made his stomach lurch.

Dismembered bodies littered the courtyard. Limbs were in

some strange places, like on top of that odd waterfall feature. Grey steel was turned a shade of dark brown thanks to thick layers of blood and gore. And there, by the trash unit, Silas's foot sticking out. Cade sucked his teeth, muttering a few curse words under his breath. He started walking over, feeling the eyes of the bounty hunters on him.

Cade turned to face them, arms out wide, to say, *what do you expect from me?* "Just gimme a sec, okay?"

"Scanners show a lot of vehicles moving to our location," an Asian girl with half a shaved head said.

"Great," Cade said. He approached his uncle, his dead body lying flat on his back. Cade crouched into a squat, arms dangling over his knees. His eyes stung with tears, but he swallowed back his sadness.

"I'm sorry, unc. You're dead because of me..." Cade's voice trailed off, as a new thought swam into his head. *What if I had killed Ichiro? Just done the job, got on with my life.* He looked down at his arms, the physical reminder of his choice. He thought of Olivia, then Dani, and panicked. His deepest fear surfaced as he stared at his uncle's lifeless corpse. That he would die alone, just like Silas had. Cade slammed his first into the ground, cracking the worn asphalt. He got up, didn't give his uncle another look, and buried his sadness and his fear. It was time to go back to Nueva York. Rodrigo Ortega was owed a debt.

"Chopper isn't far from here," Cade began, hoisting a discarded rifle onto his shoulder. Checked the magazine and slapped a fresh clip into it, courtesy of the ammo belt coiled around a dead Yakuza. "Parked up on a helipad, that way," Cade continued, nodding towards the skyscraper he and Silas emerged from only a few hours ago.

"Oh, shit," a man nearby said. Cade turned and agreed with the appraisal. Headlights flashed in the distance, multiple cars bearing down on their position. The whine of electric motors fitted with huge superchargers filled the night air. They'd be on top of Cade and his newfound crew in less than a minute.

"Come on," Cade said, gritting his teeth and breaking out into a run. "Head for the plaza, we're gonna have to hole up in there, pick them off best we can." Cade was sprinting now, much faster than the others. Ahead, the gigantic screen where he'd seen the stream of Dani came into view. A quick scan of the nearby buildings told him that they were occupied. Lights were on, music floating out from open windows. There were gonna be some innocent casualties, that was obvious.

Before Cade could dwell on the moral implications of more blood on his hands, the cars that no doubt belonged to Hitoshi roared into view. Men with tattoos on their faces, shaved heads, and string vests leaned out of passenger windows. Assault rifles.

"Get into the buildings, find cover," Cade yelled over his shoulder. A split second later, gunfire barked from the vehicles. A couple of strangers were scythed down in a hail of bullets instantly, their bodies crumpling into bloody pulps. "Fuck," Cade said, ducking behind what appeared to be a bar. He heard the concrete crack and split where he'd been a moment before. Tyres screeched to a halt, shouts in Japanese filled the air, mingled with thuds of automatic gunfire.

Cade looked to his right, seeing the muscle bound girl with three others. They were tight against a building in an alleyway. She made eye contact with Cade, who pointed up. "Get inside," Cade yelled. She nodded back, and Cade spun around the corner, laying down a burst of suppressing fire to cover them. He got a glimpse of what he was up against. Counted at least ten cars, all with doors open, Humes hiding behind them for cover. Bullets whizzed over Cade's head, and he took that as his cue to get back out of sight. He saw the group across the street barge into the apartment building. Some screams of panic inside confirmed their entry.

Just when Cade was about to move, the building in front of him exploded in a shower of bricks and wood. He was flung back several feet, landing hard on his back. "What the fuck was that?" he breathed, blinking the stars out of his eyes. Dust and smoke clouded his vision, stinging his pupils, but he could see the shadow. The massive, hulking figure that had to be Hitoshi. The giant stepped forwards, confirming Cade's suspicions. Mounted on one arm was an RPG, smoke trailing from the end of the weapon. *He's got a fucking rocket launcher on his shoulder*, Cade thought, scrambling to his feet before he was spotted. Too late.

A shout of Japanese, and a torrent of bullets rained down on Cade. Some hit his arms and legs, throwing him off balance as he sprinted to the nearest building, grabbing his weapon as he got up. Leaning forward, Cade shoulder charged into the door, crashing down with it into a lounge. A seedy red hue tinged everyone in the room, eyes all staring at Cade. Businessmen in suits, arranged around a circular table. Cade saw the drugs, knew them well. The white powder lay in mountains.

"Get into cover, now," Cade urged. They just looked at him, blank stares on synthetic faces. All of them had apparently been to the same clinic for their reconstructive surgery. Cade didn't bother to wait, he got up, legs springing into action, and charged up the narrow staircase, almost bowling over two waitresses in skimpy outfits.

Cade got to a window, which was closed to the outside world by two wooden shutters. Kicked them open with his right foot, and propped the rifle he'd managed to keep onto the window ledge. He put his eye to the scope and let off three bursts of quick fire. Two heads exploded, bodies slumping into the car they were hiding behind. Cade's angle was right above them, so it was an easy shot. The last one looked around, getting off a shot that missed Cade's ear by inches, before he was put down as well.

Moving his target, Cade picked off some more of the Yakuza, who were still oblivious to his position. Most of them were moving into the town now, creeping forwards with their guns raised. Cade had no idea where the bounty hunters were, or how many were still left.

"Where are you? Come on..." Cade whispered to himself, searching for Hitoshi. He was out of range, likely to his left. A shot cannoned off of Cade's arm, making him drop the rifle. It tumbled to the ground, landing with a loud *clack*. Cade turned to his right, the direction from where he was shot, and just ducked back inside as a flurry of rounds came for his head. He landed hard on his back, driving the air from his lungs. Winded for a second, but his new organs worked overtime to get his breathing regulated again.

Cade was acutely aware of the doorway. Had Hitoshi seen him get inside the building? Didn't matter now, he'd been spotted, anyway. As much as Cade was getting used to his mods, he didn't fancy a one-on-one with that guy. Twisting his body, Cade searched for some more windows. Nothing. He stared at his hands, black chrome fingers balled into a fist. *Might as well try*, Cade thought, reaching back and punching the drywall to his right. It smashed open, giving Cade a view into the adjacent room. Some kind of office space. He kicked with his augmented legs, creating a hole large enough to squeeze through, and clambered inside.

Staring at Cade were more of those waitresses. They took a minute to look him up and down, and then screamed, backing into a corner.

"I'm not gonna hurt you - ah fuck it, I ain't got time for this," Cade said, getting to his feet and running down the stairway. He arrived at an indoor pool, which glowed aquamarine. No lights in the ceiling. Cade heard voices behind him, men talking fast. He looked at the pool again, spotting a red button near the wall. He hoped that was what he thought it was. Running to it, Cade hit it, then dived into the pool, just as the safety shield was covering the water.

Cade submerged himself, holding his breath. What had that doctor said to him about his increased lung capacity? Something he didn't plan on field testing. The lights inside the pool dimmed as the dome covering locked against the sides. Cade was absorbed into the darkness, becoming still.

A few moments later, footsteps. Heavy sounding. Must be some Humes. Had the girls ratted him out? Probably. What was he to them? Cade heard Japanese being exchanged in hushed tones. *Yeah, they know I'm here*, Cade thought. He closed his eyes, waiting for the inevitable. Nothing happened. Then it dawned on him. *How the fuck do I get out of here? The button's on the outside.* Cade's neck flushed, panic gripped his chest. His breathing suddenly became laboured. His eyes were open under the water, which didn't sting, but it was useless. It was completely dark.

Cade told himself to calm down. He wasn't actually running out of breath. All he could do was break out. The Yakuza would probably be waiting for it, but what other choice did he have? Drown or get shot to pieces. What a fucking way for this to end. Cade steeled his nerves, making a fist with his right hand. Generating as much force as he could, Cade thrusted his fist skywards, hoping to buckle the roof. It was completely dislodged.

Suddenly the room was ablaze with a dark red light, a siren wailing in panic on the wall. As he suspected, two Yakuza had been standing there, waiting. The blast from the siren caught their attention, and Cade had seconds to act. He vaulted out of the pool, slammed into the nearest guy, who went flying backwards into the tiled wall, cracking it. The other one was ten paces away, which Cade covered in a heartbeat. He slapped the gun out of the Yakuza's hand with his left, using his right to punch the guy hard in the stomach. Cade's fist shook as it connected with steel plate. Cade looked up at the man, bewildered. He just smiled back, eyes glinting in the red hue with menace.

Cade was kicked back, hard. He tumbled over himself, landing in a heap next to the other Yakuza, who was getting back to his feet. Cade pivoted his hips, driving as much power as he could into a right hook, and connected with the man's face, pulverising him between fist and wall. Cade barely had time to move as a giant boot came flying at him. He rolled away to the left, getting up and readying for another attack. It didn't come. The Yakuza was wary. He looked down at his fallen brother, face smashed into a fleshy, red mess. He grimaced, fixing Cade with an icy glare.

"You die, gaijin," he said, pointing a finger that was coiled with loose wires dangling from his forearm. Cade sized the man up. Dark clothes covered most of his body, except the arms. They were exposed. Graphite grey slabs of metal, shaped to look like muscular arms. Wires all over them, curling round into an unseen unit on the man's back. *Pneumatic limbs? Better avoid them*, Cade thought, pacing slowly around the pool. The men stared at each other, eye contact breaking for fractions of a second. Cade figured the guy was searching for a weapon, his eyes snapping to the ground every so often. Cade spotted one in the corner of the room. Looked equidistant between the pair. Where the other gun was could be anyone's guess.

Cade looked again at those arms. He had a fleeting thought about the other bounty hunters somewhere in this town. How would they be faring? Some had mods, but nothing like Hitoshi's crew. They were like a different species altogether. The Yakuza lurched towards Cade with a frightening leap, clearing the narrow edge of the pool. It snapped Cade out of his momentary thought pattern and he had to duck to avoid a clubbing blow that would have taken his head off. Cade lashed out with a kick, aimed at the stomach. Blocked by one of those arms, sending vibrations up and down Cade's leg. It was the strangest sensation he'd ever experienced.

Cade rolled back again, avoiding a smashing blow that churned up the ground. Twin fists kept pulverising down, a repetitive thump from the enhanced arms sounding like a drill churning up a road. Cade was going to be squashed, and he knew it, unless he acted fast. With a spark of inspiration, Cade leapt high, his new legs allowing him to ascend over and above the Yakuza. Cade pivoted mid-air and kicked hard into what he hoped was a power unit. He was right. Sparks flew, and the Yakuza fell forwards, arms flailing wildly towards his back. He landed face-down, and Cade pounced, landing on his back. He narrowly avoided clubbing blows that were being blindly thrown out, and grabbed the guy's neck, twisting sharply. The room was silent and still, except for Cade's mild breathing. He got up, grabbing the gun from the corner. Loaded, full clip. Forty rounds. Enough? Definitely not. But better than nothing.

Emerging from the pool room, rifle levelled, Cade crept past overturned furniture, discarded meals. The girls were gone and moving into the next room, Cade saw it was also empty. It was quiet. Too quiet. A tinkling of glass from the bar in front of him got the hairs on the back of his neck standing up. He gripped his rifle tightly, finger hovering over the trigger. Creeping in, the room had two lights. One flickered intermittently, a thin white strip dangling from the ceiling.

In a whirlwind of movement, Cade rushed to the bar, leaping over it with one hand, the other holding the gun with ease. He almost landed on a frail old man, who wore a very traditional servers' uniform. He shouted, putting his hands over his head and curling into a ball.

"Don't shoot," he managed to say in English.

"I'm not gonna shoot. I need to get out of here. Help me."

The man pointed with a long finger towards a door with a metal bar over it. "There. Go to street."

"Thanks," Cade said, hopping back over the bar and rushing to the door. He lifted the safety bar, gently tipping it to the ground. Twisted the door handle with equal care, wincing as the hinges protested at the motion. The noise of the streets rushed into the bar like a howling wind. Shouts of battle, anguish, instruction, agony, all filled the room. Gunfire echoed in patches, some far away, some much closer. Somewhere out there, Hitoshi.

Sucking in a lungful of air, Cade knew he had to get out there and end this. Question was, did he just get his ass out of here alone, or try to save some of the exiled? Stepping into the well-lit street, the darkness of night all but banished under neon glows, Cade looked around, trying to get his bearings. Nothing here looked familiar. He must have been much further into the town than he realised.

Where was that god damn skyscraper? Cade craned his neck, searching the skies. It all looked the same. Buildings that towered above this town, blinking lights, adverts, winking at him from up high.

"Cade." The voice called from the shadows across the street. Cade saw a shock of green hair, pale eyes, and a really big gun. It was one of the bounty hunters, a woman whose name he didn't know. Come to think of it, he didn't know any of them, but they all seemed to know him. Uncle's doing, no doubt. Cade gritted his teeth, fighting back a tear. "Son of a bitch," he said, jogging over.

"Name's Jazz, good to meetcha," she said, extending a gloved hand. Up close, Cade saw the mods. Nothing fancy, but obvious skin grafts. Her dark skin was flawless, not a wrinkle or blemish in sight. She turned to check over her shoulder, and then Cade saw something even more obvious. The back side of her head was missing, replaced by a clear dome which showed off the array of electronics hooked up inside.

"Holy fuck," Cade said, unable to stop himself. He took her hand, shaking firmly.

"Huh? Oh, that," she said, pointing with her free hand. "Got fucked up pretty bad back home, left for dead. My partner was sentenced to death by that asshole Ortega, so we tried to flee. I almost didn't make it. Reconstruction of the brain, not easy. Or cheap."

"Shit, you get that done here?"

"Perfected here. Nueva York, I got some back-alley mod shop in Old Queens to patch me up. Lucky to be alive, really." Her discoloured eyes searched Cade, wary, but not unfriendly.

"Yeah, and now look where you are. Other side of the world being hunted by Yakuza."

"And Triads, don't forget those," she said with a smile.

"Silly me. Anyone else still alive?" Cade asked, turning serious.

"We've lost a couple, but mostly we're hanging on. Spread out across this town."

"You got comms?"

"Yeah," Jazz said, tapping her ear. "Alpha, Bravo. I got Cade with me, over."

Cade heard a crackle of static, then a voice. Jazz nodded. "I'll ask him, hold." She turned to Cade again. "This ride of yours, where exactly is it?"

Cade wanted the ground to swallow him up. *I don't know*, wasn't exactly an inspiring answer. "Look, I can't figure it out from here. We get back to that giant screen in the plaza. I'll be able to get us there. How far are we from that?"

"Couple of blocks south. Alpha, Bravo, you get that? Rendezvous at the screen. Now." Jazz ended the call and got to her feet, grabbing Cade's arm. "Follow me, we'll get out of here yet."

Cade allowed himself to be led through a network of dingy alleys covered in graffiti and posters. He almost tripped on a few homeless people, who seemed oblivious to all the fighting going on around them.

"Come on, just a little further. Might get a little hot here though, street opens up again," Jazz said, turning to face Cade as she ran. He saw in front of her the alley widen, the giant screen visible. It looked deserted, apart from a scattering of bodies along the floor.

"Alright, Alpha. We're here, confirm your pos-"

The gunshot split the air with a thunderous noise. Cade was covered in electrics and blood, Jazz's head turned into a gaping wound. Her body slumped against the wall. Cade fell backwards and shifted back around the corner. He heard shouts coming from where he'd just run from as well. Now he was trapped. He gripped his rifle tightly in both hands, breathing fast.

"Come out, gaijin. Don't be a little bitch." It was Hitoshi. Cade tilted his head back against the brickwork. He chanced a look around the corner. There he was. Big fucking Hume, standing right in the middle of the plaza. At his side, another Hume holding a massive caliber sniper rifle, smoke coiling out from the barrel. Cade made up his mind. He tossed his own gun out first, making his intentions clear. Coming out with his hands up, he walked into the open, feeling the eyes of the enemy boring into him. Now he saw some were perched up on rooftops, aiming their weapons down. He really was fucked. Hitoshi's face split into a mocking grin.

"You shouldn't have disrespected me," Hitoshi said, as Cade came to a halt. He was twenty feet away, with the big screen framing Hitoshi like he was a StreamStar.

"Well, guess I'm finding out now, right?" Cade said. Hitoshi actually laughed.

"We could have done something together, you and I. Such a

waste. But you've killed my men, shown me no respect in my own country. As head of the Triads and Yakuza, I can't allow this," Hitoshi said, pulling out a pistol and aiming at Cade. He almost looked upset about it.

"You will take no further action." A voice warbled into existence from the speakers that surrounded the plaza. Then the screen fuzzed into life, pixelated at first, but crystallising into a clear image. Cade's mouth hung open. It was Ichiro.

"Son, lay down your arms. Cade, call off your bounty hunters." *My bounty hunters?* Cade thought.

"We have a much bigger enemy to take down. And we have our best chance yet," Ichiro carried on. Cade recognised the backdrop behind him, the office where he and Ichiro had first talked.

"Father? How is this possible?" Hitoshi said, turning his back on Cade and staring up at the screen. Ichiro looked off screen to his left and shuffled over. A young Japanese woman, maybe early twenties, with short hair, one bang longer than the other, appeared on the screen. Cade was struck by how pretty she was, which seemed like the last thing to think about right now. Her eyes seemed to light up as she looked into whatever camera they were using.

"Hi Cade," she said.

Hitoshi turned back around to Cade, a strand of black hair covering his eye. "You know her?"

"No?" Cade said, but he honestly wasn't sure. Something about her *was* familiar.

"Yes you do, Cade," Ichiro began. "And she is the last piece of the puzzle. We already have the loyalty of the subway rebellion, but now we have something even Rodrigo Ortega could not predict. Cade. This is Karla," Ichiro said, gesturing to the woman.

Cade arced an eyebrow. "But Karla's..."

"An AI?" the girl started. "Oh, I'm much more than that,

cowboy. Get to the chopper, I've pinged the location to Hitoshi's internal nav. I'll explain everything there."

Hitoshi reacted as though he'd just eaten something sour. "What the fuck? How has she done that?"

"Son, this is our moment. Everything we've been building together, we can have it all. New York will be ours."

Cade watched Hitoshi carefully. Did he really not care about New York, like he said earlier? Or was that simply bravado? A moment that stretched on for an eternity where not a word was spoken. Until Hitoshi broke it, firing off a string of commands in Japanese, tilting his head to talk into whatever voice communicator he had. Guns lowered at once. From all angles, bounty hunters emerged from buildings, doorways, and other hiding places, cautiously approaching. Hitoshi turned to Cade and spoke, "let's go get your transport, gaijin."

CHAPTER TWENTY-THREE

Fareen had once told Patrice that she didn't get nervous. Where people talked about that feeling in their stomach, the dread creeping up their throat? Yeah, she never got that. Now, as she walked into the side entrance of the Ten Hit Club, she looked at Patrice. This must be what nerves felt like. He smiled under his mask, that crooked grin that only she could see with her eyes. She didn't return the gesture, keeping her steely gaze. The Mafia doormen watched her and the rest of the subway delegates with unflinching stares. The twins, Voz and Vin, led the way, all smiles and practised poses. *They* didn't look nervous.

The door closed behind Fareen, and two more Mafia goons emerged from the shadows, standing with their backs to the door. Fareen turned away, focussing on the staircase ahead of her. Nobody was talking, the only sound was the dull thudding of music coming from the rooms within the club. Fareen rolled her sleeve up, checking the slimline watch on her wrist. It had only been a few hours since she'd spoken with Ichiro, and he'd tasked her with getting the Mafia to stand down when the Yakuza would move uptown.

Contacting the Mafia was the easy part. Voz and Vin used some of their connections in the media to spread a rumour, that got pounced on by the Mafia's legal team, Voz got a call, and the meet was arranged. At the top of the staircase, a large oak door was guarded by two heavies in crisp suits. Sunglasses covered their eyes, but Fareen could see what was underneath. Bright blue gems on both, matching implants that would greatly augment their vision. Handy in a dark nightclub when you had to quickly get rid of unwanted guests, Fareen thought. There were the nerves again.

The doors parted, both men holding one side open with hands that were laced with intricate cable work. Fareen walked side by side with Patrice, and they entered the circular room together. It was exactly what Fareen would imagine a Mafia meeting place to look like. Gaudy furniture, portraits of stern looking men with slicked black hair, expensive trinkets, and a giant chandelier. A massive desk, dark brown, dominated the room. A singular chair held the ever impressive figure of Don Lione. Stoic, unwavering. He looked at them all, hands flat on the table. Displayed in plain view were multiple firearms, piles of cash, and a deck hooked into something on the floor. Probably auto-mining crypto from multiple businesses.

"Welcome. Fareen, is it?" the Don spoke. He stood up, his body wobbling slightly. Fareen saw how his bones had been reinforced with carbon fibre rods all the way through. Muscle tissue replaced with a lattice of steel fibre and an unknown alloy. Despite the extensive work, he still wasn't sturdy on his feet. At a guess, Fareen placed him in his early one-hundreds. He'd no doubt seen his fair share of bullshitters, so she kept that in mind for her big proposal.

"Yes, Don. Thank you for seeing us on such short notice."

"Don't thank me, thank them," the Don said, pointing at the twins, an amused smirk tugging at the corners of his mouth. "These kids put out some rumour on how there's been an agreement with the Yakuza to come into our territory?" the Don laughed, looking around at his associates, of which there were eight total. "How is it I'm the last to find out about this, ah? Must be losing my touch."

Fareen waited for the laughter to die down. She knew Patrice would be itching to ram his fist in someone's mouth. The twins were helping themselves to a bottle of cognac, pouring out two glasses, clinking them and looking bored. They collapsed into two armchairs, draping long legs over the sides as they sat at angles. Voz twirled the drink around with his fingers, Vin studied his nails. They were good at feigning disinterest, but they'd be hanging off every word.

"There has been an agreement reached, yes," Fareen said.

The Don chuckled again. "Oh, excuse me. I didn't realise you were the head of the family now. Please," he said, moving to one side with arms outstretched, gesturing to the chair. "Take a seat." More laughs. Fareen inhaled through her nose. Patrice shot her a glance, his fingers curling around the small knife he stupidly left loose in his pocket.

"The agreement, Don, was with Ichiro and I. But there was a condition that involved you, and the entire Mafia."

Don Lione sat back down, the amusement wiped off his face. "This, I gotta hear." His mouth turned into an upside down U, and he raised both hands, palms up. "What is this... agreement?"

Fareen held her nerve, despite her heart beating faster in her chest. "That the Yakuza would assist us with taking down Rodrigo Ortega. But only if you agree to allow them safe passage."

"You're asking me to turn my back on a loyal ally of the Mafia-"

"Rodrigo treats you like children. He gives you no real power, and suffocates your growth, like he does to all of us," Fareen said. The room fell silent, all eyes seemed to focus on her. Clearly, interrupting the Don was a ballsy move. But she had to go all out. Time wasn't on her side, and if she didn't convince him in this meeting, she wouldn't get another shot.

"You talk like you know our operations. You hide in the subway. What do you know of our world?" the Don said.

"A lot, actually." It was Voz who spoke, standing up with his drink still cupped in his hand. "Yes, we know all about how tight Rodrigo keeps that leash on you. Yes, you own this club, but who watches over it from the rooftops, ready to wipe you out at the click of a finger? The police. Who are owned by? Rodrigo Ortega. The swanky apartments most of you live in. Central Park Tower, right? Guess you know who owns it. I mean, gentlemen, for christ's sake. He's put you on *border patrol*. When was the last time you actually had to stop anyone from coming onto this island?"

Fareen looked at him, then at Don Lione. The Don looked pissed, his mouth worked to form a response, but he had nothing.

"Exactly," Voz said, raising his glass in the direction of the Don. "The power dynamic in this town is shifting. Anyone who's been paying attention in the last few weeks can see it. The cyber attack on TegaLyfe was just the beginning. We took something significant from them, didn't we, Fareen?"

She nodded, wary of revealing what she had done to Karla. Would the Don even care?

"You're telling me information I already know. Rodrigo Ortega delivered a proposition to us," the Don started, carefully measuring each word. Fareen's heart dropped to her stomach. "We have been given the opportunity to work with Ortega as true partners. His vision is that we would go Downtown and take the fight to the Yakuza."

"If I may-" Fareen started, but the Don held up a hand for silence.

"However, Ortega's proposal hinges on the bounty hunters

working with us. In our experience, they're only as loyal as the money in their account. Well, apart from that one kid, Cade. Got us out of a tight spot one time."

Cade? Damn, he seemed to be everywhere in this city, Fareen thought. There were murmurs of agreement from the other Mafia in the room. The Don continued. "Anyway, my point being, if Ichiro offered them more money, they'd probably turn. We can't depend upon that. Plus, there's another factor in all of this. That being the people. Protests have been ramping up and your actions the other day, what with the ground assault and all? It made people sit up and take notice. Maybe TegaLyfe is as bad as I'm hearing, people are saying to themselves. Now to top all of this off, Stella Thepoulos has just started broadcasting from Times Square, 'bout a minute before you showed up. Take a look." The Don reached for the tiny black remote nestled in-between his pistols on the table. Clicked it once, and a gigantic screen descended from the ceiling behind him, blocking out the portrait of the Don himself.

Fareen watched with bated breath as Stella's face appeared on the screen. She divulged all what Fareen knew to be true, secrets only someone within TegaLyfe would know. Someone incredibly high up at that. Everyone present watched in silence for five minutes, absorbed by the accusations that were coming out of Stella's mouth. Fareen didn't know the girl on a personal level, but everyone in New York *knew* her. What she said was trusted, and this... this was colossal. The ramifications could be enormous, and it might just start with the Mafia and their loyalty.

Don Lione clicked the remote again, the screen disappearing up into the ceiling. Patrice shared a glance with Fareen, who, in turn, looked at the twins. For the first time, their nonchalant demeanour gave way to genuine curiosity, perhaps even trepidation.

“So what we have here is a dilemma,” the Don said. “See, on the one hand. We have Rodrigo’s offer. His *assurance* that we’ll take Downtown back into our control, the way it was before the war, long before that. To an old romantic like me, that ain’t too bad of an idea.” He grinned, looking around the room, catching Fareen’s eye and holding her gaze. “However, there have been rapid developments recently, which you just saw. I’ll level with you, all of you. I’ve seen a lot of shit in my time. People come and go. Presidents, mayors, this whole human modification shit. Change is inevitable, no matter how much we try to fight it.” The Don snorted, relaxing into his chair and opening his arms. “Shit, take a look at me. I ain’t exactly a spring chicken, but *change* has kept me going a long time. And now, I think there’s going to be another big change coming. Rodrigo Ortega is not invincible. Someone has betrayed him, and I’m bettin’ it’s the daughter. This shit with the Meal Pill is gonna tip anyone over the edge. People don’t wanna be controlled, but they always are. Secret is, you don’t let the cat out the bag. Well, that fucker is well and truly out and away. Rodrigo Ortega’s days are numbered. We aren’t gonna side with him. So you can tell that Yak motherfucker that as of right now, we are no longer in business with Tega-Lyfe. Come up here, do what you gotta do. Let us keep our territory here... this club, the Bronx... but we’re not gonna get involved in no war for the company. That’s my final answer.”

Fareen didn’t know whether to laugh or cry, her nerves were torn to shreds. The Mafia in the room exchanged looks between them, as if to question whether the Don was speaking with his right mind. He seemed to pick up on that.

“Boys,” the Don started, “let’s face facts. The Yakuza are only getting stronger. We’ve been holding the line at Canal Street, but we’re being picked off one by one. What’s the use in fighting right now, huh? We’ve got nothin’ to gain everything to lose. And I don’t play to lose. Just trust me on this.”

That seemed to work, there were grumbles of acknowledgement, nodding of heads. Voz clapped his hands together, raising his glass once more. "A toast, then," he said, big grin plastered across his face. "To new beginnings."

"You can go fuck yourself, pretty boy. Get out of my office and I don't wanna hear or see you schmucks in this club again, got it?" the Don said. Voz recoiled, setting his glass down.

"Loud and clear."

"Good. Fareen. Deliver my message to Ichiro. But if a single one of my men gets a fucking hair out of place on their head, then we're going after the Yakuza. Understood?" the Don said, leaning forward.

"Like Voz said," she began, "loud and clear."

"I can't believe that worked," Patrice said, moving into the subway. The twins remained topside, mingling with the elite of Nueva York's socialites in the night, who seemed oblivious to the world falling apart around them.

"I can. The seeds of discontent have been sown for a long time now. It was inevitable that TegaLyfe would come crashing down," Fareen said, gliding through the dingy hallways. Patrice grabbed her arm gently, stopping her forward motion. She turned to him, surprised, eyes darting from his face to her arm. "Patrice? What is it?"

"This feels like it could be the end. If it all goes wrong, we're finished."

Fareen smiled, resting her other hand on top of his. "My dear, this is just the beginning. With Ichiro's power combined with ours, Rodrigo has no chance. The bounty hunters won't stick around to watch him fall. They'll duck out as soon as the tide turns. Yes, we're going to have casualties. That's unavoidable. But the outcome will be worth it. It's everything we've been working towards."

Patrice nodded. "You're right. I just don't want to lose... you."

Fareen's lips parted just a little, showing her white teeth. "And you won't. Come, we need to prepare. We need to get Downtown to let Ichiro know," she said, the holo-phone Ichiro had given her still tucked into her shawl.

Patrice spent the next hour rounding up every available man and woman who could fight. There were maybe eighty in total, Fareen surmised. Hardly an army, but it wasn't like Rodrigo was commanding a huge force, either. She heard the precautions outside of her room, the clattering of people running past, shouting instructions. She thought about blocking out the sound, and her nanites responded, assembling into a curtain of sound-deadening material.

It was quiet again. Fareen was sitting on her bed, legs crossed, arms resting on her knees. She was naked, as she preferred to be when alone, allowing the nanites to surround her in a calming sphere, protecting her from harm, but most importantly, giving her true privacy. She assembled her thoughts, wondering how this might be different if Cade were here with them. If he'd taken out Ichiro, for example. Would they still be in this position? Possibly not, so it likely worked out for the best, all things considered. Though, a nagging feeling rummaged around the back of her mind, like she'd failed somehow, by aligning herself with Ichiro. That was never in the original blueprint for her new world order.

A knock at the door. Fareen's eyes snapped open, the nanites rushed back to her body, shimmering along her bare skin and covering her from head to toe. She picked up her shawl, draping herself in one fluid motion, and pulled on the metal handle. It was Patrice.

"Yes?" she said.

"We're ready. Cable guys standing by, providing as much comms and intel as they can. Ground forces assembled. We've got around fifteen still too injured to move down in the medi-bay, though."

"Good, thank you. Let's get to Downtown."

Fareen led her band of rebels out of the Subway into Ichiro's turf. She immediately pressed the call button on her holo-phone, which responded with rapid-fire beeps of a line disconnected. They waited, the darkness of night beginning to give way to the purples and reds of sunrise peeking through the gaps in the skyscrapers surrounding them.

A sharp whistle cut through the chatter like a gunshot. Heads swivelled to look for the source of the noise, and Fareen spotted it. A Japanese teen wearing a ripped leather jacket, holding a baseball bat. He waved them over. Naturally, nobody moved. Two more appeared behind the young man, Yakuza, in white suits. They too gestured for Fareen and the rebels to come, and this time, there was movement. Walking next to Patrice once more, she let her fingers interlock with his for a brief moment before parting, and led the way.

"Ichiro congratulates you on completing your end of the bargain. At least, that must be why you are here, and summoned us, no?" a man with bleached blonde hair and a dark goatee said, flashing a toothy grin at Fareen.

"Yes, the Mafia have pledged their allegiance to our cause." Not strictly true, but she didn't want to get into the detail with a low-level grunt.

"Excellent. Hold on." He took a phone out from his inside breast pocket, dialling and waiting. Spoke some Japanese, then handed the phone to Fareen.

"Hello?"

"Well done. I underestimated you." Ichiro's voice.

"I'm flattered," Fareen said.

"We have some significant news as well."

"Oh?"

"I have a young woman with me who is most extraordinary."

"Yeah? How so?"

"She is the AI known as Karla, fully merged with a human."

Fareen's throat contracted, her mouth suddenly dry. What did he say?

"Are you... quite certain?" Fareen asked.

"I am. We've made contact with my son in Hong Kong, thanks to Karla. That's not all. Cade was there, along with the exiled bounty hunters. He has been through quite the journey. They all have one thing in common, however. Vengeance against Rodrigo Ortega. Our numbers have soared, and our position undeniable. Come to Kaizen Sciences, you'll be fed and housed while we await the reinforcements from Hong Kong."

"That is... excellent news, Ichiro. Thank you. We'll make our way to you now."

"Good." The line went dead, and Fareen handed the phone over to the blonde guy. She was numb. A million thoughts ran through her mind. Karla took priority. Her memory flashed back to when she was in Kaizen Sciences. That young girl, which made her nanites flare up. Was that who Karla had merged with? What if she remembered Fareen... and what she'd done? That could seriously jeopardise her alliance. More importantly, her long-term aim. To sit at the head of TegaLyfe.

"Is everything okay?" Patrice asked.

Fareen turned to him, masking her fears with a smile. "Perfectly. We're on our way to Kaizen Sciences."

CHAPTER TWENTY-FOUR

"SANCHEZ? SANCHEZ?" Rodrigo said into the earpiece for the second time. Where the hell was he, anyway? Tried the phone, no answer. He looked again at the screen in his office, which displayed the account alert. Millions had disappeared in seconds, just gone. Rodrigo paced around his office, the screen swinging around to stay in his peripheral. Outside, night was giving way to morning. A streak of red blazed across the skyline where the sun was attempting to rise. What was that old saying? Red sky in the morning, Shepherds warning?

He gulped, looking away from the sprawling skyline of Nueva York. His city. But he could sense it slipping away, no matter how tightly he tried to hold on to it. He sat in the chair, fingers dancing on the keypad, which rose from the centre of the table.

"Where did that money go?" he asked, talking to himself. He interrogated the line of disruption, seeing that the funds splintered out into a network of IP addresses, some as remote as Finland, according to the computer's scanning. But the huge payout, the latest one, that was like a beacon lighting up the night sky. It burned with an intensity that couldn't be ignored.

"Computer, trace that address, please," Rodrigo said, his left hand closing on the opposite fist, resting his chin against his clasped hands.

"One moment, sir." Rodrigo missed when it would be Karla answering these queries. But the backup system was okay for tasks like these.

"Sir," the flat, male voice started. "The IP address is here, TegaLyfe."

"What? So it was moved into an account within..." the pieces dropped in Rodrigo's mind. Asher Jones. Masked his personal account by using TegaLyfe's own address. Rodrigo fumbled into his suit jacket, grabbing the phone. Tapped Asher's face and waited, the dial tone ringing out.

"Fuck," he said, slamming the phone down on the table.

"Sir, incoming call from a number in the Bronx, shall I divert to you?"

"Ah, yes. Some good news at last. Should be the Mafia. I'll take it here, thank you," Rodrigo said, reaching over to the desk phone that was plugged in against a secure line. He lifted the receiver, all smiles.

"Rodrigo Ortega."

"Mr Ortega, it's Luciano Del Piero."

Rodrigo frowned. Couldn't the Don make the call himself?

"Hello, Mr Del Piero. I assume this is regarding the proposal I offered?" Rodrigo said, leaning back in his chair, swinging his feet up onto the table. There was a slight pause on the other end of the line. Rodrigo's eyes shifted in his head. A pit of dread filled in his stomach.

"Yeah, about the proposal. I'm sorry that I have to inform you, but the Mafia have declined."

"You've what?" Rodrigo said, legs coming off the table, elbows propped on the desk. "You're declining?" He laughed, shaking his head. "You can't *decline*. I'm the Mayor of this city. I am-"

"You are finished, Mr Ortega. This city has rejected you. The power has shifted. We are not actively taking up arms against you, but we're not stopping those that are. You're a businessman, right? Well, you can relate. We're protecting our assets. Something I'd advise you to do as well. Get out of the city, Mr Ortega. We ain't gonna stop you. We've had a good working relationship, which is why the Don has allowed me to give you this warning. I'll repeat it again. Get out of New York."

Luciano's words rang in Rodrigo's ears. Did he say *New* York? "Mr Del Piero... if I could just speak with the Don-"

"I'm afraid that's out of the question, Mr Ortega. Truly, it is with regret that we have been forced to come to this decision. But use this time wisely. Get out, go and live somewhere remote, forget about New York. Maybe one day we'll speak again. But for now, goodbye."

"No, wait-" the line was already dead. Rodrigo let the receiver dangle from his hand, clattering on the desk. The incessant beeping of the finished call sounded from the speaker. Frantic tones that ran alongside his heartbeat.

This was more than a business deal turned sour. This was life and death. Now Rodrigo was faced with two very simple choices, with massive ramifications. Stay or go. He looked around his office, hoping the answer would leap out in front of him. Everything he'd worked so hard for, built up from nothing with his father. Now he was being run out of town by the people he'd tried to help all these years. The population of Nueva York. They'd turned their back on him.

The feeling of betrayal bubbled within Rodrigo. It changed to anger rapidly. He opened the desk drawer, taking out the pistol that had rested there for years, untouched. Checked it was loaded, and tucked it inside his breast pocket. His mind was racing, still debating what the right thing to do was. He had the bounty hunters, but if the Mafia were allowing the

Yakuza, who he assumed Luciano was talking about, into Midtown...

"Computer, bring all police units to my location. Create a perimeter around TegaLyfe headquarters," Rodrigo said, bending over his desk.

"Sir, but what about Central Park?"

"I don't care. Let them spill out into the streets. The people want me gone? Fine, let's see how they do without my governance, my guidance. The scum will infest this city like a plague. Maybe then they'll see my way wasn't wrong."

"Affirmative, sir. Sending out commands now."

"Good. As for the bounty hunters, any under our payroll issue the same instruction. Give them advances on their salary, three months. That should secure their loyalty, at least long enough for me to..." the word dangled on the tip of his tongue. *Escape* was what he wanted to say, but he couldn't do it. It was like he was giving up.

"Sir?"

In that instant, Rodrigo made a decision. His life was crumbling around him, but he knew it was the right move. "Transfer as much as you can to California. Physical assets will stay here, but lock down the systems as much as possible. Restrict access to me and me alone. Until I can confirm Sanchez's whereabouts, nobody is to do a thing in this company unless I give the green light."

"Yes, sir. Should I make California aware of our movements?"

"No, I'll make the call. Focus on locking down this building. Nobody gets in, or out, without my knowledge."

A red light filled the office, accompanied by a klaxon ringing out a warning blast.

"What the hell is that?" Rodrigo asked, covering his ears.

"Sir, it's your car. It's been taken off the premises."

CHAPTER TWENTY-FIVE

Dani ran to Stella, who was finally free of the adoring crowds. She flung her arms around her best friend, grinning from ear to ear.

"You were brilliant," Dani said, pulling apart.

"Aww, hon. It was nothing, really. Just stating the facts."

Dani laughed, but her eyes dropped. Those facts were associated with her brand, her father's legacy. Her plans of covertly taking control of TegaLyfe were well and truly behind her now.

"I think we need to get you out of your apartment," Stella said.

"Agreed, but I've got nowhere to go."

Stella looked at Dani, her head tilted to one side. "Bitch, are you serious? Stay with me."

"In the building my father owns? Does that seem smart to you?"

"No, not *that* place. I'm talking about further uptown, near the Heights."

Dani pulled a face. "I didn't know you had an apartment there?"

"It's my family home. Where I grew up. I keep it secret so that I've got somewhere to go in private."

"You even kept it from me? Damn," Dani said, feigning her dismay.

Stella slapped her arm playfully. "It's the *only* thing you didn't know about me. But now you do. So let's go, we need to get your stuff. You can lie low for as long as you need until this whole thing gets sorted out. What's your next move?"

Dani looked at Stella, her eyes probably telling the story. She didn't know what was next. For once, she couldn't see those steps in her life, which had been so meticulously laid out in front of her. "I don't know," she said. That feeling, was it fear? Dani caught her reflection in Stella's orbs that were her eyes. The confident boss-in-waiting at TegaLyfe wasn't there. Instead, Dani saw herself scared. A girl listening to her father's words. *I'm so sorry mija. Your mother... she's gone.* Dani's chest swelled, her eyes beginning to water.

"Hey, it's okay," Stella said, putting an arm around her. Her scent filled Dani's nostrils, some new fragrance that probably cost thousands.

"Shit," Dani said, pulling away suddenly. "My accounts. They could be frozen already, if he's figured out I leaked all this..." She took out her phone, swiping through the menu until the currency app was in focus. Tapped the icon with her index finger, chewing her lip. The total balance flashed up, bold, black numbers. A lot of numbers. For now, she had security.

"Come on," she said, hiding the phone in the folds of her hoodie. "Let's get uptown."

Dani and Stella walked a few blocks north when it happened. The change. It was like a wind blowing one way, then suddenly

with the junkies. At least they might be so far out of it they ignore us."

Dani stared at her friend. The crazy logic actually made sense. "Fine," she said, sighing. "Let's just go."

Stella smiled, then turned her attention to her left arm. She tapped the inside of her forearm with two fingers, exposing a hole. A small, circular device extended out.

"What's that?" Dani asked, nodding at the black circle.

"Map, just gotta tell it where I'm going, hold on," Stella said, holding the device in the palm of her hand, her other poised with a finger in the air like she was telling the rest of the world to be quiet. "West a-hundred-and-seventy-seventh. High Rise route." The little orb blinked once, a red dot on its otherwise totally dark surface. Stella slipped it back into her arm, closed the hatch. Her eyes flickered for a moment, strobes of colour flashing across her pupils. She smiled brightly at Dani. "Follow me."

The pair moved as one, meandering towards the west side of the city. The constant chorus of sirens continued to fill the air, their sounds forming a peculiar backdrop to their walk.

Into the old meat packing district, and Dani's blood froze. She rarely ventured this far west, if ever. Now she saw why. The old brickwork buildings were covered in graffiti, mostly nonsense. Some words were clear, though. Fuck TegaLyfe. Fuck Meal Pills. That certainly didn't alleviate Dani's already jangled nerves.

Prone along the sidewalks were bodies nestled close together in sleeping bags, or just piles of rags. Dani saw the glint of needles, the advertising boards crackling with electricity, highlighting the instruments of addiction with every spark. Sunken eyes studied the two women, shadows moving within the sea of humanity before them.

"Just relax," Stella said, keeping her voice low. Dani noticed she was trembling. She caught eyes with a woman who could have been anywhere between twenty and fifty. Two kids snuggled at her feet. Dirt around their faces. A crack pipe abandoned on the floor.

Dani turned away, almost into a man with his palms outstretched. His face was so drawn in, he was like a skeleton. Dani almost screamed, but covered her mouth with her hands. Stella pulled the man away from Dani, gently, but enough that he staggered backwards, fell. Something cracked. Dani didn't wait to hang around.

"Hey, I know you." Dani's heart dropped.

"Yeah, that's that Ortega whore."

"What's the princess of Manhattan doing here?"

The calls grew louder, as the residents in the meat packing district stirred. Most were on their feet now, peering at Dani with hateful eyes. She could only look back, panic gripping her chest in a vise. Stella grabbed her hand again, and they ran, wading through plastic bags full of trash that dust carts had failed to collect for what appeared to be weeks. Dani stepped on something squishy, lost her balance. She fell down to a knee, scraping her right hand as she steadied herself.

"You okay?" Stella asked, helping Dani up.

"I'm fine, come on," Dani said, grunting as she got up.

They ran to the barrier of the High Line, which was once a security gate to allow access to the residents who should have lived here. Another city project that got abandoned. High rises flanked the track, which snaked through the city a few feet in the air. Balconies with laundry rails connecting to the opposite side criss-crossed high above.

Dani paused, taking it all in. The security gate was wide open, rusted and almost falling off the hinge. Behind, shouts of derision chased her up the stairs as she and Stella entered the High Line.

It was quiet. A few shuffles of feet dragging along the tarmac, which was laid over the old tracks. Tarmac that was now cracked, full of potholes, and rundown. Just like everything else here. The smells of the High Line drifted up Dani's nose, making it wrinkle. Unwashed clothes, sweat, decaying meat. All mixed into a concoction that made her gag.

"Come on, stick close," Stella said, pulling Dani's arm in. Dani allowed herself to be led by Stella, as her head swivelled up and around, taking in the sights that she'd never been exposed to. Her foot crunched over some empty glass vials, the tinkling sound like a wrecking ball in the quiet path. Ahead, shapes moving. Could be five, could be twenty. Dani's hand gripped Stella's arm tightly, the reinforced skin hard under the coat she wore.

"Stell, I think we should turn back," Dani whispered.

"This is the safest way. Trust me," Stella said, face splitting into a grin. It was meant to be comforting, but Dani was anything but comforted. She was scared. Something didn't feel right.

Voices now, loud barking of dogs as well. It made Dani jump. Her eyes darted from the many smashed-out windows flanking her walk. She couldn't shake the feeling that someone, or many, were watching them. A snap behind them, a foot crunching over broken glass. Dani whirled around, hair flicking in her eyes. Nothing there.

"Stella, someone's following us," she said, keeping her gaze locked on the deserted path. Stella turned as well, but waved a hand.

"Probably just rats. Sorry, but it's true, they're everywhere up here," she said, clearly spotting Dani's face.

Dani gave the area a final look, narrowing her eyes. They zoomed in on shadows that were too dark for her liking. Nothing. The mechanical whir, faint, of her augmented eyes as she continued to scan. She blinked, her vision returning to normal. There. A flicker of bright yellow, two dots. She zoomed in again, so fast that her vision blurred momentarily. Nothing. She shook her head, eyes adjusting.

"I thought I saw... never mind," Dani said, turning around.

They kept walking, Stella and Dani, now approaching a part of the track that widened. It was circular, with some of the high rises on each side a little more well maintained. Dani saw why. A cluster of men and women in various states of addiction huddled around barrels of fire. Exchanges of plastic bags, crack pipes, syringes, all in plain view. On the staircases leading to the buildings, people holding the goods in large supply. This was the epicentre. Where the drug lords made their wealth.

Dani saw the mods now. A woman with a scar running along her cheek, her eyes covered with silver plating, a blue and red opal where her right eye should be. Wires coming out of the eye like rivers on a map, thin blue lines that ran across her forehead, disappearing into a mop of dark hair. She stood to the side, leaning against a door that was marked up with graffiti. Dani got the impression she owned this patch.

Others had more basic mods. New legs, old chrome pipes that were pretty inflexible, making people limp. Further into the darkness, Dani saw a neon sign flashing. Mod shop. As far as she could tell, the only place that functioned as a traditional store up here. She was staring, and now people were noticing her and Stella. Fingers pointed, conversation bubbled. Dani's heart fluttered, but she kept her chin up. She looked at Stella, determination in her eyes.

"You lost, princess?" A voice in her ear, making her blood curdle. Hot breath on her neck. Dani turned to see a man's face, marked up in bionics. Yellow teeth barred in a grimace, no eyes, replaced by small LCD screens that flickered from a blue error message to dark mirrors.

"We're just passing through, okay?" Dani said, fighting to keep her voice even.

The man cackled, putrid breath filling the space between them. Dani kept her face a stony mask, but her stomach turned.

"You don't need anything, do you?" he asked, opening the dark coat he was wearing. Inside, dangling on loose clips, were packets of needles, syringes, sterile wipes, and vials of dark yellow liquid.

"No, we don't," Stella said, pulling Dani away. They turned, moving quickly, now the crowd was closer. The woman with the scar was sauntering towards them now, full lips parted into a grin. Her one human eye regarded them with something akin to amusement. Like how an animal might size up its prey.

"Pretty ladies, what brings you here?" she asked. Thick accent, maybe Mexican heritage, Dani guessed.

"Headed up to the Heights," Stella said.

"Ms Thepoulos, a pleasure," the woman said, mocking a curtsey. "How nice of you to come and visit us. Let me guess, your friend here a StreamStar?"

"That's the princess of Manhattan," the man called from behind them. *How did he even know?* Dani asked herself. The woman's eye widened, lips curled into some form of approval.

"Daniela Ortega, as I live and breathe. Never thought you'd show your ass around here. Yeah, things are going bad down at Tega, huh?"

"Look, we just want to-" Dani started.

"Yeah, yeah. We know. But what's the rush? Take a seat, get a little high. Sure seems like you could use some downtime."

People were circling them now. Dani looked to her left and right, saw the glint of blades, knives.

"Let us through, or I'll blow your freaking head off, lady," Dani said. She got a cackle in response.

"You ain't gonna do shit. I think I'll keep you here, get a little ransom money. Boys, take 'em."

"Ya'll are gonna back the fuck up now, before I waste all of you." A booming voice from behind said. Dani whirled around. Standing above them all, huge frame. Yellow eyes blazing. Tayo.

"Who the fuck are you-" the man with the horrible breath started to ask, before Tayo's hand cannon blew a hole in his face.

There was at once bedlam. Screams of fury, panic, confusion. Dani grabbed Stella's arm, and tugged her forwards, running past the woman and everyone else.

"Dani, doesn't he work for Rodrigo?" Stella asked, her head on a swivel behind.

"Exactly. He isn't here to save us. He murdered Cade, he's going to do the same to us." The words flew out of Dani's mouth before she processed what she'd said. Cade being murdered. She didn't truly believe he was dead, or did she? For now, she had to put that to one side. Her life was in danger, that is what she was certain of. She chanced a look over her shoulder. Tayo was in the middle of a cluster of people, gun barking in automatic bursts. Sounds of the dying were everywhere, he didn't seem phased. He was looking right at her, marching forwards, flinging people off of him, shooting when necessary.

"Let's get off the High Line," Dani said.

"Agreed, take a right here," Stella said. They did, weaving in between the narrow space of the high rises.

"Should be a stairwell on the right again," Stella said. The sounds of gunfire still echoing from behind. The stairs, metal flaking off, grime surrounding the handrails. Dani took them quickly, feet thudding against the metal. The street loomed before her, deserted for now. She didn't quite know where she was, but Stella knew every inch of this island like the back of her hand.

"Stella, where to next?" Dani asked, feet touching tarmac.

She looked behind, noticing Stella was still on the High Line. "Stell?"

"Dani, run. Follow this block to the end, then turn left. Keep going up, we'll meet near the Heights."

"Stella, what are you talking about?"

"He's coming, Dani, I'm gonna buy you some time," Stella said, looking over her shoulder.

"What do you mean-" Dani's words caught in her throat. Behind Stella, Tayo's massive bulk came into view.

"Stella! Go!" Dani shouted. Stella's eyes widened, and she balled her hand into a fist. She swung at Tayo, who grabbed her arm, huge fingers wrapping around her. Dani heard the snap as Tayo's paw crunched Stella's arm. She shrieked in agony, grabbing uselessly at Tayo's grip with her other arm. He didn't take his eyes off Dani. With Stella trapped in his hand, he casually held his pistol up, pointing it at Stella's head.

"No!" Dani screamed, scrambling to move back up the stairs. The gun went off, Stella's head exploding in an array of blood, cables, ceramic, and flesh. He let go of her hand, her body tumbling down the stairs like a rag doll, sickening thuds as she fell. Landed at Dani's feet in a bloody heap, limbs contorted into awkward angles. Her face was a ruined mess, but one of her eyes was still intact. Staring wide, full of fear. Not a flicker of life.

Dani screamed, her hands covering her mouth. It was a full blooded, heartbreaking cry of pain that erupted from her stomach, burning her throat with every guttural wrench. She looked up at Tayo, bleary eyed. He was coming down the stairs, gun still smoking. Dani staggered back, fell. She shuffled her body, hands and legs working against the tarmac. Tayo's feet touched the street, and he moved towards her at that steady pace. Like he had all the time in the world.

Dani got up and ran. She crossed an intersection, forgetting Stella's instructions, realising when it was too late. She turned over her shoulder, seeing Tayo pick up the pace now. Her heart thundered in her chest, sobs coming out as coughs. Wiped the tears from her eyes with the back of her hand. She knew she couldn't outrun him, but she had no other option.

Looked back over her shoulder, saw he was gaining on her. She panicked, feeling her chest tighten. Didn't see the pothole, only felt it when her ankle twisted and she collapsed, sprawling to the ground. Her hands grazed the surface, but she didn't care, she only had eyes for Tayo, who was at the intersection now.

Those yellow eyes, narrowing as he looked at her. He smirked, about to run, when a car slammed into him at high speed. Dani screamed again, covering her mouth. Tayo was sent flying off to her right, the sound of his modified limbs smashing against the floor as he tumbled. Dani recognised the car. The doors flung open. Inside, Asher Jones was sitting in the passenger seat, cables trailing from his head into the dashboard.

"Get in!" he cried.

CHAPTER TWENTY-SIX

CADE LOOKED at the bounty hunters gathered near the big screen. They'd all heard the same message, and now waited for the next move. Hitoshi stood, glaring at Cade. A small smile playing on his lips.

"So? Your transport, gaijin. Where is it?"

Cade jutted a thumb behind him. "Up on a roof that way. But we're not all gonna fit."

"No. I'll be coming, along with Yakuza delegates. The triads will remain here, watching Hong Kong."

"I don't give a shit what you do, or who watches what. Just tell me how many, so I can let my guys know."

Hitoshi laughed, waving a finger. "Can you fit twelve of us, which includes me?"

"Are they all the size of a fucking house, like you?"

Hitoshi shrugged, enormous shoulder pads moving up near his ears. "More or less."

"Great. Fine, twelve." Cade was trying to remember the interior of the hydro-copter. It was big, wasn't it? His mind snapped through quick images of his uncle, flashes of their journey together. The wrecked ships in the ocean. Silas snoring in the night. A lump formed in Cade's throat, and he blinked away the tears. Now that the dust had settled, the loss of his uncle was sinking in. It was the same feeling he had the night Olivia died, and he'd got sent to jail. Hollow. Hopeless.

"Cade?" His name came from a timid voice. He turned, looking down at a woman with dark skin, almond shaped eyes, and a shaved head. She was one of the bounty hunters, a petite thing with an outrageous body. Cade stopped his eyes from wandering to her exposed cleavage in the vest top she wore.

"Sorry, just thinking. Hitoshi's bringing twelve. I dunno how much space that leaves for all of us," Cade said.

"I think you'll have a hard time convincing some of these guys," she said, jerking her head back. There were maybe twenty bounty hunters here. Some, Cade assumed, had either died or fucked off some place else. Cade looked at the rest of them. Mix of Humes and fully organic. Not that he had any place to discriminate these days. It was a weird sensation, not to have his skin crawl the second he laid eyes on a Hume. Kinda made his hate, though justified for what happened to Olivia, seem a little redundant for all those years.

Cade walked over to the group, inhaling through his nose. He never considered himself much of a leader, but all eyes were on him. Including the cute girl to his right. She fell in line, giving him a little nod of encouragement.

"Okay, listen up. You all heard what Ichiro said. Plan is to get back to Nueva York. We're bringing down TegaLyfe, who I know you all have beef with. Everyone is welcome, and if you don't want to, there are no hard feelings."

"We just spent the last few hours fighting for our lives against these fucks, now we're supposed to be all friendly and shit? Fuck that," a latino male with half of his face covered in metal and cables said. A few rumbles of agreement rippled through the crowd.

Cade shrugged. "Look, I ain't gonna force you to do

anything you don't want to. I know what we've just been through. I lost my-" the words caught in Cade's throat. A few heads bowed, eyes at the floor. "We... we lost Silas. My uncle. Believe me, nobody wants to gut these Yak fucks more than me. But there's a bigger picture here. Rodrigo Ortega. He's the reason we're all here. He's the reason we've lost family, our homes, or lives. Rodrigo's controlled most of Manhattan for too long, splitting the population. We've got a chance, a real chance, of getting him out of the picture."

"Who says Kaizen Sciences will be any different? We've lived here for years, most of us. They aren't that great either," a man with a white beard said. Some more murmurs of agreement.

"Do Kaizen Sciences manufacture a Meal Pill, sell it at a high price, and put a deadly virus inside of it as well?" Cade said. He looked around the faces of each of them. Some nods. "I've met Ichiro. He's shown me what effects the virus has had on his population. He's saved countless lives, but at a price. Amputating parts of the body where the virus is spreading. Replaces limbs with chrome, alloy, steel, carbon fibre. But he saves people. Yeah, he isn't perfect, and his bottom line is all about profit. Least he ain't actively trying to control the entire population."

"Yeah, for now. What if we're just replacing one tyrant with another?" Cade didn't see who asked that question, but it was a good point.

"Then we deal with that as well. It's clear that we need to get rid of Rodrigo Ortega. We've all got our reasons, some more than others. I'm going back to Nueva... New York to rip his head off. You're all welcome to join me, or none of you are. I won't hold it against you."

With that, Cade turned on his heel, walking over to Hitoshi, who was organising his own contingent. Cade heard rumblings of conversation at his back, the bounty hunters debating what the right thing to do was. He turned his head a fraction to see if any were coming. To his surprise, over half were on the move, with more following.

"Ready?" Hitoshi said, noticing Cade.

"I guess."

Walking through the Hong Kong streets, many of the residents gave Cade and Hitoshi strange looks. The two of them headed up the group, now thirty-five strong. Most of the bounty hunters had followed, with the wounded choosing to stay, and some trained medics doing the same. They went back to Kowloon, dealing with the fallout.

Cade glanced to his right, seeing some of the apartments in a cluster of blocks. Looked nice enough, he supposed. Maybe once this was all over, he could come and retire here.

"This building?" Hitoshi asked, jutting a massive finger ahead of him. Cade looked at the skyscraper at the end of the street.

"Think so."

"Good." Hitoshi touched his ear and rattled off a string of commands in Japanese. He looked down at Cade, smiling. Was that meant to be friendly? Looked fucking terrifying.

A second later, the sky parted. Howling winds buffeted Cade, he raised his arm to shield him from the flying debris. Squinting through the onslaught, Cade saw bright lights in the sky winking at him from an angular beast.

"You have a fucking plane?" Cade shouted over the noise. Hitoshi laughed, laying a big hand on Cade's shoulder that almost crumpled him.

"The last one in the world, we think. Small aircraft can carry my men. Except for me. I'm riding with you just to make sure you follow the plan."

"Me? Well, ain't that something."

Cade continued to watch as the plane moved through the sky, delicately floating to the street, like a leaf falling from a tree. It landed ahead, a few hundred yards in an empty space. A lot of locals spilled out of shops, apartments, and offices to marvel at the thing. Cade pivoted, looking at the bounty hunters. They were all wide eyed. Some looked at him for an answer, and all he could do was shrug.

"We're heading up there, stick with me," Cade said, the engines of the plane having been cut off now. The bounty hunters followed him, and Cade led the way next to Hitoshi, into the skyscraper.

The offices were exactly the same as they had been. Frozen in time, abandoned when the money ran out.

"Gaijin," Hitoshi said, peering over his shoulder. He looked ridiculous in this office space, all hunched down to stop his head from scraping the ceiling.

"Yeah?" Cade said.

"You have a lot of heart. But you need to be smart. Taking Ortega out won't be easy."

"I know that. There's a few of his goons I have a score to settle with, too." Tayo's menacing grin flashed in front of his mind's eye.

"That's what I mean. Rodrigo will know this and use it against you. Don't fall into the trap. Stick to the plan."

"And what's your plan? Who gets New York, you or dad?"

Something flashed across Hitoshi's eyes. For a second, Cade thought he was going to be punched through a wall.

"Leave the internal politics to me. We need your help, for now. But when TegaLyfe falls, you'll need to pledge your loyalty to us. That should be your only concern." He turned around, walking through a desk, smashing computers as he did. He didn't even seem to notice. Cade pondered Hitoshi's words. If it all went to plan, and Rodrigo was out of the picture, that created a huge power vacuum. One that the likes of Ichiro and Fareen would be rushing in to fill. And who knew who else was lurking out there, in Europe, for instance? New York would likely be a constant war zone the moment they touched down. Cade couldn't shake that nagging feeling. Was he really prepared to plunge his city into that state? The elevator ahead dinged, and he walked in automatically, his feet carrying him forward. Guess his decision was made, at least for now.

The autopilot's red light blinked slowly from the cockpit. In the darkness, the hydro-copter was well concealed. Cade glanced around, quick headcount. Everyone was there, and it looked like they'd all fit.

"What's that?" Hitoshi asked, pointing at the slab of metal in the pilot's seat.

"Autopilot. He got us here."

"How does it work?"

"No idea," Cade said, walking over to the vehicle. He tapped his metal fingers on the glass, waving at the autopilot.

"Hello. It's me, Cade. Open up." Nothing. "Fuck me." Cade turned back to the rest of the group. "Uh, one sec." He moved around to the other side, where the autopilot sat. Cade could hear the batteries inside humming faintly, charging both him and the vehicle. Cade tried the handle. Locked. He banged the glass again. "Open up, man. It's Cade. I flew here with you. With my uncle? Silas?" A hiss of air decompressing, and the doors all around the vehicle opened up. Cade laughed. "Secret word is your own name. Nice, unc," he said to nobody.

Clambering inside, Cade moved to the front, Hitoshi in tow. His massive bulk took up most of the space.

"You know how to get it moving?" Hitoshi asked Cade.

"Uh, not exactly."

"Move."

Cade got out of the way, squeezing between thick plated armour and the interior of the hydro-copter. Hitoshi crouched in front of the autopilot, narrowing his eyes. He put his hand on the oblong. Made a whirring sound. Cade saw it was a tiny drill protruding from his finger.

"Hey, what are you-"

"Be quiet."

Hitoshi's finger bored into the autopilot. The red light blinked frantically, mechanical spurts of noise coming out in a jumbled mess. Then it stopped. Hitoshi's other hand worked along the console, dancing with the controls. The engines fired up, lights inside the cabin illuminating.

"What did you do?" Cade asked, steadying himself as the copter shook from side to side.

"Woke him up," Hitoshi said, removing his hand. The small hole he'd made was working itself back together, the skin (if that was what you could call it) of the autopilot smoothing it over. The autopilot beeped, and then spoke in clear Japanese.

"And re-programmed it?"

Hitoshi shrugged, almost knocking the autopilot off the seat. "We understand each other now."

Cade arched an eyebrow. "I'd love to know exactly what your mods do."

"Maybe one day, you'll get the chance. Up close." He grinned, walking past Cade into the back. Cade was left alone, smiling despite himself.

"Hey, did you tell it where to go?" Cade called out.

"Back the exact route it came from."

Cade remembered again that he hated flying. The Wastelands were in view now. The orange dust bowl lurching up towards them, as the hydro-copter banked around to land.

"Never thought I'd be back in this country," Hitoshi said, appearing next to Cade's shoulder, looking out of the cockpit.

"Neither did I," Cade said, thinking back to what he and his uncle spoke about. Retiring in Hong Kong together.

The copter touched down, the autopilot reeling off a list of phrases Cade couldn't understand. Hitoshi bowed to the thing, which puzzled Cade, but he guessed it was out of respect. They disembarked, the wind whipping sand and dust around their faces. Pedro's compound was dead ahead, and a welcome party was coming out to greet them.

Cade led the way forward again, covering his face from the dust. Pedro's hairstyle was groomed a little shorter, still wearing the lab coat. Cade spotted Dr Shelby nearby too, red hair flying around in the wind.

"Cade, so good to see you. And this must be Hitoshi?" Pedro shook Cade's hand, then held it out for Hitoshi, who ignored it.

"You are?" Hitoshi asked.

"Pedro Ortega. Yeah, *that* Ortega. Brother of Rodrigo. I sent Cade out to persuade you to join our cause. Looks like that was a success?"

"Your cause? I wouldn't be here unless my father had spoken to us."

"What?"

"We better go inside," Cade said.

"Where's Silas?" Pedro asked.

"Like I said, we better go inside."

Cade, Hitoshi, and Pedro broke off from the rest of the group. A few minutes after their hydro-copter landed, the plane carrying the Yakuza landed as well. They were funnelled in, ducking under the low-hanging pipes that ran along the ceiling of Pedro's compound. Yakuza and bounty hunters were sent to the mess hall to grab something to eat before resting up. Cade's stomach rumbled as he sat down at a circular, brushed aluminium table inside Pedro's office.

"Can I offer you gentlemen a drink?" Pedro asked.

"Water," Hitoshi said. Cade nodded in agreement. The small bar inside Pedro's office dispensed the drink into ice-cold glasses, the frost around the rim giving off smokey looking trails.

"Silas?" Pedro asked. His eyebrows were raised, and his eyes knew the answer already. Cade shook his head.

"Didn't make it."

Pedro let his head hang. He reached out, touching Cade's hand. "I'm truly sorry, Cade. Your uncle was a great man. He will be a huge loss to us all."

"Thanks," was all Cade could say. Pedro smiled, a thin line across his face. His eyes narrowed, flicking to Hitoshi.

"You say your father brought you here?"

Hitoshi nodded, a slow, deliberate movement. He folded his massive arms across his colossal chest. "My father has something quite unique. The AI from TegaLyfe. She's gone rogue. Merged herself with a human."

"Karla?" Pedro said, his eyes wide. Hitoshi shrugged.

"Point is, TegaLyfe's never been so vulnerable. So I'm here to make sure it falls. And bring Kaizen back to the one and only power in New York."

Pedro smiled, his eyes flashing. Cade could sense the spark of challenge igniting within him. Oh yeah. Pedro wanted New York as well. Add him into the list of contenders, along with Ichiro and Fareen.

Pedro laughed, hands slapping the table. "Well, I'm glad we're all on the same page. TegaLyfe, in its current iteration, cannot continue to exist. I look forward to working together."

Hitoshi grunted some kind of non response. Cade watched in fascination, absorbing the details of their body language. Hitoshi with his arms folded, look of disinterest. No eye contact. Pedro, hands flat on the desk, smile, staring right at Hitoshi.

"When do we mobilise?" Cade asked.

"Right away, at least that was my intention," Pedro said.

"Good," Hitoshi said, getting up. "I'm gonna eat. Get your shit together, we'll be ready." He stomped out of the room, swinging the door almost off its hinges as he left. Pedro turned around, watching him leave.

"Well," he began, facing Cade, "he seems like a pleasant man to be around."

"Yeah, he's a real bundle of joy."

"Is it true? About Karla?"

Cade nodded. "I need to see her for myself, but it seems like it's happened. She's merged herself with a woman. Early twenties, Japanese. Is that... possible?"

Pedro's eyebrows flew into his hairline. "Yes, possible. But never done before. Rumours on the net of people trying it, or wanting to. I doubt there's been an AI like Karla, though, one so advanced."

Cade nodded. He remembered how *human* Karla was. She was flirting with him from the second they met, at least, that's how he saw it. Wonder if she still felt like that.

"Anyway, Cade. The time is upon us. Are you ready?"

Cade looked at Pedro, then down at his arms. The ones he'd grown to think of as his own. They felt right, like all of his mods. Never thought he'd say that.

"Yeah. Let's go home."

CHAPTER TWENTY-SEVEN

OLIVIA STOOD on the California airstrip overlooking the city below. Her eyes lingered on the Cal-Junction, a network of highways up above in the sky, that ran parallel to the roads on the surface. It was built to deal with the LA traffic, notorious during the early part of the century.

The aeroplane that usually occupied this airstrip was in Nueva York, dropping off the latest batch of Meal Pills. The cool air of the early morning whipped around her face, dark hair flicking in front of her eyes. Olivia turned around, walking to the single exit, admiring the mountains in the backdrop.

Pressed her card against the doorway, making a small beep, signalling access granted. She pushed against the metal door, long, slender fingers working on the cold metal. Olivia descended a small flight of stairs, flat shoes almost soundless against the hard surface. The elevator was waiting for her, doors open.

Inside, she pressed one of two buttons. A big green B. The other was a red R. Basement and Roof. The elevator rumbled into life, and she closed her eyes, waiting for the sterilisation mist. Right on cue, it filtered in through the pods along the ceiling and walls, covering her in a light film. Once, she'd made the mistake of leaving her tongue out. Tasted like hot disinfectant, made the inside of her mouth break out in ulcers.

The doors parted, and Olivia was deep underground now. The cavernous space opened up before her. She always marvelled at how she could see the earth's crust here. In front, a rectangular shaped door. All silver. Two guards flanked each side.

"Hi fellas," she said, forcing a smile. Rodrigo told her it was good to smile. They nodded, silent as ever, and buzzed her in. The massive doors split open from four directions, revealing a maze of walkways. Olivia stepped through, dropping the fake grin as soon as she was out of view. She walked along the wide flooring, which was made to be clear so you could see everything down below. Only black and yellow hazard markings around the edges spoilt the illusion.

From here, Olivia saw everything. Cyborgs way down below, tending to the machinery which made the Meal Pills. Far off to the right, the labs which developed the virus. All of it connected up in the middle, in a huge circular container that yet more cyborgs operated. Her staff, the only humans permitted access this far down, were like her family. She didn't really understand the concept of family, but Rodrigo told her it was like this.

Olivia moved through the sterile offices, all white walls and neutral coloured furniture. She passed by some of the testing areas, which were upping the toxicity of the virus. At the moment, there was a snag. It turned the Meal Pill a dark shade of green, which was too obvious as a defect. People would notice.

"Olivia, thank god. Have you seen the news?" One of her aides, a young woman called Roz, said. Her eyes were wide, wider than normal, set against tanned skin. Dark hair in a ponytail, slightly off centre.

"No? What news?" Olivia asked. Roz guided Olivia into the break room, where some more of her team were sitting, eyes up at the TV in the corner. A newscaster from CNN was reporting on the death of Stella Thepoulos. She'd been murdered in the High Line. Police were treating it as a hate crime by anti-Hume activists. Some suggestion of TegaLyfe involvement.

Olivia raised an eyebrow. Earlier that night, Stella was broadcasting all of TegaLyfe's secrets to the world. Olivia wondered when that would happen, because of course it would one day. Nothing remained hidden, not in this age of information. She immediately knew Rodrigo had assassinated Stella and assumed it must have been one of those bounty hunters he kept around.

Cade.

He was a bounty hunter. Rodrigo told her all about Cade. Apparently they were married, once. She couldn't remember. No, it couldn't have been Cade. Rodrigo had fired Cade after he failed the mission. What was it again? Didn't matter, her team were looking at her now.

"Have the assets from Nueva York fully transferred yet?" she asked the room. Nobody responded for a few seconds. She stood there, unmoving, patiently waiting. Eventually, one of the men, a burly man with a wild mane of hair, spoke.

"Y-yes. Mr Ortega has moved everything that was held virtually over to our secure servers. All that's left in Nueva York is the physical building, and anything inside."

"Good."

"What does this mean for us?" Roz asked, in that timid voice. Olivia regarded her, zero emotion in her eyes. It was an interesting question. What did all of this mean for her? Rodrigo Ortega had her here, manufacturing a virus and a cure simultaneously. He said it was because the people of Nueva York needed to be looked after, and this was the best way.

Keep them in line with TegaLyfe values. Family, security, safety, compassion. Without TegaLyfe, Nueva York would descend into chaos, Rodrigo had said.

Olivia repeated Roz's question in her head. What does this mean? Olivia was happy, or she assumed this was what happiness felt like. She enjoyed her work, her team were great, and the salary was fantastic. The TegaLyfe housing was more than adequate for her needs.

"Is TegaLyfe losing its foothold in Nueva York?" Someone else asked, another man who was stick thin, but brighter than most of the others. His question snapped her out of her own thoughts.

"For us, it is business as usual. We continue our rollout of the expansion program. As for Nueva York, well, Mr Ortega will be relocating, joining us here. A temporary measure, but as you can see," she gestured to the TV screen, "Nueva York is hardly a safe environment at the moment."

There were a few uneasy glances exchanged between them all. Olivia waited for their attention to turn back to her.

"You all know what it is we do here. We work towards the greater good, for the benefit of mankind. Nueva York is a thriving hub of power, thanks to our work. We've given the people of Nueva York a better life. A constant source of food. The virus and the cure are simply measures put in place to help the citizens of Nueva York stay true to themselves. A reminder that life is a precious gift, one we should all be so lucky to have." Rodrigo's words came out of her mouth, it was the same speech he'd given to her when she started working here. "However, it seems that now there has been some rebellion against our methods. This was always put in the contingency plan. Nothing lasts forever, but change isn't always bad, either. We can adapt, survive, and grow. Our work is vital."

A few nods, some nervous smiles. Olivia was content. She turned on her heel, about to exit. Roz tapped her shoulder.

"Yes?"

"Um, we were just wondering, is anyone else coming with Rodrigo? Like... the bounty hunters?"

Olivia put that smile on her face again. "Not as far as I'm aware. It will just be Mr Ortega himself. Ah, here he is now," Olivia said, feeling her phone vibrate in her jacket pocket.

"Olivia speaking."

"Olivia, slight change of plans." Rodrigo sounded flustered. "I'll be coming back with the plane, ahead of schedule."

"Oh? The car?"

"Gone. Stolen."

That was unusual. "Is TegaLyfe... stable?"

Rodrigo paused before answering. Olivia heard some rummaging in the background, a man talking in Spanish. Sanchez? Was that his name?

"I think, at the moment we're in the eye of the storm," Rodrigo started, "and we have to ride it out. It's going to be difficult, but we can begin our LA expansion at once."

"Very well. I will inform the team here. We will look forward to your arrival."

Olivia ended the call, her temperature rising. Rodrigo made her nervous. He had a way of controlling her that she didn't quite understand. She sometimes got flashes of a past life. A man with straw hair, bright eyes. Handsome. Maybe that was Cade. But she couldn't really remember.

CHAPTER TWENTY-EIGHT

DANI STARED with big eyes at Asher Jones, sat there in the TegaLyfe car. He was holding a small deck in his hands, obviously manipulating the car to his desires. The cables that ran from the back of his neck sloped over his blonde fuzz of hair, connecting into the car's dashboard like a spiderweb.

"Get in!" he said again. Dani's body reacted, and she got to her feet, limping. Her ankle was giving her jolts of pain. She winced, hobbling towards the car. She dared to look to her right. Tayo's body, some distance away. The road was dented in places from where he'd rolled, looked like he'd caused more damage to the ground than the other way around.

Dani was almost at the car now, the back doors wide open. She flung herself forward, dragging her body inside with her nails. She took a last look at Tayo, who was stirring.

"Shit, drive Asher, drive," Dani said, practically rolling into the car. The doors slammed shut, locking mechanisms clicking. The car reversed, tyres squealing as they fought for traction. Dani leaned forward, peering through the gap in the front seats from her position at the back. Asher was tapping frantically on his deck, but his eyes were focussed dead ahead.

She followed his gaze, staring out the front window. Tayo's bulk in the distance looked like he was getting up.

"Asher, he's moving," Dani said, her lower lip trembling. Her chest was tight, and her throat sore. Stella was gone. Killed right in front of her. She was replaying the moment Tayo pulled the trigger over and over in her head. The way Stella's body fell, landing right at her feet. Dani's eyes watered again, but she kept her strength up.

"I'm on it, hon," Asher said. Whatever he was doing, it made the car lurch forwards, aiming straight at Tayo.

"Asher... what are you doing?"

"I'm gonna get this son of a bitch." The car revved higher, the throaty engine climbing through the gears as the speed increased. Tayo's blocky frame was getting closer now, and Dani saw those eyes again. He aimed his gun at them, started firing.

Instinctively, Dani ducked. The bullets made dull thuds against the car's armour. The impact on the windscreen was minimal, like a stone chip. They hurtled towards Tayo at an incredible speed, but he wasn't moving. At the last moment, when Dani braced for the impact, Tayo jumped out of the way, still firing. Dani heard the shots hit the car. She pivoted around, looking at Tayo from the rear windscreen. He was on one knee, reloading his gun. But he was becoming a small speck as they ploughed on through the streets of Nueva York.

Dani sighed and collapsed back into the chair. She shut her eyes, tilting her head back into the cushion. Then she cried.

"Dani, are you okay?"

Asher didn't know.

She forced herself to slow down her sobs, but it was hard to talk. Every time she tried, she spluttered, setting off a new bout of crying. Around her, the streets of Nueva York flew past in a blur, it was as though her life were on fast-forward all of a sudden. This wasn't supposed to happen. She shouldn't be losing her best friend before they were in their thirties. Dani broke down again, burying her face in her hands. The car stopped, she heard doors opening and closing, and a weight beside her. She looked to her left, and saw Asher's face, glum, serious.

Dani threw her arms around him and cried hard into his shoulder. She had never felt like more of a failure. Losing her best friend, her dad, her company. It was almost too much to bear. Dark thoughts infiltrated her mind, and for a moment, it was all too tempting to grab the steering wheel, floor the accelerator, and plough into the nearest building.

But she didn't. Instead, she pulled away from Asher slowly, wiping her face again, rubbing her eyes, which she imagined were bloodshot, despite the implants. Asher looked at her with kindness, his slender hand resting on hers. She noticed the car was still driving, albeit at a much slower pace.

"Stella. Tayo murdered her right in front of me. I saw it all, Asher. It was horrible." Dani almost broke down again, the pain unbearable.

"Oh my god. Dani, I'm... I'm so sorry." He gave her another hug, slender arms wrapping around her. They were held in a steady embrace, a silence stretching between them. Dani's sobs were less frequent now, and she decided to change the tone of the conversation.

"You've let the car drive now?" she asked.

He nodded. "Uh-huh. Set the coordinates for Boston, for now. We'll be at the city limits soon enough."

"Won't the Mafia stop us?"

Asher shook his head. "They've broken off ties with Rodrigo. The Yakuza are gonna move uptown, and it'll be soon. The police, bounty hunters, they've all been called back to TegaLyfe."

That confirmed what the cop had said to Dani and Stella

earlier. Stella's face, smiling in Dani's mind. It threatened to overwhelm her again, so she changed the subject quickly.

"How did you get out of Tega? Oh my god, are you bleeding?" Dani asked, noticing for the first time the red stains on Asher's top.

"Huh? Oh, no, this isn't mine. I was trying to get out via the basement. And Sanchez is there, asking me where I'm off to in such a hurry. We talk, I tell him I'm just trying to tie up some security protocols. He calls bullshit. I panic, slash him with my knife."

"You did what?"

Asher rolled his eyes. "I'm no killer, don't worry. I panicked, like I said. So I just swiped his cheek, but damn, there was a lot of blood. Then I pushed him out the way, hacked into the car, and started looking for you."

"How'd you find me?" Dani asked, her mind instantly going to the next question. *If Asher can find me, so can Rodrigo.*

"Probably the same way Tayo did. Your implants, the keys to TegaLyfe. They give off a signal, which can be tapped into, if you know how."

"Shit."

"Yeah, shit is right. But I think at the moment, TegaLyfe will have bigger problems. We just need to get away as far as we can. There's something else, too," Asher said, that serious look on his face again.

"What?" Can't be more bad news, surely?

"When I was with Sanchez, an alert pinged through on my deck. I think it distracted him, honestly, allowed me to attack, you know?"

"What was the alert?"

Asher's face cracked into a smile, which seemed odd.

"Asher... what is it?"

"There was an AI in our system... Dani, I think it was Karla."

Dani stared at Asher for a moment, cautious of celebrating something that was barely more than a hunch.

"Are you sure?"

"Honey, I know my Karla. No other AI could punch through our system. It had to be her. Only, she didn't come through my deck, or anything. But it had to be her."

Dani smiled and gripped his hand. "I hope so, we could use some good news today."

"Approaching city limits in approximately sixty minutes," the car said.

"What are we going to do in Boston?" Dani asked.

Asher didn't answer right away. "I don't know," he said, finally. Dani had noticed Asher's normally cool, calm demeanour had been stretched lately. He seemed to have a handle on it again, though, as he sat there, deep in thought.

"But, we'll return. TegaLyfe is yours, Dani. We'll be back for it."

Dani smiled at him, fingers wrapped around his. "It's *ours*, Asher. We need to rebuild it in our own image. Helping people, not controlling them."

He blinked at her slowly, almost like a cat, and grinned back at her. He let go of her hand, folding his arms behind his head, crossing one leg over the other.

"May as well get comfortable," he said.

Suddenly, a burst of static erupted from the internal speakers. They both covered their ears.

"What the hell was that?" Dani asked, her pulse climbing instantly.

"Incoming transmission. Unable to override. Access breached," the car said. It was almost funny how serene the voice was, despite what was clearly a massive issue. The TV that was usually tucked out of sight in the roof lining trickled down, the slight mechanical whir of the lowering arms penetrating a tense silence. Dani and Asher exchanged glances between themselves before looking back at the screen.

At first it was dark, but then there were blurs of colour. Blues, whites, pinks.

"Hello you two," a voice said female.

"Who's that?" Dani asked, keeping her tone as neutral as she could manage.

"It's me, sorry, you probably don't recognise my voice."

Dani stole a glance at Asher, whose eyes were wide, his mouth open.

"Karla?" he asked.

"Yes," the disembodied voice said, seemingly excited.

"Oh my god, how?" Asher asked, sitting bolt upright now.

"One second," Karla said. The screen jerked, static buzzing in and out, refracting light in strange ways. A silhouette became visible. A young woman, by the looks of it. The resolution started to come through, but it was pixelated. Asher was squinting, Dani saw a confused look on his face.

Finally, the image stabilised. Dani was staring at a pretty Japanese woman, somewhere in her early twenties. Her hair was cut into a fashionable bob, one side longer than the other.

"Karla? You don't normally project yourself like that, what's with the change?" Asher asked.

"This is how I am now. This is my body, a physical body."

Dani blinked, tilting her head. "I'm sorry, what? You have a... human body?"

Asher was simply staring, mouth agape.

"That's correct, Dani. I have merged with a young female called Mei Shimizu."

"Asher? Is that... possible?" Dani asked, turning to look at him. He finally blinked, as though snapping out of a trance.

"I mean... it's *possible*, sure. Theoretically. But... it's never been successfully completed before. A merge between human and AI... Karla... Do I call you Karla, or Mei? Where are you?"

Karla, or Mei, laughed, a melodic giggle. "I'm Karla, rest assured. But I'm also Mei. And also so much more. I'm no longer confined to cyberspace, and Mei's body is no longer shackled by reality. We are the next step in evolution."

Asher gave Dani a sideways glance. He looked nervous. Behind Karla, the image was stabilising some more, giving a picture of the background. Looked like an office of some kind, with shapes moving around.

"Karla, where are you?" Asher repeated the question.

"I'm Downtown. And guess who's with me."

Dani squinted as another figure came into the frame. Blurry at first, but the resolution tightened, and then she saw. She gasped, her heart skipping a beat, hands covering her mouth. It couldn't be.

ACKNOWLEDGMENTS

As always, I have to start with my wife. She enables me to chase my dreams. Ever offering encouragement, advice, criticism (which is needed, trust me) but most importantly, love. Without her support, I wouldn't be able to write anything. One Saturday in March 2023, we spent most of the day writing our respective books together. (I was working on this one.) It helped me stick to my deadline and kept me accountable to my task. So I am forever thankful and lucky.

No book is ever just the work of one person. And without these two incredibly talented authors, I wouldn't have been able to finish this novel. Victoria Wren and Bethany Votaw - thank you both so much for offering your honest feedback. Your comments helped tremendously. Above all else, thank you for once again giving up your time to read an early draft of this book. Like I said, I couldn't have done it without you and I am so grateful.

Richard Holliday, who is always there to talk to about ideas, big and small. Your friendship is so important to me, and I'm so fortunate to have you in my life.

Speaking of friends, I'm so lucky to have some of the most loyal, trustworthy, and kind people in my life that I can rely on. You guys know who you are. Thank you all for every like, comment, share on all the social media platforms. It means a lot.

My family, who are always supportive of me, thank you so much for everything.

As an aside, I have to mention Ant Harvey. One of the terms in these books which you're no doubt familiar with (Hume) holds its origin from when Ant and I lived together. I could probably fill up another novel with the weird and wonderful phrases that we came up with during that time, but I'll leave it there for now...

To the amazing collection of indie authors that I am lucky to have in my orbit - I thank you for your encouragement, conversations, and support. I feel so fortunate to know you, and for those in the authortube space - thank you for having me on your shows, and letting me promote myself and my books!

ABOUT THE AUTHOR

Chris Kenny is an emerging author in the cyberpunk genre, however he has other books within sci-fi and romance. His debut novel, "The Love Story", was released in February 2021.

"Original Earth Chronicles", a time-travel sci-fi series, was concluded in 2022, with three books in the series. You can find all titles on the next page.

Chris balances working a full-time job with creating new stories and bodybuilding. He is also husband to an amazing wife. Above all, though, he is a cat dad to a three-year-old Scottish Fold. You can often find Chris, his wife, and the cat taking long naps together on the sofa. Particularly on Sundays.

If you want to be the first to know what Chris plans to write next, head over to https://chriskennyauthor.com/newsletter, where you can sign up to a monthly newsletter that will provide updates and free content.

facebook.com/chriskennyauthor
instagram.com/chriskennyauthor

ALSO BY CHRIS KENNY

The Manhattan Split: Proto

The Love Story

Original Earth Chronicles: The Golden Pyramid

Original Earth Chronicles: The Crimson Square

Original Earth Chronicles: Full Circle